Birthday Party

By the same author

Bad Manners
Curtsey
Tramp
Nothing but Gossip

Marne Davis Kellogg

Birthday Party

A Lilly Bennett Mystery

Doubleday

New York

London

Toronto

Sydney

Auckland

PUBLISHED BY DOUBLEDAY
a division of Random House, Inc.
1540 Broadway, New York, New York 10036

DOUBLEDAY and the portrayal of an anchor with a dolphin are
trademarks of Doubleday, a division of Random House, Inc.

Library of Congress Cataloging-in-Publication Data

Kellogg, Marne Davis.
Birthday party: a Lilly Bennett mystery/Marne Davis Kellogg.
1st ed.
   p.   cm.
I. Title.
PS3561.E39253B5   1999
813'.54—dc21   99-17174
CIP

ISBN 0-385-49333-9
Printed in the United States of America
January 2000
First Edition

10   9   8   7   6   5   4   3   2   1

For my beloved husband—Peter—who keeps me on my toes every single second

For Duncan and Delaney

And with enormous respect and admiration for showgirls everywhere, especially Aki, Anne-Margaret, Courtney, Delores, Marlene, Mary, Mary Lou, and Pam.

Birthday Party

One

Tuesday Evening • Roundup Country Club

The video, saluting Adelaide L. Johnson as the Roundup Cancer Institute's Citizen of the Year, began with Adelaide's parents, Maude and Henry Johnson, who had moved to Wyoming from Ravensden, Arkansas, sometime in the late thirties, after the Great Depression. Henry had been a moderately successful shopkeeper, and he brought all his savings in cash, formed the Henry Johnson & Son Land Company, and began to buy open range, which he leased back to the cash-strapped ranchers.

"Henry got the cash in the first place because he was the only white man in that part of Arkansas who would lend money to black people," my brother Elias told me behind his hand. "At about fifty percent a week interest."

They also brought their two children: a son, Jefferson Davis "Jeff" Johnson, for whom they had large expectations, and a daughter, Adelaide, from whom, I suspect, they expected nothing.

The video, of course, provided none of Elias's editorializing, showing instead old cracked photos of the sturdy, courageous young Johnson couple—Adelaide must have inherited her horse-teeth from her father, since her mother didn't appear to have any teeth at all—standing by their Model T pickup, hands on their young children's shoulders, Jeff standing straight, already a bully, Adelaide squinting, her face crinkled up, her choppers lying like sun-bleached paddles across sun-blistered lips, in front of a newly painted sign hammered into the open space, announcing that the big nothing behind them was owned by the Henry Johnson & Son Land Company.

A loud whistle split the air. "Hot dog," Clay Parker bellowed down the head table at Adelaide over the strains of "Happy Days Are Here Again." "Look at those damn legs. Those are Saturday-nighters if I ever seen a pair."

Uncomfortable laughter and a few appreciative whistles ruffled through the crowd. I think Clay, an aged cowboy movie star and the television spokesman for Johnson Land, might have drunk his limit.

Directly across from us, the floor-to-ceiling picture windows reflected back dozens of blurred images of Adelaide and her brother growing up. It was a typical rags-to-riches story, a real "Beverly Hillbillies"/"Ma and Pa Kettle" deal. Old Maude still scrubbed her wash on the back stoop, while Henry wore sleeve garters and scooted a toothpick around his mouth faster than a tennis match, looking to me as though he were rummaging around for missing crown roasts and sandwiches.

They'd sent their son, Jeff, to Dartmouth, and, in 1940, he married a seventeen-year-old New Hampshire girl, Theresa Collacello, whom we saw waving wanly from the steps of the *Wyoming Zephyr* as she took the train out West to live with her new in-laws.

"Barmaid." Elias sneezed. "Shotgun."

"Will you stop," I whispered back as quietly as I could. "You're making me laugh. Show some respect."

"*Moi?*"

"What is wrong with you tonight?"

My husband, Richard—who was chairman of the board of trustees of the Cancer Institute, and with whom we were sitting, on show, at the head table, unobtrusively reached his hand around behind me and smacked my brother on the back of his head.

Chastened, Elias slid low in his seat, crossed his arms over his chest, and sucked in a long, disgusted breath. "It's not like any of this has anything to do with reality."

I took a large bite of cherry pie to keep from laughing. I could tell Richard was starting to get mad.

By the mid-fifties, the company also had an office in England, where the Johnsons made a fortune building ramshackle low-cost housing. A black-and-white photo showed them and their English office staff smiling at the camera in front of Buckingham Palace, holding a sign that said HENRY JOHNSON & SON LAND COMPANY. Ha. Ha. Ha.

At some point, the video was vague, everyone but those left at home in Wyoming: Adelaide, and Jeff's three small children—Tom, Dolly, and Frank—died in a plane crash. Overnight, Adelaide not only assumed the role of the orphans' mother and father, but also, according to the narrator, "bravely" stepped into the position as chairman and CEO of the newly named A. L. Johnson Land Company. Henry & Son had vanished from the face of the earth.

"Oh, brother," my brother muttered.

Today Adelaide was in her eighties and had been bleaching her hair for so long that it now looked like a flock of peach-tinted chicken feathers. But her eyes—big, hyperthyroid bug-eyes—were still sharp, as cold and flat as a grouper's.

I glanced down the table just as she tugged up the front of her dress, possibly to keep out the prying, rheumy eyes of Monsignor Abbott, who sat next to her. But he had Tom Johnson's wife, the wondrous former showgirl Lucky, on his other side, and even though he was a priest, he was still a man, and knowing men as I do, I think if he were going to peek down someone's dress, he would pick Lucky's not Adelaide's.

Video reflections in the windows now showed our once-beautiful state choking to death on houses as far as the eye could see—A. L. Johnson Land Company houses that were packed tight onto curvy streets that all had the same name and, from a distance, looked like rows of cheap embroidery on some drugged-up hippie's psychedelic vest. Not a tree anywhere in sight.

And the houses were inhabited with the Chamber of Commerce types who were at tonight's dinner and had lived in Wyoming for only three or four years at the most. Slicked-up, jacked-up, done-up pseudo cowboys and cowgirls who bought their boots in Aspen or Jackson Hole. Flatlanders who wore Bermuda shorts and Reeboks to do their chores instead of Levi's and roughouts. Who spent their Saturdays watching their children play soccer or lacrosse instead of teaching them to rope and ride. Who had e-mail and faxes in their cars and drank their coffee out of quart-sized plastic Starbucks jugs and didn't teach their children table manners because they had none themselves. No one smoked. They all drank white wine spritzers or club soda with just a squeeze of lime. Spritzers. In Wyoming, for God's sake. What a bunch of geeks.

Give me a crowd of killers, corpses, felons, or socialites over this bunch of cheerleaders any day. My jaw was becoming as tight as Adelaide's dress, and probably just as unflattering. I considered going to the ladies' locker room and having a cigarette, except I didn't smoke anymore. So I drifted off and stared across the tops of the heads of the rapt audience, into the darkness, to where I thought I could just make out the top of our helicopter's rotors beyond the putting green. I imagined we were sitting in the big Sikorsky on our way home to the ranch, holding hands and kissing.

Suddenly, out of the corner of my eye, I saw a figure pop up more than halfway down the center aisle of the darkened banquet room. Clothed completely in black: commando-style trousers caught at the ankles by soft-soled lace-up boots, a turtleneck beneath a black Kevlar vest, a ski mask covering his head, he had smeared black makeup around his eyes and the flash of the whites of those eyes was sinister and chillingly determined.

I was caught totally off-guard.

The intruder was sprinting now. Moving toward us faster than I could find my purse, which held my small Glock. He stopped directly in front of Clay Parker, jerked a twelve-gauge sawed-off shotgun into position, and blew such an enormous hole in Clay, we could have shaken hands through it. The explosion lifted the drunk old cowboy's whole body up and off his chair and shot his beating heart, several ribs, and a five-inch section of his spine right out his back and into the wall. The rest of Mr. Parker followed a split second later, slamming hard into the damaged plaster. A gooey, sequined, sluglike trail on the silver-and-peach wallpaper pointed the way down to where he'd crumpled into a lifeless heap on the floor.

By then, I'd recovered myself and vaulted right over the top of the table, spilling and smashing everything in my way, and went after him, screaming, "Freeze, you son of a bitch," and "Somebody call the police—officer in pursuit on foot," at the top of my lungs. But the killer had a big jump, probably because he was wearing trousers and flat, gripper-soled shoes and I was wearing a tight skirt and high heels and had large glops of cherry pie glued to my legs and thighs and ground into my St. Laurent aubergine shantung.

The shooter sped unimpeded past the tables of stunned guests like a high-speed pinball and out a side door that led to the club's main entrance, leaving behind ghastly glittering images of Adelaide and her nieces and nephews still whooping it up on the video screens and a dead land developer on the floor. Which, I thought as I sprinted into the main lobby, was like the joke about dead lawyers: It's a start.

I flew in pursuit—racing down the curved staircase two at a time, through the front door, into the night. The doorman lay just outside in a soft heap. The back seam of his red jacket had split open and his braided hat had rolled off the curb and rocked slowly on its brim.

I stopped and listened, not breathing. Nothing. Everything was still, even the wind. The exaggerated silence was eerie. Even the traffic on Cheyenne Boulevard seemed to have evaporated.

The gunman had been fairly tall, I thought as I caught my breath. Maybe more stocky than lithe, but of course that was hard to determine with the bulky protective clothing. It was a crude, coarse, ham-handed murder, done by a person who maybe could not be sure of his aim. Someone who needed foolproof weaponry. But it was also focused and quick, and the killer never wavered or tripped as he dodged through the tables. Never an easy target. Pretty agile.

I had no idea which direction to go, and as I started down the curved sidewalk, along the snowy beds of frozen geraniums, and ahead of the shrill wave of panic that had begun to engulf the ballroom and would soon billow into the quiet night, I knew my chance had escaped me. This person would not be hiding in the bushes. Whoever this was, was a planner, and long gone.

And then, the ear-splitting scream of the helicopter's huge twin Pratt & Whitney turbines sliced through the air and by the time I could backtrack and make it to the putting green, the S-76, after a couple of awkward farewell heaves and dips, was seriously airborne. It steadied itself and moved quickly into the night sky. No lights. Gone. I couldn't believe my eyes. Someone had stolen our ride. Where were the pilots? Skyjacked? In Wyoming? They were Marines, Gulf War veterans, not some sissy corporate types who'd hand over the controls without a fight.

"Over here," Richard called from the bottom of the stairs.

The two aviators were slumped on a garden bench. Spilled coffee blackened the thighs of their navy twill uniform trousers. They had been drugged.

I looked back at the sky and couldn't help laughing, it was so incredible. So audacious. Plus, the chopper belonged to my younger brother Christian. He was really going to be pissed.

Two

Within minutes, patrolmen were everywhere, mostly trying to get the hysterical crowd calmed down and get a handle on what had happened. I was a little disappointed in the crowd's behavior—not especially surprised, because shootings were not an everyday occurrence in their lives—but they were adults and business leaders, and most of them were acting like a bunch of terrified idiots.

When I was a brand-new patrolman in Santa Bianca, California, as green as Celestina's chili behind the ears, I was called to assist in the investigation of a shooting at the Pink Lady Cocktail Lounge. By the time I arrived on the scene, the bagged-up body had been heaved onto a gurney and was being wheeled out dribbling a mixture of bodily fluids. A large puddle of blood thickened on the dirty linoleum floor where the victim had fallen. There was a smaller pool where his face had hit the deck and apparently smashed up his nose and knocked out a few teeth, not all of which, unfortunately, had been gathered up and removed along with the body.

My job that day had been to interview the regulars at the bar, get statements from the witnesses. They were lined up like Kewpie dolls in car windows, balancing on wobbly oxidized-chrome-pedestal stools with cracked, red Naugahyde, padded seats. They'd been hunched over the bar, minding their own business, cupping their drinks with both hands and staring blankly at the smoke-blackened bar mirror. Weak light, as dingy as the floor, fought its way out through red plastic Budweiser shades and turned the customers' faces into masks. The place reeked of stale beer, cigarettes, and deep-fry fat, with a little dried vomit and urine-soaked trousers thrown in for good measure. My greatest urge when I go into places like that is to start cleaning. But I guess that's just my mother in me. "If they'd just clean up," I used to figure, "things would go so much better for them."

I started my questioning with a hard-boiled, aging hooker: too much bleach, too much coke, too many cigarettes, too many bruises and split lips. "Did you see anything unusual here tonight?" I asked.

"Nah." She shook her head. Her hair was so dry it didn't move. But the sparkles on her silvery blouse, which matched her eye shadow and go-go boots, did.

"What about the shooting?"

She shrugged. "Nothing new." She took a long drag of her Virginia Slim, and I'll never forget her fingernails. They were about an inch long and had naked women painted on them. I was so young then, such a kid, only about twenty-two, I was always having to bite my tongue to keep from saying things like, "Wow, where did you get those nails?" Or, something helpful like, "That's not the way we do it in Wyoming," as if the people I was saying it to actually gave a shit about how we did *anything* in Wyoming.

But tonight, back at the shooting of Clay Parker, this Chamber of Commerce/country club group was totally uninitiated and unprepared for such a shock as a banquet shooting, and they simply fell apart and stampeded for the doors. Some of the women were actually crying, for God's sake. What did they think? That the gunman was going to come back for them? Couldn't they see this was a pretty darned specific deal? Reminded me of my little wire-haired fox terrier, Baby, who the second there is a streak of lightning and rumble of thunder in a five-hundred-square-mile area, begins to shake and shiver and run for cover because she is positive that particular lightning bolt has her name written right on it. I wondered if these gals were going to try to keep the tears going for the television crews who were setting up at the front door. They were no longer business executives, they'd become the Professional Hysterics that TV people seek out and thrive on. Even if only one person out of ten thousand is crying, that's the one the TV people want to put on the air to give the impression of wholesale panic and disaster. Give me a break, girls. Get a grip.

Until the officers could get them roped off, it was all we could do to try to protect the lawn and gardens, where we might possibly—but probably wouldn't—find footprints. Richard stood at the top of the staircase that led to the putting green. He was cool, calm, authoritative, directing people back across the terrace and down the other stairs, just as though they were leaving the opera house during a fire drill. Elias waited for them at the bottom of the steps. He spoke into his phone, trying to get a fix on the helicopter, at the same time shooing guests away from the flower beds and out into the parking lot.

I waited on the pathway, knowing that at any second Jack Lewis, Roundup's chief of detectives, would appear through the trees, thank me, and tell me he'd take it from here. I'd have to wait about forty-eight hours for him to figure out he needed my help and by then a lot of important information would already have gone by the boards. But that's the way I had to play the game. It was, after all, his town and his jurisdiction. In his eyes, I was a lowly U.S. marshal, which he considered a complete joke, and a private investigator, which he considered a threat. I've always believed his animosity toward me stemmed from two areas: One, before moving back home to Wyoming, I had been chief of detectives in Santa Bianca, California—a much bigger town than Roundup—and two, we were the same height. Pretty short.

I watched Jack pass through the police line, followed by his yes-man, young Lieutenant Evan, and stride briskly toward me in his controlled, cocky gait, his black eyes taking in everything in the harsh, white halogen emergency lighting that now illuminated the scene. His whipcord suit was pressed to a T, his white shirt crisply starched, black tie precisely knotted and tucked into his jacket, and his boots buffed to a high shine. He looked like an Alberto VO5 ad.

"Do you have a dressing room in your car, Jack?" I asked.

"Never know, never know what's in store." His voice was surprisingly deep and resonant. "Gotta stay sharp. What happened to you? You the victim?"

It was true. For starting out so totally chic and pulled together, I looked as if I'd been mugged. My skirt was torn. Mud and leftover dessert splattered my legs. "Very funny," I said.

"So what have we got here, Bennett?" Jack pulled out a

pad and pencil. So did Evan, who mimicked Jack's every move and drove me nuts. I was always expecting him to start chattering like a little monkey, jump up on Jack's shoulder, screaming and spitting at us, showing little pointed teeth and a bright pink tongue.

I canned the image and briefed Jack on what had gone down, all the way to the escape.

"He stole your helicopter?" Jack stopped writing and gave me a look over the top of his half-glasses. His black eyebrows knitted together in a straight line and his eyes flashed.

Evan brayed out a dull-witted laugh, sort of like a mule.

"Hey." Jack whipped on him like a thunderbolt. "Put a lid on it."

"Yes, sir."

"He stole your helicopter," Jack repeated without intonation. "Well, I'll be damned. What about your crew? Take them, too?"

The two pilots, now recovered, stood nearby, ready to answer questions. They didn't have much of a story to tell: A waitress had brought them each a club sandwich, potato chips, coffee, and cake. They'd eaten on the garden bench where we'd found them. The forensics team had already photographed, mapped out, and bagged up the remains of their supper.

The waitress had been tall.

"About half a foot taller than you, ma'am," one of them said to me. "But plump."

"I'm going to tell my brother to double your salary," I said, flattered he didn't find me plump or, if he did, was too smart to say so.

Jack frowned. "Let's keep this on a professional level, if you don't mind. This is not a comic situation."

"Excuse me?" I said sarcastically. "You're telling me, who

sat through a *horrible* dinner, had a fellow turn into Flying Wallenda Swiss cheese practically in my lap, ripped a two-thousand-dollar skirt all the way to Christmas, ruined a pair of three-hundred-dollar Chanel pumps chasing a perpetrator through the geraniums, and had my *helicopter* stolen while you were changing your shirt for the tenth time today, that I am not being professional? That this is not funny? I'm terribly disappointed in you, Jack. What's happened to that great sense of humor you're so famous for?"

Jack Lewis could antagonize me faster than anyone I'd ever known in my life, mostly because I was irrationally jealous of his power. I had grown so accustomed to it out there in Santa Bianca, and now I had none and I hated him. My hands kept balling into unintentional fists and I had to force them to relax.

"Let's get the staff pulled together," he said to a nearby investigator after we had shared a moment of hard eye-to-eye. "Get this waitress ID'd."

In my opinion, what he needed to do was question everyone who'd been at the head table, including the entire Johnson family. *They* would be the ones with the insight, not the Roundup Country Club kitchen crew.

"Jack," I said, "I think Tom and Lucky Johnson are leaving. I'll go see what light they can shed."

"No thank you, Bennett." His voice was prim and condescending.

"But they were there," I began and then closed my mouth. This was an argument I could not win. I'd only end up humiliating myself further.

Within minutes, all the kitchen and wait staff had lined up in the now-empty ballroom. They giggled nervously as the two pilots slowly inspected each of them as carefully as Alec Guinness did his troops in *The Bridge on the River Kwai.* They went down the line twice, three times, and finally said the woman who'd served them was not there.

Well, whoop-di-doo, I thought. No kidding.

"Is this your entire crew?" Jack asked the anxious club manager.

"Yes, sir. It is."

It didn't take any great brain to figure out the waitress and the shooter were the same person.

"Thanks, Bennett," Jack finally said. "I'll be in touch."

"Right," I growled. Jerk.

Three

Help yourselves to drinks," Elias called back to us—us being Richard, the two pilots, and me, being driven home from the dance like a bunch of sluglike loser lumps, major screw-ups in a high school football game who had blown a twenty-one-point lead in the last five minutes, our perpetrator escaped, our eight-million-dollar helicopter stolen via spiked club sandwiches.

We all slumped in the plush, cavernous cabin of Elias's maroon Suburban, which smelled of saddle leather, manure, and wet dogs, while Elias's Australian shepherds, Gal and Pal, snuggled with him up front. No wonder he'd always had trouble with women.

Richard snapped open the top of the burlwood cabinet that

contained a full bar and poured us each a shot. He was in shock, I think. Decidedly and dejectedly at sea.

"I'm trying to make up my mind whether this is more positive or negative," he said as he sipped his whiskey.

"Well," I volunteered, "I'd say it is pretty negative for Mr. Parker, and it might be hard to get anyone to be your Citizen of the Year next year."

"That's what I mean: Will it? There's going to be a lot of publicity, and frankly I'd much rather have someone shot at a banquet than in the opera house. Hey, Elias." Richard leaned over the front seat. "Where's the television set?"

Elias handed back a large-screen laptop.

"Cool," said one of the pilots and within a minute we had the live, local news tuned in. Marsha Maloney, coanchor of the "Live at Five" broadcast (which actually went from four in the afternoon until eleven at night), was on the scene at the front door of the country club. She had on a black suit that was so tight she might as well have painted her skin black and left the suit at home.

"God," I muttered. "Do you think that suit's tight enough?"

"Yeah," Richard said, perking up. "She's in great shape, isn't she?"

Give me a break. That's her job.

Marsha was starting to spool up. "Here's what Richard Jerome, chairman of the board of trustees of the Roundup Cancer Institute, had to say earlier about the shooting incident that left veteran movie star Clay Parker, Vice President of the A. L. Johnson Land Company, dead. Cut down in the prime of his life."

What was she talking about? The guy was a seventy-five-year-old lush.

Tape rolled and there was my beloved Richard with Marsha staring deep into his dark blue eyes, licking her glossy lips. Her face was so smooth, it looked as if she'd put on her makeup with a plaster trowel. "Any comment on who might have done this, or why?" she asked.

Richard shook his head. He looked so handsome on that screen, with his weather-beaten, craggy, windburned face and sun-streaked hair, I couldn't believe he was mine.

"I have no idea what could have motivated someone to kill Clay," he answered somberly. "He, the Johnson family, and the Land Company are so admired and respected, such outstanding community leaders. We were here tonight to pay tribute to them for their generosity to the new Cancer Research Institute. Clay Parker was a highly regarded member of that team, a major contributor to their success. His loss will be felt."

"Where's the shovel?" Elias said.

"How long ago did you write *that* speech?" I asked.

"We're back live," Marsha warned, "with Roundup's chief of detectives, Jack Lewis. Chief Lewis"—she stared intently at him, her expression now serious—"any leads?" She thrust the microphone into his face.

"All we know at this time is that an unidentified gunman entered the banquet room at approximately eight-ten this evening and fired one round, point-blank, at the victim, killing him instantly, and then escaped by stealing one of the guests' helicopters."

The pilots groaned.

Marsha turned her face back to the camera and began to speak, but I slapped the computer closed. I'd seen enough.

"Is there anything, anything at all you can think of?" I asked the two angry, humiliated young men. "Anything you might have forgotten earlier that you can remember now about the waitress? Any distinctive gait or manner? What about her shoes? Her makeup? Her hair? Did you notice her hands? Anything unusual about her voice?"

"Like I said, she was fairly tall." The captain, Brian Nelson, was the first to speak. "Gray hair, sort of curly. It looked like it could have been a wig. Overweight, bulging over her belt."

"I think she had on too much makeup," his copilot, Joe Carter, said. "Bright pink lipstick, lots of rouge. I didn't see her legs. Did you?" He turned to his boss, who shook his head. "Her uniform was kind of long."

"What did her voice sound like? Did she have any kind of identifiable accent?"

They both thought for a moment. "Sorry," the captain said.

"What time did she bring your dinner?"

"Seven-forty."

"Are you sure she was a woman? Could she have been a man?"

"These days, anything's possible."

Lots of possibilities, I thought, as I looked out the window at the passing countryside.

"This is going to be a good case," I said to Richard. "Jack's lucky."

"Why?" He had rifled through Elias's console until he dug out a cigar.

"Because there are so many connections: The Cancer Institute used the evening as a fund-raiser to thank the Johnson family for the gift of the site for its new headquarters. The Johnsons used the evening to unveil their High River Ranch project. Lots going on."

"Plus," Elias said, "everyone's saying how generous they

are but, come on, Richard, you know as well as I do they made a back-door deal with the feds: They had to give the institute the hundred acres to get permission to use federal land to develop High River Ranch."

"So?" Richard clipped the end off the cigar and fired it up. "Not every philanthropic act is motivated by philanthropy."

"Yeah, well, the access the feds gave them blocks the Hewitt family's access to federal grazing land from the Broken Arrow, and I understand William Hewitt has declared war." Elias turned practically all the way around in his seat to face me. "Did you know James was working for the Johnsons?"

"Wait. Hold it," I said. "You're going way too fast. You've lost me completely. What does any of this have to do with the *Hewitt* family?"

"You know the Broken Arrow," Elias said, scarcely able to conceal his impatience with my ignorance. "The Hewitts' ranch. You and William and I grew up together. Are you with me?"

"So?" I felt like punching him when he acted like this.

"Like all the rest of us, the Hewitts use federal land for grazing and the Broken Arrow's primary access—for the last hundred and fifty years anyhow—was through what has now become part of the Johnson project. The feds horse-traded them that piece of property and effectively eliminated the Hewitts' access to open range because the city is encroaching on it from the other direction."

"How can they do that?"

"Happens all the time. The government gave the Johnsons land in exchange for a comparable land somewhere else. It's no big deal, except in this case, it's a body blow to the Broken Arrow's cattle operation. So"—Elias paused and puffed on his cigar—"William, who now runs the Broken Arrow, has filed every possible sort of lawsuit and injunction, but it's a tough go because his younger brother, James, is helping the Johnsons and providing them with inside information. He's a turncoat," Elias snarled. "Selling his heritage."

"So what you are really saying is that the Johnsons are trying to steal the Broken Arrow by isolating it."

"Yup."

We all slumped back into silence. The never-ending process of our vanishing range was devastating.

I could picture James Hewitt perfectly: he'd always been a stupid little weenie who had halitosis and acne and tried to French-kiss me at dancing school. I wasn't even slightly surprised at his duplicity.

I closed my eyes and decided to concentrate on the perpetrator. It was probably one person, I thought. One person who could shoot and fly. That was not an especially unusual combination.

Ten minutes later, we turned into the private airport where all the local corporations kept their aircraft. Elias cruised to a stop in front of the Bennett Corporation hangar. The ramp director was sitting in his Blazer waiting for us.

"What's up?" Captain Nelson said to him as he exited the Suburban's big side door.

"That's what I was going to ask you," the man said. "What's the big idea?"

"What idea?"

"What the hell's your chopper doing on top of the Johnson Land Company's hangar?"

"What?"

"Follow me, I'll show you."

We piled back into the Suburban, while the pilots jumped into the ramp man's vehicle, and tore across the tarmac to the opposite side of the field where Johnson Land housed its Gulf-stream-Four and three Lears in a massive, five-story-tall hangar. We couldn't see anything from the ground and had to climb, single-file, up a metal ladder to the roof. There, sitting in the center, was our beautiful navy blue and gold Sikorsky S-76, the Cadillac of corporate choppers, twinkling in the moonlight like an ad in *FYI Magazine.*

Four

Thursday Morning

'm not at all surprised," Mother told me over the phone two days later. The shooting was still the hottest topic in town. "I've always found all the Johnsons particularly tiresome. They're such publicity hounds. Adelaide or that repulsive boy—what is his name?"

"Tom."

"Whatever. He probably staged the whole thing."

It was early. I had been sitting in my office trying to get some work done while it was still quiet when she called up and decided to chat because it was too early to call her friends. I knew my father had already gone to his office at the bank and she was sitting in a lovely peignoir in the sunny breakfast room sipping English breakfast tea and nibbling dry toast with a tiny taste of Fortnum & Mason thick-cut marmalade, or maybe a soupçon of Tiptree Little Scarlet, and killing time until her masseuse arrived.

"What became of the other boy? Tom's brother, Frank Johnson?" I asked.

"Oh, he never amounted to anything, just follows his wife around. She's Connie Johnson. You know who I mean: She's the Minority Speaker of the State House, just as tough as nails. I suppose that dreadful Adam Garrett was there, too." She was referring to Wyoming's notoriously promiscuous former senator.

"Yup."

That's all the opening she needed on that subject, and while she spent the next few minutes loudly eviscerating the Democrats, my secretary Linda Long thumped in on her sturdy heels and laid a fax in front of me. I pushed the mute button on the phone and lifted Baby off the desk, where she'd been sleeping in a slice of sunlight.

"No caller ID and no home number identifier," Linda explained as she pushed a stray wisp of wild, reddish-gray hair behind an ear.

Linda was a divorced ranch wife from Riverton who'd escaped to the city and ended up in the wasteland of Bennett's Fort working for me and being romanced by my brother Elias. I hadn't the nerve to ask her how old she was, because I had a feeling she was younger than I, even though she looked older. Meaning, I think she might be about forty but looks about fifty. Most people don't believe it, but a ranch wife's life is one of the toughest, loneliest, and most aging roles a girl can choose. So when Linda caught her husband in the hayloft with the neighbor's daughter, she was delighted. She threw her purse and her little house dog into her metallic teal blue Dodge Ram pickup and was down the road before her husband could even get his jeans pulled back up over his long-johns.

"Of course, they were just down around his ankles. That man never took his boots or trousers off for anything. Just poked his pecker right out through his underwear," she told me one time when we were straightening up a stack of old case files. "Except when he took a bath, which was far too seldom for my taste. Good riddance to bad rubbish."

Well, she had me there. I could honestly say I'd never done it with a man who left on his long underwear. Or to my knowledge even *had* any long underwear. Jeans and boots, sure. Sometimes there's simply not enough time to take all that stuff off.

I looked down at the handwritten message on the fax while Mother continued to hold forth.

In precise, tortured, second-grade printing the note read:

William Hewitt did it.

William Hewitt. *William Hewitt?* I laid my glasses on the desk, rubbed my eyes, stretched, and looked out the tall window down to Main Street, where my cousin Buck was directing the unloading of what appeared to be at least one million pumpkins for his YE OLDE PUMPKIN PATCH display, yet another way to fleece the handful of tourists—mostly retirees this time of year—gullible enough to wander through in the late fall on their way from the Grand Canyon back to Nebraska, where the pumpkins had come from in the first place.

The sky was unbearably blue and if it got any colder we'd have another snow.

Elias's faded Ford pickup appeared at the far end of the dirt street, going about sixty. He roared up and slid to a show-stopping four-wheel drifting stop—better than Marlon Brando on his bike in the *Wild Bunch*—that blanketed the pumpkins with dust.

"You stupid son of a bitch," Buck yelled at him. "What in the hell do you think you're doing?"

"Sorry, didn't see those there." Elias laughed.

Then, Gal and Pal jumped out of the truck bed and relieved themselves.

"God damn," Buck said. "Your dogs are goin' on my pumpkins. I don't even want to see what's going to happen next. Come on in and have a shot."

"William Hewitt?" I said, turning back to Linda. "I don't think so."

"He sure doesn't seem like the killer type to me," Linda agreed.

I disengaged the Mute. "I've got to go, Mother. I'll check in later today." I hung up before she could respond and went to see my boys: Elias and Buck.

My office was directly above the Golden Nugget Saloon in an 1880s pine-board building. Buck kept everything in Bennett's Fort as authentic as he could—except for the rest rooms, which were plentiful and as state of the art as Wolfgang Puck's new kitchen. Access to my second-floor international headquarters was via a rickety, dangerous wooden staircase, tenuously mounted to the back of the building with nails so short you couldn't even get a decent case of tetanus from them. I knew this because, in some places where the stairway had pulled back, the business side of the wood looked about as lethal as a curry comb. In my opinion, it should have been attached to the building with railroad spikes.

We don't have OSHA in Bennett's Fort.

□ □ □ □

"William Lethbridge Hewitt the Fourth?" Buck belched out a rumble as he slapped an empty shot glass on his desk, which also happened to be the table in the front booth of the Golden Nugget. He ran a balled fist across his lips, which were pressed shut in a straight line between his close-cropped, gray-blond beard and mustache, wiping off stray drops of whiskey.

"That gun is bigger than he is," Elias said and polished off a shot. "The recoil would have blown him halfway across the room."

I laughed, picturing the diminutive William trying to quick-draw a sawed-off shotgun. That was more in the purview of his Amazon wife, the superstar trick rider of the Roundup Rodeo, Miami McCloud.

"Couple more shots over here, Ec," Buck yelled to his hippie sister-in-law Ecstasy, who had misplaced her brain along with her name at a Steppenwolf concert in Boulder back in the late sixties. "Sure you don't want anything, Lil?"

I looked at my watch. Seven-thirty. "Just coffee."

I'm not particularly opposed to drinking at seven-thirty in the morning, but I also work. These guys, a couple of middle-aged, overweight Vietnam vets, had somehow figured out a way to drink *and* work and still have it all come out all right. Of course, their interpersonal skills sucked: Buck had been divorced a couple of times and Elias had never married. In fact, we were all astonished when he found the nerve somewhere to propose to Linda. So was she. And neither one of the guys wandered too far from home unless they absolutely had to, or for family affairs, because their lives away from the ranch and the Fort had a way of turning into alcoholic blackout Steven Seagal movies, and they'd wake up in emergency rooms with the daylights kicked out of them.

"Tell me more about the Broken Arrow and the High River project." I dumped a shot of Jameson into my coffee. What the hell. It was as cold as Mars outside, I didn't have any appointments today, and Jack Lewis wasn't exactly breaking down my door asking for help. And then, with my brain enlivened by the spirits, I thought maybe I'd just go visit William and Miami. I hadn't seen them since my wedding.

Five

I know I carry on about how much the architecture out West stinks, but it's true. Because there's nothing indigenous or historical except log cabins and teepees, mud huts and hogans, architects have unloaded ridiculous contraptions and concoctions on us thinking that we simply don't know any better—or have absolutely no standards at all. So our major Rocky Mountain cities like Roundup and Denver look like the Brothers Grimm meet Salvador Dali—adventures into surrealism.

I believe our architectural troubles began back in the 1800s, when the white man started showing up from England and Scotland and Ireland and Germany and Poland and Mexico, bringing along what he knew. The Hewitts came from

Scotland and started the Broken Arrow Ranch in the 1860s. They brought a castle.

A big one.

Their place is about a hour south and west of the Circle B and takes up around fifty thousand acres of spectacular river bottom land and thickly wooded foothills, which provide picture-postcard mountain and prairie vistas. A residential area lies just outside a piled rock gateway crested with an arch that announces in large wrought-iron letters you are entering the Broken Arrow Ranch, and once you've rumbled across the cattle guard, it's another three or four miles of rough road before the flags flying from the battlements appear across the valley. Shortly, the entire granite castle emerges. Unobscured by its natural habitat of gentle highlands mist, it appears in super-high definition in our clear, sharp, high-altitude air. It is so specific there across the valley, so perfectly delineated and three-dimensional, it looks for a moment like a computer-generated photograph.

The second I stopped the car, a pack of unkempt blue heelers, Australian shepherds, and Border collies surrounded it, leaping, barking, trying to jump through the windows in their joy at a visitor until suddenly, with the loud slam of an iron bolt, the giant, iron-banded, spike-studded front door flew open, and an ancient figure in knife-starched blue jeans, a plaid cotton shirt with a Peter Pan collar, a pearl necklace, and large pearl and diamond earrings, crabbed out with a twelve-gauge, which she discharged into the air with a deafening explosion.

"Shut your damn yappers," she yelled at the dogs, who shot past her into the house without another sound. "Or I'll blow your goddamn heads off." Then she aimed the twin barrels directly at my forehead. "State your business," she wailed, "or I'll blow your goddamn head off, too."

29

It was Victoria Hewitt. William's and James's mother. I'd heard she was dead. Victoria Hewitt always made my mother look like Mary Poppins.

My arms shot into the air like Atlas missiles. "It's me, Mrs. Hewitt. Lilly Bennett." And then I remembered. "Jerome. Lilly Bennett Jerome."

"Well, my goodness." The Browning over-and-under was lowered to my knees. "Why didn't you say so, you darling girl. I was afraid you were some trick sent by that no good son-of-a-bitch son of mine."

"No." I lowered my arms slowly and then, before I could stop myself, blurted out, "I thought you were dead."

She laughed brightly and her blue eyes twinkled. Victoria Mead Hewitt's face was a lesson in Wyoming history: lined and weather-beaten, elegantly featured, betraying the utterly unforgiving, underlying bedrock. Her thick snow-white hair was drawn into a loose topknot showing off a sharp widow's peak above her deeply wrinkled forehead. I think she was about eighty. Like my family, the Bennetts, the Meads and the Hewitts had been in Wyoming since the middle of the nineteenth century. We are indistinguishable from the land, and—as with all true Westerners—innately suspicious, steely-eyed, contentious, and wildly independent.

"He wishes I were dead," she hooted. "That would make his dreams come true. He thinks. I've still got a few tricks up my sleeve, enough to catch his damn tit in a wringer at any rate." She squinted over at me and reshouldered the gun. "Who'd you say you were?"

"Lilly Bennett, Mrs. Hewitt, and I'd sure appreciate it if you'd put that gun down."

She looked at it as though she'd forgotten about it, too. "Oh hell, probably scared the damn panties off you. All right, you'd better come on in instead of standing out here in this boiling sun. You want a Dr Pepper?"

"Sure."

I followed her through the huge front door into a slate-floored entry hall that smelled strongly of mold and faintly of incontinence—presumably the dogs'. A half-dozen, high-backed, carved wooden armchairs lined the walls, and above each hung a careful arrangement of shields, spears, swords, and banners with Hewitt clan insignias. I knew they were from the Hewitt clan because when William and I were little, we used to ride our horses right into the great hall, stand on their backs, and help ourselves to a couple of relics—generally swords and standards—then gallop them around the ranch like the cavalry, looking for Indians. Victoria would stand on the front porch and fire off her shotgun yelling, "Get those G.D. flags back here. I've got Ike and Mamie coming to dinner tonight."

She was so beautiful then. A brave, young widow with two strong sons. And whenever Ike and Mamie were in Wyoming, they'd always have dinner with Victoria at the Broken Arrow, where she would assemble a glittering, glorious crowd of power brokers and major donors; nobody had ever seen anything like it. However, even though the Eisenhowers might have *supped* at the Broken Arrow, they *stayed* at the Circle B. My mother was always quick to point that out, so I just thought I'd go ahead and save her the trouble.

But now, Victoria had developed a wild sort of glint to her eyes, maybe a little too much white catching the light or something. Maybe they moved a little too fast or were open a little too wide. Something wasn't quite right.

It didn't look as though anything about the house had changed since I'd last visited, probably thirty years ago. Not necessarily a good thing. It still felt like a museum, but now instead of a *living* museum, it seemed more like the great hall of an abandoned castle readied for a summit of clan leaders who would never arrive. And while the Wyoming Hewitts kept close business and family ties with Scotland, I had the feeling the Wyoming staff had let the hearths go cold. That they'd been left waiting too long for Mel Gibson to come walking in draped in his tartans singing "Brigadoon," and they'd all drifted off into the hills, disheveled, disheartened, doing their own thing.

We passed into the study, a dank room with heavy velvet curtains that could make you sneeze just looking at them, and dark paneled walls. A brooding stone mantelpiece framed the cold hearth. Daylight scarcely eked through the dirty leaded-glass windows, and the shapes of a few Black Angus grazing outside were simply smudges from an Impressionist painting. I wondered which wing of the house William and Miami lived in—it certainly wasn't these oppressive rooms—because William and Miami were full of life and love and Miami always had to have everything white.

Victoria pushed an old-fashioned button on top of the desk and a bell clanged and echoed so loudly it made me jump. At the same time, she yelled at the top of her lungs, *"Laird. Laird. Where in the hell are you?"* making the dogs scatter yet again, this time off the furniture.

"I'm here. Here I come," a Highlands accent responded calmly from the doorway, and I turned to see a surprisingly young man, maybe thirty-five or forty, with the cumbersome, rolling gait and physique of a bodybuilder. His arms bulked out directly from his neck, and his thighs were so thick they forced his shins to tilt out from his knees. Laird's black hair was shiny clean, cut short on top of his head and around his ears, but falling long down his back in the style of a country-western singer or a tow-truck driver or someone who wears a baseball hat most of the time. The discrepancy between his appearance and his clothing was even more curious. He was dressed like a butler in daytime housework attire: striped pants and a pristine white shirt with the sleeves meticulously rolled up. A green butler's apron hung from around his neck and was tied neatly around his waist.

"Well, don't take so long next time. We're dying of thirst. We'd like some Dr Peppers, please." She had thrown back her head and now glared at him imperiously down her chiseled nose.

"Certainly." He turned to me and I saw that his eyes were surprisingly gentle, velvet brown and definitely twinkling. I could tell he wanted to explain. "Would you like a lemon or a lime with that, miss?"

"Lime, please."

"Certainly." Laird evaporated in his black, high-top, weight-lifter Nikes as soundlessly as he had appeared.

"Please." Victoria indicated a lumpy love seat, which three of the dogs had vacated. "Make yourself comfortable." She settled herself in a straight-backed chair and crossed her bony legs.

I wondered what I was doing there on this beautiful sunny day, sitting on a grubby sofa caked with dog hair in a cold, clammy castle before a dark, cold hearth, talking to a batty matriarch, ordering Dr Pepper with a wedge of lime, and wondering which son she considered a son of a bitch. It must have been James, because William didn't have a mean bone in his body.

"Laird."

God, I wished she'd stop doing that.

He reappeared with the drinks on a rimmed silver tray. "Yes, Miss Victoria."

"I don't think we need a fire, do you?"

I didn't know which one of us she was addressing, but it was about five degrees in there and I said, "Yes," at the same moment Laird said, "No," and Victoria said, "I agree. Stop hanging around me. Don't you have any work to do?"

"Yes, I do. Will that be it for now?" Laird turned again to me. "Can I bring you anything else?"

"All set," I answered.

"I drink only Dr Pepper until three o'clock in the afternoon and then I switch to champagne. French champagne if I have company and the domestic brew if it's just me and the kids."

"Sounds like a good plan," I said, pulling my sweater around me. "From now on I'll remember to call after three."

"Smart girl." She sucked the savory pop through a straw and then smacked her lips.

"What 'kids' do you mean, Mrs. Hewitt?"

"William and Miami, of course. James is a dead man as far as I'm concerned. Is that why you're here? Has he done something? If you've come to tell me he's dead or in jail, don't expect me to lend a hand or shed a tear."

"Neither. Did you hear about the shooting at the Cancer Research dinner Tuesday night?"

"Sure. You mean old Clay Parker? He was a Nazi spy, you know. Sneaked over here during the war. Even so, I don't see why you'd pick him to kill when I understand all those Johnsons were lined up at a table like ducks in a gallery. Miserable bunch of bastards. I would have mowed down the whole lot of them. If you're here thinking James had something to do with it, you'd be wrong, because he's one of them. That's what this mess is all about."

"What mess?" I asked innocently. I wanted to hear her version.

"What mess? Gadzooks, girl." She blinked her eyes a number of times and the whites got bigger. "Where are you from? Jupiter?" She'd fixed her eyes into a scary stare. "James is trying to have me declared incompetent, you idjit, so he can sell the Broken Arrow to the Johnsons for their High River project. This is a struggle to the death. We're living in a Greek drama out here. Where in the hell have you been?"

"I'm sorry . . ." I began.

"You youngsters are all a bunch of brainless, gutless wonders. All you do is watch television all day and try to grab all the money and land you can get your hands on. Here's how it works, although you probably won't understand it." She drew herself up straighter, her eyes got bigger and bigger, and she looked more and more like Hermione Gingold in *Gigi*. To tell you the truth, I would not have been a bit surprised if she'd broken into a round of "The Night They Invented Champagne." But she stayed on track. "This is my ranch and I'm leaving the whole thing to the Nature Conservancy. That's what I need to do. It's the right thing. Have you taken a look around here? It's wall-to-wall shacks. All these new people from who knows the hell where. There's no room to breathe. I'll tell you another thing, Miss Whoever-You-Are." She leaned forward and frowned at me. "Who in the hell are you anyway?"

"Lilly Bennett."

"Oh, sure." Victoria slapped her hands on the chair arms hard enough to lift her off her seat and howled like King Henry the Eighth. "You *wish* you were Lilly Bennett. She's much younger and prettier and thinner than you are. Good Lord."

She shook her head with disgust. "Lilly Bennett, my foot. If you're Lilly Bennett, I'm Dorothy Lamour. Whoever the hell you are, if you're here to try to get the Broken Arrow, get the hell out. You'll get this ranch over my dead body. Literally."

"I'm not here to get the ranch, Mrs. Hewitt," I said, trying to calm her down. "And I'm not here about James . . ."

"Call me Victoria, dear girl." She picked up her highball glass, tossed the straw over her shoulder, and took a ladylike sip. "I've known you your whole life. How are your parents? I never see them anymore."

". . . I'm here about William. I received an anonymous fax saying that he killed Clay Parker. And actually, it's William I'm here to see."

She slammed the Dr Pepper down on the coffee table so hard it sounded like a gunshot. "Well, that's a good one. Why didn't you say so in the first place. William'd never hurt a fly. Besides, he was home here with me all night. We all had dinner together. *Laird. Laird. Where in the hell are you?*"

Listening at the door as usual. "What?"

" 'What?' Are you taking the day off or something? Get William in here."

"He's gone to the rodeo grounds with Miss Miami. They left about an hour ago."

Victoria snorted. "*Miss* Miami. Don't you just love it?"

"How do you and Miami get along, anyhow?" I asked.

"I love her like a daughter. *And* a son." She and Laird howled like dogs, showing off their bad English teeth. "Get it?"

Before her surgery, Miami had been a Texas football star named Scott Powers or something. Maybe Laird had been his sister. Now he was Victoria's attendant. And brother, she needed one, too.

Six

No wonder Victoria's vanished from sight, I thought on my way to the Coliseum, home of the Roundup Rodeo, which was clear on the other side of the city. She should be in a straitjacket. And the more I thought about it, the more I imagined that was exactly what Laird would be doing now, wrestling her into one and attaching her to a stake in the yard with a big chain so she could wander around the Great Lawn.

The cell phone rang as I pulled into the rodeo grounds. It was Jack Lewis.

"What do you think you're doing?" he yipped. Jack always sounded like his shorts were too tight when he talked to me.

"Excuse me?"

"We're just leaving the Broken Arrow, where we've been informed by some muscle-bound houseboy that old lady Hewitt's sick and in bed and that she already talked to the police half an hour ago. You know anything about that?"

"So I went to call on Victoria Hewitt. So what? I've known her my whole life and she's a lonely old woman and I dropped in for a cup of Dr Pepper. I visit shut-ins all the time."

"Spare me."

I could tell Jack had no idea what to do next. He always locked up around rich people. Starting with me. "Need some help on the Clay Parker case?" I asked innocently.

"Nah. We'll have that wrapped up by lunchtime. Incidentally, you wouldn't by any chance have gotten an anonymous fax this morning about William Hewitt, would you?"

"No," I said. "What'd it say?"

"Nothing. Say, one more thing: You ever get that fancy whirlybird off the roof?"

"Yes, thank you, we did." He was such a jerk.

"That was sure some kind of pathetic show. Sure gave everyone down at the station a good laugh, though."

"Fuck you, Jack." I slapped my phone closed and then flipped it right back open and dialed Paul Decker's office. I told his secretary to tell him to get over to the rodeo, that I thought I had a pretty interesting, pretty imminent client for him, Paul being Roundup's big-time, fancy defense lawyer.

Jack's biggest problem, I thought as I hung up, was that he was always underestimating me.

William was sitting in the stands watching Miami astride her warhorse-sized, snow-white gelding, Trooper, rehearsing for the afternoon show. The Coliseum was dark except for the brightly lit ring, and silent except for Trooper's thundering hoofbeats and occasional grunts and groans as Miami moved through an intricate series of tricks.

William jumped to his feet and embraced me. "Hear you were out at the ranch. Saw Mother."

I nodded.

"Laird called. He didn't know whether it was all right for him to let you see her or not." William smoothed his tie down his chest and buttoned his tweed sport coat. "I told him no problem. I told him right, didn't I?" His eyes were hard to see behind the thick glasses. "I mean, she didn't chase you around or anything?"

"Well, for starters, I think you ought to take that gun away from her."

"Laird didn't tell you?"

"Tell me what?"

"They're blanks. We took the real bullets away years ago. She's a little unpredictable to be walking around with live ammo."

"Tell me about it."

Miami, who was six three and weighed about two hundred pounds and, as usual, all in white, including her cotton candy hair, galloped past balanced on her head. Both her arms and her legs were fully outstretched.

"Hi, darling. Hey, Lilly," she managed to burp out before Trooper charged down the big ring and she did a handspring back onto her feet. Her buttery-soft, high-top ballet shoes made up to look like white leather cowboy boots with fringe and silver medallions, had about an inch of stickum on the soles.

"You look wonderful, darling." William waved back to her.

"Actually, I'm not here about your mother's gun, William," I said. "You're about to experience some major action any second, and I want to ask you a couple of questions before the police arrive."

"The police?"

"I got a fax this morning, an anonymous fax, that said you're the one who shot Clay Parker."

"I what?" William gasped.

"Look, I know you didn't shoot him, but it's a lead that has to be followed up, and the police received the same information. As a matter of fact, Chief Lewis just told me over the phone that he expects to have the case wrapped up by noon, and that can only mean one thing—he's coming to arrest you."

Miami zoomed past again, this time doing a spiral from Trooper's rump. "Hi, Willy-Billy," she called.

"Looking good, my angel," William called back absently. "What do you mean, they're coming to arrest me?"

He could not have been more at sea if I'd smacked him over the head with a frying pan.

"Where were you on Tuesday night at eight-fifteen?" I asked.

His mouth had gone dry and he licked his lips and sucked in his breath as though he were fighting to get his brain to work. "Well, I, uh, let me see, uh, we, we were at the country club for dinner. I mean, we were there. Miami and I. But we had dinner back in the Cheyenne Room. I guess we left just about the time it happened, but we went out the back entrance. We didn't even know anything about it until yesterday morning."

"You know how to fly a helicopter."

"Sure I do. I flew Hueys in Vietnam. But—" The light dawned and William laughed. "God, Lilly. If you think for one second I'd shoot someone at the country club and steal your chopper . . ."

"I don't think that but I want to explain a few facts to you right now: You had the motive and the opportunity to shoot Clay Parker, and I'm telling you, Jack Lewis is going to walk through that door any second and arrest you for murder."

Somewhere along the way Miami had picked up two flaming hoops and she stood in the saddle, holding one in each hand. I guess she planned to jump through them or something. "Hi, honey-bunny," she yelled as she zoomed past at a dead run.

"Looking good, lovey," William tossed over his shoulder, a memorized line. "Well, hell," he said to me. "What am I going to do? I didn't have anything to do with killing Clay Parker."

I started to answer, but one of the stadium steel doors screeched open and Jack Lewis and little Lieutenant Evan appeared like a couple of back-lit thugs from a Grade-B gangster movie. All they needed were violin cases.

"William Hewitt?" Jack called, the heels of his black snakeskin boots hitting the cement floor like tap shoes.

"Yes?" William answered meekly.

"I'm placing you under arrest for the murder of Clay Parker."

"Not so fast, Chief Lewis." A deep, stagy, resonant voice thundered from a darkened staircase and then another figure in a big cowboy hat and long Western coat emerged from the gloom. "My client has nothing to say until I've had an opportunity to consult with him."

It was Paul Decker, there to save the day.

William smiled like Christmas. He looked just like Joel Gray.

Seven

On his way out the door, William Hewitt asked me to discover who was trying to pin the murder on him, and naturally, I accepted. Nothing made me feel better than accepting large retainers from rich clients.

The next logical move seemed to be for me to drop in at the A.L. Johnson Land Company headquarters and see how they were dealing with the loss of one of their key executives. I called my office on the way downtown. "What's up?" I asked Linda.

"Mickey Giardino just called from Las Vegas. He said some, and I quote, 'real, first-class antiques, I mean stuff worth a fuckin' fortune,' were stolen out of his office at the hotel and, I quote further, 'I need someone classy like my Bennett babe to get them back, 'cause these people have class written all over them and before I remove their fuckin' kneecaps, I want to be sure it's not a fuckin' misunderstanding we're dealin' with here.' "

" 'Babe'?"

"His exact words."

"I like that. Guy's got good taste for a mobster." I grinned, recalling a wild evening spent in bed with Mickey after a boxing match in Detroit a hundred years ago, before I knew he was the heir apparent to the Giardino Family fortunes. The Giardinos being one of the most powerful mob families in the country. At the time, I thought his name was Michael Ellis and that he was a model for Ralph Lauren. That's what he said. I've always been such a sucker for a handsome face and a big bank-roll, and boxing turns me into a complete animal. Conse-quently, Mr. Ellis/Giardino and I never had anything that could be described as an actual in-depth verbal conversation, unless you count saying yes a hundred and fifty times in a row, each time louder than the last, as a conversation.

"I'm not even slightly interested in getting into any sort of mob-related business," I told Linda. "That's a whole different deal. Call him back. Thank him for his inquiry. Tell him we're booked up at the moment and refer him to Triple-A Smack Security in L.A. What else?"

"That's it."

"Okay. Get a retainer agreement with an invoice down to William Hewitt's office in the Prudential Building. Jack Lewis just arrested him, but William should be back at work in about an hour."

"Great," Linda said enthusiastically. She loved to send out invoices as much as I did.

□ □ □ □

There are certain irrefutable facts we all learn as we get older, and one of them is that how we look, how we're dressed, how we present ourselves, determines how we're treated. For instance, whenever I travel—even on our own planes—I always wear a good suit, pearls, and all my makeup, because I never know when something is going to go wrong—like a mechanical problem or weather—and I'll get stranded and need to throw myself on the mercy of a power-crazy airline bureaucrat who has dominion over the last seat out of town, or the night manager of some sort of lodging—doesn't matter if it's a five-star resort or a roadside motel—with only one room left and twenty people screaming for it.

Here's the criteria they use to choose: They always pick the person who looks as though he or she can pay the bill, is someone they would want as a return customer, and is someone who looks like he or she will do the least amount of damage to the premises. What's always incredible to me is how the gorilla wearing the high-tops and tank top and baggy shorts, displaying more hair on his back than most people have on their heads, never understands this particular bit of logic. But he doesn't and he's always getting cut out, and consequently he's always in a state of rage, and then he gets home and beats up his wife and kids and girlfriend. And he blames it on the rich people.

The other night at a dinner party, one of the women guests got into a big harangue over something like: Why are women judged by the way they look? She ranted and raved about how people, especially women, should not be judged by their appearance, that it was vastly unfair, that some very special women were completely overlooked because they didn't take especially good care of themselves. Since I was a guest at this particular event, I refrained from saying something like, Get a life. Or, Did it ever occur to you it is possible to have brains *and* beauty? Or, We all have standards. I might have passed along those comments if I'd gotten any sort of indication she had even the slightest interest in anything anyone besides herself was saying.

What had gotten her wrapped around the axle in the first place was a crack someone had made about Hillary Clinton's legs and did you notice that men are never judged by how their legs look? Well, I think that if you don't want to be judged by your legs, you should keep them covered up, the way men do. And that's the end of that damn subject.

Just for the record, I happen to like Hillary Clinton, and the fact is, everyone can't have everything. She got to be First Lady so she didn't get killer legs, too. I, on the other hand, have lovely legs, but I will never be First Lady or President. And there it is. I'm just so grateful to have Richard.

I believe form and function, style and substance, whatever you want to call them, can go hand in hand.

The reason for all this weighty discourse is that I had begun my day in the office with nothing much planned, made a move downstairs to the saloon, where I had a couple of cold-fighting shots of whiskey with my breakfast coffee, paid a visit to Victoria Hewitt's Wild and Nutty Kingdom out there at the Broken Arrow, and rescued William Hewitt at the Coliseum while his wife flew through flaming hoops. I had on a pair of jeans, caked-up roughout boots, a red cotton turtleneck, a heavy wool plaid shirt, and pearl earrings. I was clean but I didn't look that great and, believe you me, the receptionist at Johnson Land noticed.

When I stepped from the elevator into the executive penthouse and waded toward her through waist-deep, dark red carpeting, she didn't say anything. Just regarded me suspiciously across the bleached-pine rampart of her horseshoe desk with a bored expression that said, This must be another one of those cud-chewing invertebrates from Arkansas who're always showing up claiming to be related to the Johnsons.

Life-sized photographic portraits, printed to look like oil paintings, of Adelaide and Tom Johnson hung on the wall behind her. The photographer had drabbed down their teeth, minimizing them somewhat, but Tom's toupee—a glossy acrylic brown pompador shimmering over a fringe of gray—was unmistakable. Also, in the picture, his sunburned face looked open and friendly, but my first impression when I'd met him Tuesday night was of menace, possibly a wife-beater.

The place was as quiet as the bottom of the sea. When I arrived directly in front of the receptionist, she still didn't talk, and I wished I'd had my hat so I could have turned it in my hands.

"I, uh, I'm, uh," I began. "I'm Letitia Vanderbilt." The name flew out unexpectedly and I almost burst out laughing. "But everyone calls me Tish. I'm down from Montana," I added, which would explain why I looked the way I did, which was pretty good for Montana.

She looked at me with glassy, violet eyes. Either she was wearing wall-to-wall contacts or she was from a different planet. Her nameplate said La Donna Baker. She had a ring in one of her nostrils. "What is it you wanted?"

"Well, La Donna—what a pretty name that is—I'm only in town for today and I wanted to see about a couple of places in that new housing development you've got."

What I wanted to say was, What do you do when you sneeze? How do you blow your nose with that ring in it?

"You mean Buckingham Terrace?" She flipped a yellow pencil back and forth, clicking it on the top of her desk. Her long, pale, lime-green and lavender acrylic nails looked as if she'd stuck pointed jelly beans on her fingers.

"Doesn't sound right."

"Windsor Greens? Mayfair Close?" The words tumbled from her cherry lips like salads on a list of daily specials she was sick of reciting. A tongue-piercing stud clicked against her teeth. "Kensington Mews?"

What in the hell were these Johnsons thinking with these stupid names? "No, it had the name of a river in it."

"High River Ranch?"

I snapped my fingers and pointed in her face. "That's the one." At least I didn't say, hot damn. I couldn't believe how quiet the place was—no phones, no people. Just plain silent. As far as I could tell, she was the only one there. I supposed the sales department was on another floor. "I'd like to buy a couple of those."

"There's no one here who can help you today. You'll have to come back next week."

This was very strange. All the real estate salespeople I know would crawl off an operating table in the middle of open-heart surgery if they thought you'd buy something.

"Like I said, I'm only in town today and I've already got up to a half-million in financing approved."

For the shacks the Johnsons built, that would come to about five houses, and even La Donna, with her string of kiss-shaped tattoos climbing up her neck like a little red snake, knew it would be a mistake to send me away. She knocked her tongue against her front teeth like someone knocking on a door while she considered my request. Another child raised under a rock.

"Come on back," she said, "I'll show you the stuff. I can't tell you everything about them, but I know pretty much."

"Where is everybody?" I asked as I followed her down a silent, red-carpeted corridor decorated with a series of phonied-up photographs showing how beautiful the Johnsons' developments were and how good-looking everyone who lived in them was.

"Las Vegas. American Homebuilders' Convention."

"And they take the whole company?"

"Pretty much."

"No kidding. So why didn't you get to go?" I felt as if I were stumbling through Times Square like Dustin Hoffman in *Midnight Cowboy* next to a prostitute whose platform shoes were higher than her skirt was long. "I'd say you got shafted."

"Tell me about it." She swept an errant lock of zebra-striped hair back over her shoulder. "I always get screwed."

Sooner or later, you ask enough questions, people give you their map. I didn't tell her that maybe if she fixed herself up a little, tried to look like a member of the human race, she'd get invited along more often.

"That's lousy."

"Adelaide says I can go next year. I've only been with the company for three months. But I don't think it was very fair. T.J.'s secretary's only been with him for two months and she got to go. I'm planning to quit."

"T.J.?" I asked.

"Oh, sorry. Mr. Johnson. Stands for Thomas Jefferson. Like the old-time president. Thomas Jefferson something or other. Know who I mean?"

"Yes, I do. Thank you."

"I just call him T.J. Everyone else calls him Tom. He's the number-two person after Adelaide. You want a cup of coffee?"

"That'd be great." I followed her into a small catering kitchen. "Yeah," I commiserated as she filled two turquoise Johnson Land Company mugs that had old lipstick smudges around the rims. "You definitely got screwed. My sister and me, we go to Vegas three, four times a year. Stay at the Sands."

"I thought they tore that down."

Hell. What did I know? I haven't been to Las Vegas since 1971 when Mark Rothberger and I got drunk at lunch celebrating his fifth divorce, rolled on to Frontier Airlines, and flew to Las Vegas. This was before both Mothers Against Drunk Driving *and* ATM cards, and neither one of us had any cash. All he had was his American Express card and a twenty-dollar bill. So we ended up eating some big, disgusting, unbelievably expensive dinner in a French restaurant in a hotel, I think it was the Sands, where he could use his AMEX card. It was a totally weird experience. There we were in this hermetically sealed room that was supposed to be the Tour d'Argent or something. Like the Tour d'Argent, tall windows wrapped around the corner, but instead of looking out on the Ile de la Cité, they opened onto the gambling floor—five million slot machines and gaming tables lost in a fog of blue cigarette smoke, flashing lights, and ringing bells announcing jackpots.

"Yeah," I said to La Donna. "That was a real tragedy. We went to watch them implode it. You know, when those famous brothers from Fort Worth, or Amarillo or wherever, glue dynamite all over the inside and then the whole thing collapses inward and the next time you see it, it's in some Bruce Willis movie."

"Cool," she said. "Here's the stuff." She extended her hand to indicate I should step into a large conference room.

"So where do the Johnsons stay?" I asked.

"Well, Adelaide and T.J. have their own houses there— they go all the time—but they keep the company people at the Mirage."

"My sister and me always stay there now. It's nice."

"I wouldn't know. I heard Garth Brooks stays at the Bellagio."

The posters in the conference room were different from those at the banquet two nights before, showing the project was almost double the size of the one they'd unveiled. The model, which was maybe eight by twelve feet, showed every cut, groove, and gouge in the land and about seventy-five-thousand three-bedroom ranch houses. The streets were named after birds: Mockingbird, Finch, Raven, and so forth, and each one had eight versions: Mockingbird Lane, Street, Way, Court, Place, Terrace, Mews, and Cross. It looked like the old Anaconda copper mine in Butte—a Westerner's version of the Circles of Hell.

"Wow," I whistled. "This is ten times bigger than I thought. How in the world did they put all this land together so close to town? You'd have to pull some serious strings to do something like this where I come from."

"Yeah, it's pretty cool, isn't it?" She walked slowly around the table, which was surrounded with a foot-high, Plexiglas fence. "Tom made some special deal with the Secretary of something, that Nicky guy, about getting rights to some national forest land. It was all very hush-hush, cost him a bundle from what I heard, had to make all sorts of promises and stuff. The Vice President even called up here one day," she bragged. She had no idea of the magnitude and the illegality of what she was telling me. I assumed "that Nicky guy" was the Secretary of the Interior, Nicky Harmon. "Do you know Senator Adam Garrett?"

"Well, I wouldn't say I know him, but I've sure heard of him."

"He's real cute. Real cute. Always brings me a box of candy." She seemed to get lost in a reverie of real or imagined trysts for a moment or two. "Anyhow, they gave a couple of acres to the Cancer Institute or something to get the government land approved, keep it all on the up and up, and then they bought a big old ranch, it's called the Broken Arrow."

"Really? I've heard of the Broken Arrow. That's a famous ranch."

She nodded. "Actually, it's not completely done yet, but old Mrs. Hewitt's crazy and her son's going to get her some help and put her in the hospital so he can sell the ranch to Adelaide and T.J. Supposed to be wrapped up pretty soon. All this stuff's real hush-hush."

"I guess."

"Yeah. I probably shouldn't be telling you all this but I could give a flying you-know-what. I'm handing in my notice as soon as they get back. These are the nicest houses, up here on this hill, I think. See? They look out on the mountains and all." She reached over the glass wall and wistfully clicked a silvery-green fingernail across a dozen construction paper roofs. It sounded as if she were shuffling a deck of cards.

"Didn't someone get murdered or something?" I asked.

She paused and looked up at me, slightly blank. "Oh, you mean Clay?"

I shrugged.

"Yeah. That was something, wasn't it. He got shot at that party the other night. His funeral's today."

My antennae shot up. I should have known this, but it's exactly the kind of information Jack Lewis loved to keep from me. "Oh?"

"They're burying him in Vegas. He was from there. Well, as much as anybody can actually be from Vegas. He was pretty old anyway."

"What time is the funeral?"

She looked at her watch. "Pretty soon, I guess. It's supposed to be at four, I think."

My heartbeat went off the charts. I glanced at my watch—almost one o'clock in Roundup. Noon in Nevada. I took a deep breath and forced myself to stay on-track. "Jeez. That's kind of fast. I'll bet his body's hardly even cold."

La Donna shrugged her disinterest. "They all had to go to Vegas anyhow, so I guess they just decided to take him with them."

"Man, that'd be something, be buried in Las Vegas. Do you suppose they have funeral chapels there like the wedding ones? Like Elvis can be your minister or something?"

"Cool." She laughed. "Except this place is called Wood-lawn or Forest Lawn or something. Doesn't sound too Elvis-y."

Eight

I looked around the big Bennett Corporation hangar. The Gulfstream was gone. That meant Christian was off somewhere on business and I could help myself to whatever was left on the line: a couple of Lears and the chopper. The small Lear was perfect for a quick trip to Las Vegas. "Vegas" to the cognoscenti.

"The boss must have forgotten to tell me you were traveling today," one of the senior company pilots said as he walked around the sleek little corporate jet, which had just been towed outside from its berth next to the reclaimed helicopter. "I would have had her all ready to go."

"No problem," I told him. "You know how busy Christian is."

I was grateful there had been pilots already on duty and not rubbing sleep out of their eyes. Christian got pretty steamed when I rousted flight crews out of the sack without checking with him first. Sometimes he treated the company fleet as if it were his own personal, private property, which basically it was, since my business did little, if anything, to enhance the family coffers. At least they all admitted that my career—which they thought had something to do with law enforcement of one sort or another—was vastly more interesting and productive than if I'd been flying around being a golf groupie or a party girl or simply a shopper.

Through the cockpit window, I watched the copilot flipping switches. She and the captain were both so good-looking, I wondered if they kept their hands off each other up there on those long flights when the autopilot was in charge and there wasn't anything else to do. I mean, one can study Mr. Jeppeson's navigational charts and boring computer readings just so long.

"You going for a stock sale or something?" He interrupted my thoughts, and it took me a second to figure out what he meant. Then I realized that, dressed as I was, a stock sale would be the only appropriate reason for my trip. At least I'd hidden my hair under my Stetson.

"Yes," I lied. Close enough.

"We're ready when you are." His jaw was as square and sharp as a Cracker Jack box.

"Let's go."

Not so fast.

A gleaming black Jaguar XJ-6 convertible screamed around the corner at about a hundred miles an hour, heading straight for us, and skidded to a teeth-rattling, ear-piercing, hair-raising, tire-burning stop just inches from the plane's stairs.

Oh, my God, I thought. What in the world is she doing here?

"I didn't realize your mother was coming along."

"I didn't either."

Mother tossed open her car door as though she were jettisoning the emergency window of a commuter plane during a safety demonstration, and gathered up her purse and fur coat before alighting. As usual, she looked like a picture from Suzy's column in W—as though she'd just attended a benefit luncheon at the Armory in New York City. Today she had on a peach-colored Rena Lange suit, which, with her pale face and silvery hair, made her look practically angelic. Sort of like a human Venus flytrap. One of the ramp boys ran out of the office and moved her car.

"You're a darling boy," she told him. "I hope you don't mind too much, Lilly, dear, but when my duplicate game got canceled and I heard you were going to Las Vegas, I just had to come along because Selma Colombo has been after me for months to come out and have lunch with her at the Bellagio—she's been so lonely since Tony died—so I called her up and she was free, so I just thought I'd hitch a ride."

"Selma Colombo?" I couldn't quite believe my ears. "How on earth would you know one of the Colombos?"

"Why wouldn't we? It's a perfectly lovely family. Your father and I have known Selma and Tony for years."

"Mother, they're mobsters."

"Oh, that is such a ridiculous rumor. I hope you don't pass it on. You think everybody Italian is in the Mafia? All that gangster stuff in Nevada is finished. Your father and I have gone to Las Vegas twice a year for thirty years for banking conventions and everything's been completely cleaned up."

I decided to drop it for the time being and asked her instead how she had discovered I was going to Las Vegas in the first place.

"Linda, of course."

"My Linda?"

"I hope I didn't get her in any trouble."

"What did you threaten her with?"

"Don't be silly. I didn't threaten her with anything."

Mother and I stared hard at each other. And, by God, she blinked. It was a miracle.

"I simply mentioned I hoped she'd be able to join us on the cruise for Christmas."

"Let me tell you something, Mother. This isn't a vacation; I'm going to Nevada on business. If you get in my way or slow me down, I'll have to leave you behind."

"Oh, I understand completely. Your father always says the same thing."

"But I mean it."

"Of course you do, darling. Well, I'm ready. Let's go." She disappeared into the small aircraft, trailing Miss Balmain and a fluttery chiffon scarf.

I smiled at the pilot, who had an awkward grin on that chiseled face, and shook my head. He and I both seemed to take a deep breath at the same time. Then he followed me silently up the narrow steps and pulled the door to behind him. I ducked into the tight little compartment, which could accommodate six passengers—four facing each other and two single seats behind—and buckled myself into a calfskin seat, facing forward. Mother sat across the aisle behind me. She always made a point of saying that the forward seats were for the businessmen and she, the lowly wife, would take the most inconspicuous, the most out-of-the-way seat where she would be the least trouble. She began immediately to work on her needlepoint: a petit-point purse she'd been working on for approximately six years.

I buckled my seat belt and sighed. Why couldn't anything ever be easy?

Blasting off the ground in a Lear Jet is as close as a civilian can come to blasting off on a shuttle mission or riding in a fighter jet. Free from the restrictions forced by the sensitivities of the paying public, the plane hurls itself off the ground in seconds and screams into the sky at an extremely steep angle.

I closed my eyes and let the solid blanket of G-forces embrace me, holding me helplessly in place while the giant hand of God flung us into the heavens like a comet headed for Jupiter instead of Las Vegas, which I admit is sort of a different planet.

"There's fresh coffee in the thermos, Miss Bennett," the captain called back once the elegant little craft leveled off and we were zooming through the stratosphere straight and steady—an invisible speeding arrow painted navy blue and gold from Apollo's giant bow. "And a couple of sandwiches."

I opened my eyes and watched Baby standing on the seat across from me, her front paws on the windowsill. She had leaned into the climb as the world grew small. She was an old hand at this stuff. Astrodog. She took virtually everything for granted.

Mother had stopped needlepointing and taken out her book—a biography of Queen Mary—and gave the appearance of someone reading with placid rapture. I could hear her brain telegraphing mine, "You will notice I'm not making a sound back here. Not a sound."

I called Richard.

"Where are you?" he asked. "Sounds like you're calling from a plane."

"I am."

"Oh?"

"I'm going to Las Vegas."

"Excuse me?"

"Las Vegas. I'm going to Las Vegas to a funeral—Clay Parker. Remember him? The guy whose brains are splattered all over your suit pants? I just happened to find out his funeral is at four o'clock this afternoon. I would have invited you to come along but I didn't think you'd be much interested. What with your sex kitten and all."

"She is not, I repeat—*not*—my sex kitten. I went out with her a few times when I was working at the Met. We signed the contract with her two years ago, before I'd even heard of you. End of story." I could hear the exasperation in Richard's voice and it made me feel like a real dip.

Several years ago, Richard decided to leave his safe, profitable spot at Morgan Guaranty in Manhattan, move West, and change his life. He became a champion team roper and general director of the Roundup Opera Company, in that order. He had resigned not only his business career but also a number of board positions, including his slot as a trustee of the Metropolitan Opera, whose staff he joined to learn the ropes. That's when he met the notoriously difficult prima diva Kaleen Warhurst, who was now starring in the Roundup Opera Company's high-risk, obscure season opener, Carlisle Floyd's *Susannah*.

A recasting in the American South of the biblical tale of Susannah and the Elders, *Susannah* contrasts, according to the official write-up, "virtue among the fallen with falling among the virtuous." The church elders catch dishy young Susannah bathing in the pond, watch her for a while, get more excited by her than they probably should, get ashamed, and then say it's all her fault, that she's the devil. When in fact, she is just a very nice, naïve, God-fearing young woman who didn't even know they were there. But the elders are afraid someone might have seen them, so, being men, they blame their presence on her. The ability of the soprano to convey Susannah's virginality and innocence is very, very important.

Rehearsals had started on Monday, and Richard couldn't believe what was going on with Diva Kaleen.

"This fine Bible story has degenerated into a peep show starring four horny elder tenors and a sex-fiend soprano," he said. "I knew she was juiced-up—I mean, she's got a reputation—but I had no idea. Even the stagehands are following her like dogs. It's like watching Russ Tamblyn and the Jets circling her, snapping their fingers. I just dragged her and the stage manager out of the broom closet."

"I still don't see why you don't just cancel her contract."

"Cancel her contract?" Richard's tone was uncharitable. He was always frustrated by my lack of business sense—negotiation had never been my strong suit. "On what grounds? Because my wife doesn't like her? She's doing her job, just a little too enthusiastically. Besides, when I booked her, I thought it would be fun to have her out here. She sings like an angel. When will you be back?"

"Probably not until late. I'll call. Oh, if anyone, such as my father, is looking for my mother, she's with me."

"Are you serious?"

"Yes." I whispered into the phone. "She just showed up. She's having lunch with Tony Colombo's widow."

"Won't it be kind of late for lunch?"

"Las Vegas."

Before we signed off, I told Richard that if Kaleen Warhurst even so much as looked at, or south of, his belt buckle, I would personally rip all of her famous hennaed hair out of her head.

I looked out the window. We had passed Salt Lake and entered the moonscape of the American desert. Magnificent ancient canyon lands wound like serpents through the red stone.

My next call was to Linda, to thank her for telling Mother where I was going and to have her line up a car since I didn't want to waste any time getting lost in Las Vegas.

"This is a new one," she said a couple of minutes later when she called me back. "There's only one limo service in Las Vegas, Bell Transportation, and they don't accept credit cards or checks. Cash only."

Mob.

"Name's Grady," said the driver, who had shown up in a six-door, white stretch limo instead of the black Town Car I'd requested. Mother had already been whisked away in a silver Bentley.

"Do you know where the Woodlawn Cemetery is?" I asked.

"Sure, I do." He grinned back at me in the mirror. He had on Blues Brothers dark glasses, jagged teeth, a friendly face, and a hat and collar that belonged to somebody two sizes bigger than he was. "Other end of the Strip."

I glanced at my watch. It was only two—I'd moved to Pacific time and gained an hour—and the funeral wasn't until four. "Is there by any chance a Chanel boutique on the way?"

"You bet your life. Best shopping in the world's right downtown at The Forum. I sorta thought you'd like to do a little shopping. Most of the women who come here," he sniggered, "first thing they want to do is go shopping. My wife's the same. Far as I can tell, you gals are all the same."

Maybe I was slightly oversensitive about how I looked, but I'd had it with first the receptionist at the Johnson Land Company, then the captain, and now the driver, suggesting I might want to clean up a little. I pulled out my badge and flashed it under his nose. "I'm nothing like any gal you ever met, Grady. Do me a favor, keep your eyes on the road and take me to Chanel as fast as you can. Don't worry about tickets. This is official business."

"Yes, ma'am." He spun in his seat, turned on his high beams and flashers, whacked the car into drive, jammed the accelerator to the floor, and away we went like a Russian premier in Moscow's famous Center Lane. Everything Grady knew about high-speed driving, he'd learned on television.

Nine

Unfortunately, anybody who's ever been to Las Vegas knows you can't get anywhere very fast, even with all your flashers going and Grady at the wheel. The traffic is ridiculous, especially on the Strip, which is, hopefully, unique in the world. This place is so weird, all I could do was squint out through the darkened car windows as we passed all five boroughs of New York City. Literally. There is a hotel named New York-New York and it is a reduced version of the New York skyline.

"That there's Brooklyn, and there's Grant's Tomb, and Ellis Island, and the Statue of Liberty, Harlem, and Central Park," Grady explained. "Inside, parts of the hotel are all done up like the subway. They've even got graffiti."

Graffiti on purpose. Get a life.

Then we arrived in Italy. "This here's the Bellagio, our newest, finest hotel, and over here's the Venetian."

We passed a place called Treasure Island, where two full-sized pirate ships were in the process of having a cannon battle. One of them sank. Next we arrived at a skyscraper tower where columns run from the bottom to the top ending up in what looked like under-scaled rooftop Roman temples: Caesar's Palace. And just beyond that, The Forum, where a young man in a toga held my car door.

Best shopping in the world? Depends on what you're after. It's true, all the top designers have boutiques there, but they don't exactly sell the same kind of gear in Las Vegas that they do on Avenue Montaigne or Fifth Avenue or Worth Avenue or Monte Napoleone. More like Rodeo Drive on drugs. Everything in every boutique is a Versace knockoff: serious S&M straps and rivets. Except, thank God, Chanel, which—if you go to the back of the boutique past all the nutty stuff—still has a few good suits and has maintained some sense of propriety. Ropes of pearls and chains of sparkles, while still ropes and chains, connote a different sort of lifestyle from steel links, black leather straps, and diamond-studded dog collars. Way different.

Thirty minutes and a few thousand dollars later, I walked out in a deep sepia suit with onyx buttons, black suede pumps, a smart black hat, and a triple strand of dime-sized pearls with earrings to match. And a tote bag full of disposable cameras.

Grady puckered up and whistled when toga-boy opened the door. "Why're you going to Woodlawn?" he asked once we were on the road again.

We passed more and more unbelievable sights, like for example the tallest space-needle-ish tower in the world, two thousand feet tall or something ridiculous, and on top it has a restaurant, a roller coaster, and this horrible ride where thrill-seekers strap themselves into greasy, sweaty harnesses in an elevator cage—that has vomit on its ceiling—and get raised five hundred feet in the air (remember, they're already two thousand feet up), wait for the attendant to cut the brakes, and scream like crazy, throw up, and wet their pants while they free-fall five hundred feet, and then bounce up and down on a stack of giant tires until the cage runs out of momentum. I kid you not. It made me gag just to look at it.

"You got kin there?" Grady asked.

"Yes." I answered without listening. I was still thinking about a two-thousand-dollar nightie I'd seen in the window of the Prada boutique. It was made out of two pale, pale pink organza panels—one front, one back—connected over the shoulders by thin pink satin ribbons. I was wondering whether, if I turned out all the lights, I could get away with it. Possible.

"It'll probably be pretty crowded this afternoon on account of Clay Parker's services being today, too."

"That's the one I'm attending."

"He was one hell of a guy. Excuse my cussin', Marshal, but he was. Everyone here loved him. So you was kin to Clay?"

Well, I was in it now. "Not blood kin," I said. "He was like a brother to me, but he wasn't my actual brother."

Grady nodded. "A lot of people felt that way about him." He looked at me in the rearview mirror over the tops of his glasses. His eyes were dark and bright and sharp as Baby's.

"You German?"

"Excuse me?"

"They say he was a German spy, a Nazi, but we never could hear any accent or nothin'."

"No, I'm not German. And frankly I don't think Clay Parker was German either."

"Me neither. I think it was just something someone made up. Everybody's got a story here in Vegas. A past. They catch the guy who did it yet?"

I shook my head. "Did he have any enemies?"

"None I ever heard of. Well, here we are. Old Woodlawn. Just in the manner of tourist info, in case you're interested, it's the oldest cemetery in Vegas. Only one with a few upright headstones."

Even in Roundup, where the oldest things are only about a century or so, when you say oldest cemetery, the image connotes large, leafy elms, peaceful family crypts, and mausoleums with statues of placid angels and weeping Madonnas, winding lanes, gentle hillsides, and quiet beauty. It's not like that in Las Vegas.

Woodlawn Cemetery is a large field of patchy dead grass, maybe eight city blocks square, surrounded by a sometimes wrought-iron, sometimes brick, fence with a few lonely headstones jutting up here and there like lonely sentinels on Easter Island. The landscaping consists entirely of a handful of scrub pines so wind-whipped—they only have needles in one thin row on one side—that they look like a bunch of cheap toothbrushes stuck in the dirt, along with a short string of bare cottonwoods.

The fancy entrance with a big sign on the main drag was padlocked shut with a rusty chain, so we circled around until we came to a side gate.

Grady stopped at what I assumed to be the location of the Parker funeral, since it was the only area that appeared to be ready for any sort of activity: a pile of claylike dirt covered with a sheet of Astroturf and a half-dozen crepe-paper flower funeral wreaths on stands. No one had arrived yet. I got out of the car.

It was hot. There was no wind. Not even a breeze. And as I wandered around, scoping out the place, the sun poured out of the sky like unbearably heavy buckets of quarters from a slot machine jackpot.

Sad. This was a very sad cemetery. A cemetery of mostly poor people whose names were painted, not carved, on the headstones. Few loving messages, no tender good-byes. A cemetery of people either too broke to go home or too unwelcome there, whose families would not or could not pay their way back for a proper burial. Dozens of headstones from 1930— victims of the Great Depression who had gone to Las Vegas in one last, desperate attempt to win it all back in one big roll of the dice. Stockbrokers. Bankers. Businessmen. Tycoons. Shop-keepers. All in 1930. All suicides. What incredible tragedy.

Occasionally, there would be a more prosperous-looking family plot, such as Clay Parker's, but they were few and far between, and they were all mixed together, the plain and fancy headstones. No preferred plots in evidence, just first come, first served. Just line 'em up and bury 'em. Cemetery salesmen must have it tough in Las Vegas.

I settled on a cement bench, its green paint peeling away in the heat, and brushed the dust off my new skirt.

Ten

Clay had a history here. Judging by the grave-stones. He'd been well established and I re-membered reading somewhere that after all we little cowboys and cowgirls had stopped going to the Saturday movies back in the fifties when he galloped at jaw-dropping, edge-of-your-seat speeds—so impossibly accelerated we all forgot to breathe—across the badlands and through the rocky draws and around the giant rock formations, he'd moved to Vegas and made some deals, bought some land, protected himself. Those were the big Mob days and I wondered who the partners were who had given him their blessing to prosper in this town where only the most connected and courteous survived. It looked as if he'd brought his whole family with him and buried them in Woodlawn: his parents and grandparents, maybe a brother who'd been a World War II veteran. They'd all died in the early fifties, and maybe a young wife and child, both dead in 1963, maybe in an accident or fire since they'd been buried at the same time. That's the problem with headstones—you can only learn questions from them. The Parker graves were well kept and had a large brown cement horse looking over them. Maybe the horse was buried there, too.

I glanced at my watch. Four o'clock. Grady had gotten out of the car and was peeking around a tree.

"I'm just keepin' an eye on you from over here, ma'am," he yelled. "Got my cameras all ready to go." He patted his bulging pockets.

Shortly, a thin wail of sirens, lots of them, warbled through the air with the lonesome, far-away, middle-of-the-night sound of distant fire trucks that have nothing to do with you. Two men in suits materialized from a grounds-crew truck at the far end of the cemetery, down where the Strip was, and unlocked the giant padlock on the rusted main gates. And finally, after much heaving, swearing, and cursing, as the sirens grew closer and closer and had almost reached air raid levels, got them wrestled into place. One of the men leaned back against the gate and mopped his face and head with a large white handkerchief. He looked as if he were having a heart attack. It was hotter than Hades.

Moments later, Clay's cortege turned in at a pace slower than stately. It was a dead crawl. Slower even than a New Orleans funeral when all those ancient black men stagger the casket down the street behind the jazz band and it looks as though they're all going to teeter over to the curb and die of old age before they get where they're going.

Slow. Three cops on shiny white motorcycles led. They

had to drag their feet on the ground to keep from tipping over. The white leather tassels on their handlebars dangled like wet spaghetti, not even a little flutter. Then came the white hearse, its windows solid with flowers, followed by several limousines, a horse trailer, and maybe sixty cars, all with their lights flashing. They bumped over the graveyard's potholes until they came to a silent, shimmering cinema verité halt worthy of a low-budget, black-and-white, B-grade *Godfather* knockoff. Waves of heat shimmered on the hoods of the limos—the big engines running silently to cool their occupants while invisible, unbreathable exhaust fumes thickened the air. Car doors slammed as stone-faced funeral home men—burly flatfoots with all the buttons on their dark suit jackets buttoned— showed the sweating audience of mourners where to gather around the grave. Masses of flowers were carried from the hearse and the trunks of the limousines and plopped down among the funeral wreaths. Nobody said a word. Just slammed down the trunk lids.

When the funeral director determined the stage was properly set, he directed one vehicle at a time to advance to the gravesite and spill out its VIPs.

The first person out of the lead car was James Hewitt, Victoria's errant son and brother of the accused, my client, William Hewitt. He helped Dolly Johnson—who appeared unsteady on her feet and laughing hysterically—with such unctuous solicitude it made me want to throw up.

I hated James Hewitt. How could he be such a traitor? How could he not want to fight to the death to protect his family's ranch instead of colluding to sell it? He'd always had an attitude problem—always felt the world owed him a living instead of the other way around. Hypercritical, ultradefensive, mean-spirited, and cynical. I'd never liked him as a child and I wondered if I'd always seen that turncoat in him, seen the warnings, the potential for major damage, for relishing the role of spoiler? He broke other children's toys, but never his own. He was rich and handsome but he liked to pinch girls and make them cry.

Next came Tom Johnson, smoothing his cheap shiny toupee into place over a telltale border of gray. He was a string-bean of a fellow, his face and ears were elephantine, and the full family banquette of teeth was nestled into chapped lips like slabs of cement on a sandy beach. His wife, Lucky, who had legs as long as stilts and a black hat as big as a saucer sled, followed him out of the car. The way Tom looked at her, I could tell he was the one who thought his name should be Lucky. He was as besotted with her as a mewling, drooling calf with its mother's udder.

Adelaide was the last out of the first car.

"Leave me alone," she barked at the driver, who'd offered his hand. She'd slid her way across the leather seat, so her skirt was completely around her waist, and drilled her high spike heels into the dirt like tent stakes, three feet apart. Her lobster claw fingernails were dug into either side of the door and she heaved herself into the light like Mama, the mean, chunky, drunken prison matron in the musical *Chicago,* who sings to the jailbird girls, *You be good to Mama and she'll be good to you.* Yowie. Made me clammy. Who did Adelaide think she was? Sharon Stone? This move does not work on an eighty-five-year old woman.

The car door slammed and the limo moved forward as the second and third cars took its place.

Well, I thought, isn't this interesting? If anybody wanted to pull off ranch heists or land grabs—especially with Wyoming's Land Use Bill the subject of a special legislative session and due for a vote any day—the group that bailed out of the next two cars would be the ones you'd want to have on your side. They represented America's most liquored-up, crapulent, crapulous, wenching, whoring, dipsomaniacal, and just plain crooked politicians: Our own former United States senator, Adam Garrett, whose trademark leonine hair, now flecked with gray, flew back from his chiseled, clean-cut face with studied carelessness—"I'm more sensitive than Alan Alda," he liked to claim; a couple of senior senators from New England; Secretary of the Interior Nicky Harmon; the lieutenant governor of Wyoming, the state treasurer of Nevada, and the congressman who represented the Third District, home of the High River Ranch.

Each was accompanied by a working girl, working in the world's oldest profession.

It was hard to decide which man was the most dissipated or degenerate. They tugged and buttoned their jackets around their girth and squinted their bloodshot eyes into the blinding heat. None of them put on dark glasses because for some strange reason, the media, or possibly media consultants, have declared that anyone who wears dark glasses is suspect. Innocent people have nothing to hide. Only guilty people wear shades. So politicians and people on trial always stand around in blinding sunlight, squinting, wrecking their eyes, and looking completely guilty. And like they're too stupid to put on their dark glasses.

Grady was snapping pictures mindlessly fast—like a grandfather watching his grandson on a new trike—and tossing the used-up cameras into a bush as though he'd done this a hundred times before. He made a good deputy.

The next seven cars carried recognizable mobsters and their top bosses, including my old friend from the Detroit boxing match, Mickey Giardino, who had become the chairman of the board, the Capo di Tutti Capi, last year when his father Sam died—ostensibly of natural causes—in a Staten Island steak house with a cigar clenched between his teeth and a bullet hole in his left eyeball. All the old families were represented, but there were no mob wives, no mob girlfriends, no mob women at all in sight. I studied Mickey. Even from where I was sitting on my bench twenty feet away, he still had it. The guy was a walking sex machine—a human neutron bomb that vaporized all the women he touched. He looked like a model or a sophisticated Wall Street banker. As a matter of fact, they all did—not a broken nose, black silk shirt, or scarred cheek among them. The Mob had gone mainstream. One of the bodyguards crossed over to Grady and made a big show of confiscating his camera, unaware there were a dozen, already exposed ones hidden in the weeds.

Two convertible Suburban limos proceeded to the head of the line. The pièces de résistance. The guests of honor. The showgirls. A total Las Vegas experience. On cue from a tall man in a white suit—he looked like Tommy Tune, but I don't think that's who it was—two dozen of them stood and emerged from their white carriages like the earth's most rare and exotic birds stepping gracefully from jeweled nests—all legs and feathers and bijoux. Each of them was well over six feet tall.

Japan has its geisha who can tell jokes and play those dinky long-necked guitars. Big deal. So what. We've got *showgirls* and they adorned the gravesite like elegant white cranes with their gigantic feather headdresses swaying gently and their long legs sprinkled with stardust. While Clay's white horse, its flashy regalia blinding in the sweltering sun, was unloaded from the trailer, the girls split into two lines, forming a corridor from the hearse to the grave. They solemnly escorted Clay, who had been laid out in a glass-topped shiny white casket, to his final resting place.

These would be the sort of honorary pallbearers Richard or Elias or Buck would like to have. I think they would think it would be worth dying for.

Clay Parker had been loved in Las Vegas. He was an important man, and I assumed his friends—who had substantially more connections and money than the Roundup Police Department—would be doing some serious investigating of their own. Poor Jack Lewis, I thought happily. Outgunned again.

The minister was in a plain old white surplice with a collar and a gold cross and conducted a regular Christian burial, which he concluded with, "The Johnson family invites you all to come by Clay's ranch at 53198 Blue Bird Drive for a short reception."

"Do you know where that is?" I asked Grady.

"Sure. Everyone knows where Mr. Parker lived."

The cortege left the cemetery and we crept across town at ten miles an hour—anything faster would have blown away the showgirls' feathers—into the setting sun. Headed who knew where.

I wondered what my mother was doing.

Eleven

Grady had slipped smoothly into the line, so when we pulled up at the entrance to Clay Parker's spread out in what used to be the desert, with palm trees and a white rail fence circling several acres and a horse ring with a couple of Grand Champion–quality Arabians looking curiously at the goings-on and hoping for some sugar cubes, the man at the gate had no reason to stop us.

I signed the thick guest book and joined the crowd inside. Nobody knew who I was, with the exception of James Hewitt, who hadn't spotted me yet. None of the Johnsons would recognize me, we'd only met for a couple of minutes Tuesday night, and today, with the hat and dark glasses, I could remain anonymous for as long as I liked. For instance, I could gawk at Wayne Newton all I wanted.

I've always liked Wayne Newton. I spent many happy hours slow-dancing to "Danke Schoen" with my B-57 pilot-lover in the Doom Pussy Club at Clark Air Force Base in the Philippines during the Vietnam War. So when I realized he was all by himself next to the Beluga caviar and smoked salmon, I decided to tell him so.

"Thanks," he said. "I appreciate it. Who are you?"

"My name's Lilly Bennett." I stuck out my hand and took off my glasses. "I'm from Roundup."

"Roundup, Wyoming?"

"Yup." Yup? Yup? What was that? I had butterflies and felt silly as a schoolgirl visiting with Wayne Newton—he really is almost larger than life—and so *nice*—and here I was sounding like my brother, or Buck. Like someone from Roundup, Wyoming. Like some kind of hick chick.

"I played at a county fair there a long time ago. Nice town. Or at least I thought it was until you shot my friend Clay. I understand they've arrested the man who did it." He reached for another toast.

"Here," I said, taking it from him. "Let me fix that for you."

It was a reflex from the dark ages of my upbringing, a Neanderthal move no hip twenty-first century girl would ever undertake, having to do not only with good manners but also with following the advice of my mother and grandmother, which was basically: Never let a man do anything for himself. Let him be Tarzan. You be Jane. Because believe you me, girl, if you don't, some other girl will. Granted, this message was delivered in the days when a woman's wagon was hitched to a man's star and he was as esteemed as the British monarch and the Church of England: the Provider. The Protector. The Defender of the Faith. She kept the home fires burning. The "keep your man happy" philosophy is so deeply ingrained in me, I couldn't shuck it if I wanted to, which I'm not especially interested in doing, since it's also always been a great way to get great men—they like it. Besides, I don't need to prove how tough I am. When it needs to, my rubber hits the road just fine.

My friends like to give me a lot of crap because, for example, whenever Richard and I are going through a buffet line, I fix his plate for him. Well, bottom line, I waited my whole life to meet Richard Jerome and now I've got him and they don't and I don't intend to lose him over something as silly as begrudging him gracious service that takes five seconds of my time and makes him, and therefore me, feel good.

I piled on the caviar for Wayne Newton. I squeezed some over the top and handed him the finished product. "The man the police arrested was for show. He's out on bond and didn't do it anyhow. The book is wide open and from what I've seen here today, it's hard to tell if Clay had any enemies. It doesn't look like it."

Wayne accepted the plate of toasts and sipped his champagne. "You know, you're right. That's the truth. Nobody can figure out why somebody'd want to kill him. He was just the nicest, most straight-ahead, honest-as-the-day-is-long kind of guy. And, of course, they say this Johnson bunch is the same."

I almost choked. "Really?"

"They're from Roundup, aren't they?"

I nodded. "Yup." What more could I say? "Have another."

"I don't know them very well. Clay was their spokesman

and, from what I've heard, he was pretty key to their success. Tom and Lucky built a house on the other side of me—I live right over there. Casa de Shenandoah." He pointed out the window. "You can just make out the lights. So when they're in town, we wave hello over the fence every now and then. Lucky's a great gal, and Tom seems nice enough. You probably know them better than I do."

"I really don't know them at all." I arranged a few capers on top of a salmon canapé. "I gather they have a lot of business around here."

"Johnson Land did a couple of big developments out by the dam, and I hear the houses are okay, for what they are. I know they're sold out. I haven't been out to see them." Wayne traded his empty champagne glass for a full one. "How long are you in Vegas?"

"I'm not sure. I just came for the funeral."

"Have you seen my show?"

I shook my head.

"I'd like you to see it. Be my guest tonight."

"I'm married," I blurted out. What in the hell was wrong with me? Did I take stupid pills for breakfast or something?

Fortunately, Wayne had the grace to laugh. "I'm not asking you to marry me. I'm asking you if you'd like to see my floor show."

I could tell my face had turned lobster red and was so hot I was pretty sure steam was escaping from my ears and eyes and nose and mouth. I looked at Wayne, completely horrified.

"Forgive me," I gasped. "I'm acting like a complete jerk. I don't know what's wrong with me. You probably wouldn't believe I've had dinner at the White House a dozen times, same with Buckingham Palace, met a lot of important people, been a lot of places, and meeting you has reduced me to a total idiot.

Let me begin again." I took a long belt of my drink. "Thank you. But no. Much as I would like to, I cannot see your show tonight. I truly am in Las Vegas on business and I'm going back to Roundup as soon as I'm wrapped up here."

"Last flight to Roundup goes at eight."

"I have my own ride."

"Oh?" I could tell he wanted to know what kind of ride. He knew I wasn't flying it myself, since I had about four ounces of Jameson on the rocks in my glass. But Wayne Newton was way too cool to ask. "What business are you in?"

"I'm an investigator, working on Clay's murder."

Wayne sipped his drink and his eyes twinkled good-naturedly over the rim of his glass. "You think I did it?"

"Hardly."

I looked over at Lucky, who was talking to three of the showgirls. The four of them were laughing and seemed to be good friends.

"How long was Lucky Johnson a showgirl?"

Wayne tilted his head back and dropped a handful of cashews into his mouth. His teeth were beyond perfect. "She performed at the Stardust for about ten, twelve years, I guess. She was basically Miss Las Vegas. Came from Monte Carlo and before that, as I recall, the Crazy Horse in Paris. She was Top Girl here for quite a while. She met Tom a couple of years ago and got married and decided to retire. Lots of the girls are married."

"They are?" I couldn't believe it.

"Sure." Wayne laughed. "Showgirls are the queen bees in this town. Super elite. They live in a world of their own—make a lot of money—they're the untouchables. Most of them—most, not all—live pretty normal lives. Those girls she's talking to? They're the Big Three right now, the prima donnas. Suka,

Martine, and Lana. The youngest one, Suka, with the platinum hair, she was Miss Israel and then Miss Universe. She's been voted Top Girl for three years now."

Suka was so exotic, she looked to me as if her name could have been Sheba, Queen of the Giant Cat Women. The angles in her face were carved from unblemished white marble, culminating in lips so perfect they could only have come out of a doctor's office.

"Martine is French," Wayne continued, "and does all the international Convention and Visitors Bureau work. She represents Vegas all over the world—same thing Lucky used to do. And Lana, she's English, and was married to a high school principal. I think she's divorced now. She was Sam Giardino's girl for about fifteen years."

"How old is she?" She looked about thirty.

Wayne shrugged. "I don't know. Forty. Forty-five maybe. Lana's considered old Vegas royalty."

"I didn't look that good when I was *twenty*," I said.

Wayne smiled. He had the warmest eyes.

Just then, an arm circled my waist and a man who smelled reminiscently of Vetiver pulled me close and whispered in my ear, "I thought that was you. Your secretary said you were busy."

I had been expecting him, but nevertheless, a jolt of electricity froze me in place as his breath brushed my neck.

"And I thought your name was Michael Ellis." I twisted out of his armhold.

"You might not have come to the fights with me if you'd known who I was."

"You can say that again." I laughed. "You had me convinced that brooding aquiline look of yours had to do with some kind of WASP emergency, like losing the America's Cup or being jilted in Newport or getting your Top-Siders scuffed or something. It never occurred to me you'd been brooding about how to whack your first cousin for stealing your numbers or some other family no-no."

"You . . . are . . . lookin' . . . good . . . babe." He said it slowly—every word enunciated. "Real . . . real . . . good."

Wayne was taking it all in like crazy.

"And now you're here." Mickey's fingers stroked my cheek. " 'Member that night in Detroit?"

A few months ago, this would have had major potential for turning into a seriously good time. I have always been attracted to men like Mickey, who have a hard, dangerous edge. Who slaughter the king's English but have Midas's Touch. Whose Savile Row bespoke suits veil a current of sexuality that makes them relentless animals, in and out of bed. Men who are bold and aggressive, who aren't afraid to roll the dice and take the big risk. These men make me melt like grappa gelato on an August day in Palermo.

I took Mickey's hand, removed it from my face, and kissed his fingers good-bye. "Forget it, honey. Party's over. I'm a married woman."

He nodded sagely. "A married woman with a badge. It's good. I like it. Well, at least you got my message this morning and you're ready to go to work—catch that fuckin' slimeball that stole my Fabergé eggs."

"No, Mickey," I told him. "I'm here because of Clay Parker's murder. The man accused of doing it hired me."

"You're not here on Giardino Family business?"

I shook my head.

"I'll tell you what. I'll scratch your back. You scratch

mine. I'll help you with this Clay Parker situation and then you'll help me with my eggs."

"I don't need any help, Mickey."

"Oh, babe." He kissed my palm. "That's what you think. Everybody needs my help."

Twelve

In the beginning, the mob families tacitly agreed—back before Michael Milken turned over the apple cart and screwed up the status quo with his junk bond flood of money—that they would all operate in Las Vegas as in neutral territory, sort of like a Switzerland of the desert: no wars, everybody equal. But the reality was, Mickey Giardino was unquestionably the Most Equal of Equals, the Top Man, the Kingpin. In spite of the town's newly acquired, cheesy veneer of respectability and family-oriented casinos—whatever that means—and we're-all-so-squeaky-clean-and-happy-here lovey-doveyness, the Mob still rules, and the Giardinos own a little of everything.

Although all the families were represented at the funeral

reception, it was Mickey around whom those Top Girls fluttered and chirped like bluebirds around Uncle Remus.

When Mickey introduced me to them, the fascination was mutual: They'd never met an heiress who was also a cop and I'd never seen any creatures so beautiful in my life. I studied their makeup like a scientist looking at amoebas under a microscope. Like a fourteen-year-old examining the cover of *Seventeen* magazine trying to figure out what made Claudia Schiffer look so good. What did I think? That if I tried this at home I'd look like them? That if I did a few ballet exercises I'd grow a foot and have their bodies? Yes. Of course that's what I thought.

And what did they think? That if they bought a warm brown Chanel suit and suede pumps and pearls, they'd be me? Yes. That's exactly what they thought, too.

"You are from Roundup in Wyoming?" Martine's French accent was mild.

"Yes. Have you been there?"

"No, but we will be visiting there next week."

"For Lucky's fiftieth birthday party." Lana said.

"Wait a minute," I said to Lucky. "You're going to be fifty? Really?"

"Yes." Lucky smiled and I could tell she felt sorry for me, because she was older than I and she looked so much better. I realized what it was like to be on the receiving end of how I felt about Linda, and I didn't like it. "Tom is bringing in the whole show."

"How long will you be there?" I asked the girls.

They looked back and forth at each other, but it was Suka who answered. She puckered her lips and frowned. "Maybe three days. I'm not sure." Her words were strongly accented. Her skin was as lustrous and translucent as alabaster and her body as lithe as a swan's, but her green eyes betrayed that under all that ephemeral facade, she was strong as a running back.

"We'd love it if you had time to come out to the ranch for a steak fry."

Their faces brightened. "Really? Do you mean it?"

"Absolutely. Maybe on Wednesday."

"Wednesday would be perfect," Lucky said.

Oh, boy. I forgot: Elias and Linda's engagement party was Wednesday. Linda would have a heart attack.

"Have you seen our show?" Lana asked. I was trying to figure out how she got her hair, which was pulled straight up and back, to hold on to all that plumage without tipping her over backward, and then I realized there were two sections of feathers, a smaller one in her hair and a whole shoulder rig that carried the grand array.

"No."

"Please come and be our guest tonight."

"You remember that man," Suka said to her buddies in her throaty voice, "I date from Wyoming? So handsome. Elegant beyond everything. And reesh."

"I'd forgotten about him," said Martine. "He was superb. What was his name?"

"I never forget him. Reeshard Gerrome. My Got. He was a *man.*"

Once it sank in and I got my heart to start beating again, I was about to ask, "You mean Reeshard Gerrome, as in my husband? *That* Reeshard Gerrome?" But a loud, drunken voice interrupted my train of thought.

"What do you think you're doing here, Miss Rich Bitch? Out slumming?"

James Hewitt.

I took a deep breath and then grinned at my new friends.

"Excuse me," I said and turned to face him, my brain still swamped by Suka and Richard. How old was she anyway? Twenty-five? She was just a kid.

James's eyes bulged belligerently from his head and a sneer contorted his face. It was easy to see, if you knew the signs, that the guilt was eating him alive, from the inside out. He had betrayed his mother. His brother. His heritage. And therefore, himself. These were unforgivable sins and he knew it and it was killing him.

"I'm here, James, because I'm working for your brother." My voice was calm, but inside I was seething.

"You mean the man who murdered Clay Parker?" James crowed and looked around the room, like a school-yard bully warming up the lynch mob. "He's no brother of mine."

"Funny," I said. "He says the same thing about you. William Hewitt did not kill Clay Parker and you know it as well as I do."

"The hell he didn't. He had motive, opportunity, all those things you cops need. He had 'em all."

"Let me get my facts straight here. Take this opportunity to ask you a couple of questions—it'll save me from having to come to your office." I removed my notebook from my purse and flipped a few pages. "Where were *you* Tuesday night? I didn't see you at the dinner."

"I was there. I just wasn't up front with all you swells."

"Are you sure you weren't back in the country club kitchen sprinkling sleeping powder on club sandwiches and spiking coffee with knockout drops and pulling a ski mask over your face to kill your old friend Clay? You're about the same height as the killer."

"I'd never kill Clay," James said. "He and I were on the same team."

85

I stared into his firebrand eyes and gaping red mouth. All I could see was infamy. "You're on the losing team, Hewitt, and one way or the other, I'm going to make sure they bury you so deep you'll never see the sun again."

Everyone around us was silent, and then Dolly Johnson tugged on his arm. "Come on, Jimmy," she said. "Let's get a drink."

"Where were you Tuesday night?" I repeated.

He gave me a look so hate-filled it poisoned the air around him, and then, like nuclear fallout, he dissipated and disappeared into the quiet crowd.

"Whoa," Wayne said when we'd all had a chance to catch our breath a little and settle down. "This Lilly girl means business."

"She always did." Mickey grinned at me proudly.

Just then, my pager went off. "Excuse me a minute," I said. "I have to make a call."

"Hurry back," Mickey said. "We'll be waiting."

I stepped out to the dark, empty patio to return the page. The evening had turned cold, and I hugged my arms around myself and held the phone to my ear.

The glass walls of the simple, U-shaped house framed the large patio and turned the guests inside into an exotic *tableau vivant*. Royal palms towered overhead, their fronds rattling in the breeze. To my left, I could see an empty corridor, punctuated with small, dim spots of light on the soft carpet and works of Western art on the wall, and what I assumed to be the closed doors of Clay's bedroom and a guest room. To my right was the bright white kitchen where the large catering crew moved quickly and professionally to stay on top of the party. And, in the center section of the house, the rhinestone-studded crowd flowed through the living room and dining room in waves of glitter, like schools of silvery fish.

I watched Mickey motion an aide to his side and speak quickly to him. Wayne Newton said something that made the showgirls laugh. Dolly dumped James Hewitt into a deep arm-chair and whispered something to Adelaide, who nodded and whispered to Tom, who said something back to Adelaide, who nodded emphatically. I felt like a voyeur, as though I were watching some sort of high-camp, arty Spanish movie while I shivered in the cold and waited for the pilot to answer the phone.

"I'm sorry to disturb you," he said without preamble, "but I'm in a challenging situation here. Need you to make a decision."

"Shoot."

"Your mother is on board and wants to take off. Now."

I watched Adam Garrett, a smug, satisfied look on his face, step out of the guest bedroom, square his shoulders, admire his reflection in the darkened glass wall, check his zipper, and start down the corridor. So what else was new? He was always sticking his business into someone or other. Nicky Harmon, the Secretary of the Interior, was waiting for him. He handed Garrett a drink and then led him into a corner for a private huddle.

I checked my watch. Six-thirty. "Tell her I'm on my way," I lied. No chance I was leaving this shindig—someone in the crowd had murdered Clay Parker and I had lots of questions. Lots. And I hadn't even spoken to any of those whom I considered to be suspects yet.

Whoa! Lucky Johnson came out of the same bedroom Adam Garrett had been in. Holy cow. This was the most over-sexed investigation I'd been involved with in years—Las Vegas showgirls, libidinous high-level politicians, and mobsters—all in one room. I still couldn't get over the fact that Jack Lewis and his boys weren't here, and I wondered if Mickey Giardino and his friends had stolen Clay's body from the Roundup morgue. Maybe Jack et al. still thought it was there? Yes, I realized. That's exactly what's happened.

Seven-thirty back home.

I decided to call Richard and let him know I'd be a few more hours. As I punched in our number, I remembered what Suka had said about him: "My God. He was a man." James Hewitt's shenanigans had blown it right out of my mind. I knew Richard had not sat around twiddling his thumbs and waiting for me to walk into his life. I mean, Jeez, neither one of us had—I mean, when you get right down to it, it would almost be easier to make a list of the people we *hadn't* slept with when we were single. But, Suka, the Miss Universe Queen of the Giant Cat Women? And Kaleen Warhurst? Who'd show up next? Pamela Anderson Lee?

Unfortunately, just as I'd finished entering the number, a thick-skulled goon in a baseball cap and satin motorcycle jacket materialized from around the left side of the house. An old-fashioned, gorilla-type bodyguard, with a big nose and thick glasses.

"The boss thinks it would be a good idea if you was to leave now," he told me.

"Really?" I pushed Send.

"He axed me to see that you get to your car with no problem, 'cause it can get dark on this side path." He grabbed my phone and smacked it shut and, at the same time, with a fast, professional, and painful clench, twisted my arm behind my back. I tried to shake him off, but his giant mitt had my hand bent almost parallel with my wrist. It hurt like hell. "And he didn't want you to trip or nothin'."

"I'm a guest at this reception."

"Boss says to tell you this is a private party and the family wants you to leave."

"What family?" I was waving frantically over my shoulder trying to get Mickey's attention, but no one could see into the dark outside. "Clay's family is all dead. Which boss?"

My escort was duck-marching me along the uneven flagstone path. He held me close and for a moment I felt giddy and hysterical, almost laughing uncontrollably, because his breath was like being taken prisoner by a hot dog with mustard, relish, and onions. Underneath all that I could have sworn he was wearing Coco perfume.

"The boss says to tell you this is a private party and the family wants you to leave," he repeated.

I felt a needle jab me in the butt and suddenly I was drenched with mind-freezing fear. What had he done? Oh, dear God. Not a shot. To be incapacitated by drugs was the stuff of my greatest nightmares—the midnight sweating terrors that paralyzed my lungs and jammed my voice. He dragged me off the path and held me in place until the drug took effect. Panic seized me. My heart started to pound uncontrollably, and my legs wobbled. I heard myself speak but the words that came out didn't make any sense. I'd become a movie in my head: I saw Grady running around the car to open the door. The man telling him the lady had had a little too much to drink. Grady helping load me into the backseat like a Ziploc bag of jelly as my head spun out of control and I rolled helplessly to the floor.

"Take her to the airport," came through the door as it slammed shut with a distant thud.

Thirteen

The shriek of the wheels as they touched down awakened me from far, far away. I thought I must have had a stroke—I was heavy, deep-down, lost, aged.

"Well, it's about time you sobered up," Mother said.

I fell back and closed my eyes and tried to remember what had happened, what I was doing on a plane with my mother, and it came back to me slowly as Baby crawled up my front and started licking my face.

"I wasn't drunk, Mother." The inside of my mouth was glued together and the words came out with dry smacking sounds. "I was drugged."

"What?"

"Somebody gave me a shot of something." I reached down

and gingerly rubbed my left buttock. A tender, apple-sized lump had risen where he'd jammed in the needle. It hurt. My head pounded like a jackhammer.

"Are you all right?"

I rubbed my eyes and shook my head and looked out the window. It was snowing, and I couldn't tell if it was the snow blurring the blue taxiway lights or my eyes. "Yeah, I think I am. How did I get to the airport?"

"The same driver you left with. He was very concerned. Very nice young man."

"Was there anybody else with him in the car?"

"Not that I could see." Mother actually seemed worried. "Are you sure you're all right?"

I nodded.

"I paid him myself."

Well, whoop-de-fucking-doo, I thought. Give me a fucking break. "Thanks," I said. "I hope you gave him a big tip?"

"Fifteen percent. Always sufficient."

Poor Grady. He deserved fifty percent—minimum. Oh well, I had to call him anyway about the cameras and to find out what had happened. I'd catch up with him in the morning.

The cabin lights came on and stabbed my brain like ice picks, making me wince. I groaned.

"I don't think you should drive, Lilly," Mother said. "I think I'd better take you home."

"I'm fine," I answered, not at all sure if I were fine or not. "If I have a problem, I'll pull over and call Richard."

We went back and forth a few times, but ultimately she got into her car and headed into town, and I got into mine and headed back to the ranch. I opened all the windows. It was freezing outside. Freezing. And the snow blew into the car and whirled around my face, but the air sharpened me up. After a while I felt well enough to turn on a little Gloria Estefan to help me through the curves and over the icy patches of Crazy Squaw Canyon. Before long, Buck's giant, lighted billboards emerged through the storm: HAVE A SHOT OF SASPARILLY AT THE GOLDEN NUGGET SALOON IN BENNETT'S FORT WITH WYATT EARP—ONLY $5. VISIT YE OLDE CHRISTMAS SHOPPE—WYOMING'S BEST DECORATIONS.

It was only October.

My tires hummed over the cattle guard as I raced under the wrought-iron arch at the entrance to the Circle B, and ten minutes later, my house appeared across the stormy valley—sparkling, warm, fires flickering through the windows, Richard waiting.

I never tire of coming around the bend and seeing my house sitting there on the riverbank. Built by my great-grandfather for his mother, the cabin was constructed of chinked logs and stone chimneys and had a tin roof. When Richard and I got married and decided to keep this house instead of building a bigger one, we lengthened it by twenty feet, adding a study downstairs and an upstairs bath and dressing room for him. The ground floor now contains the living room, dining room, kitchen, library, Richard's study, guest room and bath, and now has four, instead of three, sets of French doors on each side that open onto a wide, surrounding veranda. Upstairs, where our bedroom and baths and dressing rooms are, French doors with little balconies are cut into the sloping roof in each direction. There are fireplaces in every room.

I was so cold when I walked in, I was as blue as my eyes. Richard wrapped me in a soft blanket and put me on the sofa in the living room in front of a roaring fire. Then he brought me a large glass of water, two aspirins, a mug of Campbell's tomato soup laced with a little sherry, and a plate of chicken quesadillas he'd heated up.

"Who's Mickey Giardino?" he asked once I'd had a couple of bites.

"Why?"

"He's been calling every fifteen minutes."

I told him the whole story—about all the people at the funeral, including the bought-and-paid-for politicians, all the Johnsons, all the mobsters, Wayne Newton and the showgirls, and their upcoming visit to Roundup. About James Hewitt and my confusion over who had drugged me: Who was the boss the thug mentioned?

"Whoever murdered Clay Parker was at that funeral and reception. Somebody there wanted him dead but I can't figure out who or why. Why Clay Parker? And why at a dinner at the Roundup Country Club? What kind of message was that?"

"You mean Mickey Giardino, the Mafia don, was the guy you told me about at the boxing match?" Richard said.

"Have you heard anything else I've been saying? Like for instance someone drugged me unconscious and ran me out of town?"

"Sure I did. But I mean: The most erotic evening you ever spent? That's a fairly broad statement."

"Yup." I grinned at him.

"What all did you do?"

"Come upstairs." I laughed. "I'll show you."

But unfortunately, between the knockout drug and the warm soup, Richard had to carry me to bed, where I burrowed into the down puff and pillows like a hibernating bear cub. I can't be the life of the party every second.

Fourteen

Friday Morning

When the alarm went off at five-thirty I lifted my head and looked out the doors. They were covered with frost but from the early golden light that filtered through the starry designs, it looked as though the day would be a show-stopper—warm and bright. Richard and Baby were cuddled up tight.

"I'm not going riding," I groaned and burrowed back into my pillows.

"Why not?" Richard mumbled.

"Because my head feels like it's going to explode from whatever they put into that shot and my bottom feels like someone has implanted a grapefruit under my skin where he jammed in the needle." I snuggled into him. "I'll give you a hundred dollars to build the fire."

Silence.

"Five hundred."

He and Baby were pretending like they'd gone back to sleep, so I got out of bed and tiptoed over the painted wood floor, stepping from rug to rug as best I could, and built the damn fire myself.

At six, I heard Celestina's truck drive up, and at six-fifteen she came into our room with a pot of coffee and a plate of tiny warmed orange rolls. *"Buenos días."* She smiled and handed me the tray. "Time to get up. The day is a-wasting. We all have work to do."

I love Celestina. We grew up together. She is my sister and confidante. She is the fourth generation of Vargases to live and work on the Circle B, and after her divorce, when she told me she'd decided to stay on the ranch and marry the new manager and not move to town and open a restaurant, I burst into tears. She was the wife and mother every busy household wants and needs. She was worth her weight in gold and that's how we treated her.

"Up. Up." She clapped her hands. If the bedroom windows had had window shades, Celestina would have been snapping them.

"I didn't get home until midnight," I said. "And I was drugged and I'm not getting out of bed until I feel like it."

"Everybody has excuses." She tucked Baby under her arm. "Come with me, my little angel. You are the only good one in this house."

"You were a big help," I said to Richard after she'd closed the door and gone back downstairs.

"I'd like to get back to that boxing match conversation."

"*Wait a minute.*"

Richard jumped back as though he'd been shot. "What? What happened?"

I started to laugh as the memory from the night before came back. "Nothink, darlink. Come here. Let me kees your leeps. You *man*. You *reesh* man. Sound familiar?"

Sunlight flooded the valley, turning the white meadows and snowy treetops in the dense forest into a Christmas card. It would all be melted by noon. Even now the dirt roads were clear, and judging by the amount of mud thrown by the tires of Elias's old pickup as it bucked and banged up the road to our house, they were starting to get sloppy.

His cab door slammed shut with a familiar hollow rattle and he stamped the mud off his boots at the kitchen door. "I had a feeling Celestina might be making pancakes this morning," he said by way of hello.

"For you, anything," she told him.

Minutes later, while I ate my peeled grapefruit sections and prayed they wouldn't add another five pounds, Richard and Elias poured rivers of melted butter across their short stacks just the way sunshine poured through the breakfast room window.

"Doesn't it ever bother you guys that maybe all that fat is bad for you?"

"Nah."

They each grabbed a section of the paper. Our family owned the evening paper, the Roundup *Evening Star,* but the *Morning News* was owned by the Butterfield family. Ellen Butterfield, the publisher, was an old flame of Elias's. For years we all thought they'd get married.

"Have you seen Ellen lately?" I asked.

Elias shook his head, not raising his eyes from the front page.

"What do you suppose she's up to?"

He shrugged.

"Excuse me. Hello? I'm here talking to you. And I would think that since you've invited yourself to breakfast when Richard and I are still practically on our honeymoon, you could at least talk to the bride."

Both men looked at me with expressions so bored and blank I could have smacked them silly.

"This is the breakfast table." I sounded so much like Mother it was great. "This is where we have conversation."

"You're right." Richard put his paper down. "What would you like to talk about?"

"Well," I began, then noticed a picture of Connie Johnson on the front page. "Let me see that." I grabbed the paper from Elias and scanned the article about the Land Use Bill—State Minority Leader Connie Johnson's legislative masterwork, which had turned her husband's family and all land developers in the state against her because it would force developers to allocate eighty percent of their property to open space. It was a great bill, and I was astonished it had been hatched by a Johnson—even if she was a Johnson by marriage. The vote was scheduled for next week and it was still too close to call.

"I don't understand, how Tom's and Dolly's brother could end up married to someone with a social conscience. How could he tolerate something so positive for our state and so negative for Johnson Land?"

"Frank doesn't have anything to do with the family company—he's got his own and he's probably keeping quiet so he can get his new golf courses approved outside of Dubois."

Richard took a bite of his English muffin. "It's total self-interest, which just happens to have a long-term benefit to the state. Short-term thinking on his part, though, for the business he's in."

"He's just as big a slimeball as the rest of them. He's probably planning to cash out and leave," Elias mumbled through his eggs and sausage. "I heard he has a lawyer on his staff who does nothing but pay off prostitutes who threaten to file charges because he likes to play a little rough. So, was there anything else you wanted to talk about?"

"Well," I began and the phone rang.

"Good, give me back the paper."

"I guess I'll have to tell you about the showgirls later."

It was my Moscow office.

Elements of the fallout following the collapse of the Evil Empire—the Soviet Union—bear unsettling similarities to the fall of Nazi Germany after World War II. Thousands of treasures: paintings, sculptures, jewels, and porcelains were missing, and now, with dollars starting to flood the Russian economy, the families of the previous and rightful owners of these objects wanted them found and reclaimed.

The result of all these missing goods—whose trails were cold, to say the least—was that my business in Russia was booming. I had sizable staffs in Moscow and St. Petersburg. My director in St. Petersburg was the former chief curator of Old Masters seventeenth-century at the Hermitage Museum. In his mid-fifties, he was widely regarded as a genius, the world's leading expert in his field. But his vast knowledge of fine and decorative arts extended far beyond his specialty, and once I had set him up as a private dealer, people brought him objects and told him things in confidence. His degree of success was astonishing—not only was he returning pieces to their true owners, but also, after only six months, the shop itself was making a fortune.

The director of Bennett Security International in Moscow was a beautiful and savvy young Frenchwoman, a former Sûreté chief inspector, whose taste, Russian language skills, and contacts, were impeccable. It was an outstanding team.

"So how are Boris and Natasha?" Richard asked when I hung up. He was having a last sip of coffee.

"They're not Boris and Natasha. They're Natalie and Dimetriev. And they're fine."

"That Natalie is extra fine," Elias said. "When are you going to bring her back here for more training?"

"Not in your lifetime. Aren't you announcing your engagement in a few days?"

"So what's with the showgirls?" Elias asked as he started in on another short stack.

"Tell you later." I pulled on my jacket and walked with Richard down to the helipad, where the chopper purred slowly. I watched it thunder into the sky with a lot of flame and glory, bearing him and Christian away like the dei ex machina they often were.

"What did happen yesterday?" Elias asked when I got back to the house.

I took my time hanging up my jacket and pouring myself more coffee, trying to gather my thoughts. "I'm not exactly sure," I finally answered.

I described to him the funeral and the reception. Wayne Newton's invitation to his show. Mickey Giardino's request for assistance. The three showgirls who were coming to the ranch for the party on Wednesday. James Hewitt's drunken accusations and his rescue by Dolly Johnson. Former senator

Adam Garrett and Secretary of the Interior Nicky Harmon. Adam Garrett and Lucky Johnson's tryst. The goon on the patio and the hypo in my bottom. "The boss says to tell you this is a private party and the family wants you to leave."

"None of it makes any sense," I concluded. "And when I got home, Richard said Mickey Giardino had been calling. Now, we all know when it comes to bosses, Mickey is it. But if he were the 'boss' the goon was talking about, he wouldn't call to see where I'd gone because the injection would have been his warning to stay away. Adam Garrett and Nicky Harmon might be up to some questionable hanky-panky but they're not going to go around shooting up a federal marshal—they might be dopes but they aren't stupid."

"Who's left?" Elias said. "Wayne Newton doesn't know you well enough to run you out of town, and even though you're still pretty good-looking, I don't think the showgirls would be exactly threatened by your presence. No offense. Maybe it was the Johnsons."

I recalled watching through the window as Dolly whispered to Tom and Adelaide, followed by some conspiratorial nodding. "Why would the Johnsons do this? And who killed Clay Parker? He was their corporate spokesman. They could have just fired him if they wanted to get rid of him."

"Let it rest for a while," Elias said and lost himself in thought. Presently, he drummed his fingers on the table, blotted his mustache with his napkin, folded it, and placed it squarely next to his plate. "Better get to work. Keep me posted on the showgirls. You would come across them just when I'm getting ready to hitch up." He hefted himself to his feet and pulled on his jacket. "Thanks for the chow, honey." He kissed Celestina and left.

I called Linda and asked her to see if William Hewitt could come to the office after lunch. Maybe he'd have some answers.

I didn't return Mickey Giardino's calls. I didn't want to owe him anything. Yet.

Fifteen

I think William Hewitt was born in a coat and tie, he was always so dapper. He arrived in a tweed sport coat with a yellow silk handkerchief, a starched white shirt, a red twill tie decorated with feathered fishing flies, flannel trousers, and cordovan brogans. He might have been little, but he looked and acted big—unlike my nemesis Jack Lewis, who was little and acted like a little weenie firecracker, piss-ant, pipsqueak. I wondered if Jack knew about Clay Parker's funeral yet, or if he still thought the old cowboy's body was enjoying its safe repose in the city morgue.

"Let's review," I said once William had taken a seat at my scarred-oak conference table, which Buck claimed was actually the table where Doc Holliday had operated on Wyatt Earp—

same claim he made about the table in the jail, along with what he claimed was Wyatt Earp's desk. I believed him about the desk—the rest of the stuff I knew he'd picked up at barn sales around the state because I'd watched him haul it all in, in the back of his pickup. I think Buck, in his slightly zapped brain, thinks I look out the window only when he's looking up at me. The rest of the time I just look at my desk or the floor. This ostrichlike shortcoming may provide some explanation of why he kept getting shot out of trees as a spotter in Vietnam: He thought he was invisible. Which also explains why he's happy here in Bennett's Fort playing the Wizard of Oz, poking his head under his table in the saloon until reality blows over.

I showed William a copy of the handwritten fax that accused him of shooting Clay Parker. "Have you seen this before?"

He picked up the sheet and studied it. "They showed it to me at the police station."

"Do you recognize the handwriting?"

"No."

"Could it possibly be your brother's?"

William scanned the characters again. "I don't have any idea. It looks like it could be anybody's."

"It doesn't make sense." I took the page back and reviewed it once more, hoping some new clue had appeared in the last five seconds. "What's wrong with James, anyway? What made him turn against you and your mother, all of us for that matter? It's as though he's declared war."

William shook his head. "I know. I don't have any idea what his problem is."

"William, honey, you and I have known each other way too long for you to think I'll buy that. Something happened, a long time ago, to make him act this way. What was it? You have to tell me because it may have a bearing on why you would be the one accused of killing Clay Parker. And if he tried to pin this on you, he'll try something else. Believe me, whatever you say does not go outside these walls. Give."

William scratched his cheek and looked out the window, where Buck appeared to be explaining to a tourist that she'd have to buy five dollars' worth of something if she wanted to use the bathroom. She was yelling. He was shrugging.

"It happened when we were in our twenties." William's face was closed, his lips tight. The words squeezed out as though each one cost fifty bucks. "I'll remember it as long as I live. The three of us were at the dinner table, fighting. Mother and James fought constantly. That particular evening the subject was how James wanted to move to Edinburgh and run the office there. Mother was telling him he wasn't ready, and he was demanding it as his birthright. That he was entitled to manage the Scottish holdings. Then she said it."

William stopped talking and looked out the window.

"Said what?" I prodded.

"She said, 'You have no birthright.' Then she told him he wasn't a Hewitt."

"What?" My reaction was so loud, it made Baby jump off her down-filled cushion and start barking.

"Then, she had to make it worse by saying she wasn't certain *who* his real father was." He gave a disgusted snort. "Can you imagine? There was no reason for her to tell him that, even if it's true. Which, if it is, answers lots of questions about why he and I are so different."

"You're right. I've never known two brothers so different from each other."

"All the same, it was just mean as hell. She was drunk, as usual, and let fly and got him right between the eyes. The damage was done—there was no way any of us could ever go back."

"She really doesn't know who his father is?"

"I hate thinking about it," William said. "It was one of those family crises when the world as you've known it changes irrevocably, forever, for the worse. When you find out nothing is as it seems, and has seemed, for your whole life. I'll never forget the look of betrayal on James's face. There was so much pain, she might as well have stabbed him. And then she realized what she'd done, and tried to take it back. Tried to turn it into some kind of bonanza for him, saying his father had been a high-ranking officer, because that's all that visited the ranch during the war. 'Some divine general or other,' she told him. 'Maybe it was Ike. Or Douglas. Or George.' "

"Poor James," I said, trying not to laugh, because truthfully, although the tragedy itself made my skin crawl, at the same time, I could also picture Victoria whooping it up with all the great generals of World War II. "No wonder he's in such a state all the time."

"It's pretty obvious he's never going to get over it. He's basically dedicated his life to getting even."

"But why would that make him want to kill Clay Parker and blame it on you?"

"I don't think he killed Parker. My brother may be bent on revenge, but I don't think he's a killer. And to answer your question: He blames everything on me. He is Cain. I am Abel."

The office door flew open and Linda zapped on the television set. "You've got to hear this," she said as the screen filled with what appeared to be the wreckage of a two-engine aircraft splattered over a field and several people milling around the debris. "It's Frank and Connie Johnson. They crashed."

"Are they alive?"

Linda shook her head. "No. Killed on impact."

We watched quietly as Marsha Maloney, who stood at the edge of the wreck site outside Cheyenne in her special KRUN-TV Nike disaster suit, told all into her wind-whipped microphone.

"Minority Speaker Connie Johnson and her husband, Frank, estranged member of the A.L. Johnson Land Company family, commuted in this King Air"—she indicated with her arm the field of twisted metal parts as though she were a restaurant hostess showing customers to a table by the window—"between Roundup and Cheyenne most weekdays during the session. Sources close to the couple say both Mr. and Mrs. Johnson were highly experienced pilots and had just taken off from the Cheyenne airport for the fifty-minute flight to Roundup when what one eyewitness described as loud popping, backfiring noises came from the plane before it nosedived to the ground in what another observer described as 'a desolate, godforsaken piece of nowhere' between Cheyenne and Roundup.

"Connie Johnson has been in the national spotlight lately as the lead legislator on the controversial Land Use Bill, which is scheduled to go to a vote next week. There have been rumors of a possible presidential Cabinet appointment. The landmark legislation has been a lightning rod for the entire state, driving the wedge deeper between two historic enemies: ranchers and real estate developers. We are joined now by Lieutenant Governor Wally Oates."

As Oates stepped into view, and started blabbing about what a great guy Frank Johnson had been, I recalled seeing him get out of one of the limousines at Clay Parker's funeral. I wondered how he'd gotten to the plane crash site so fast, unless he'd known about it in advance. The "desolate, godforsaken piece of nowhere" wasn't anywhere near the state house, and while the television stations had helicopters to get to disaster sites quickly, the state didn't. It could scarcely afford gas for its Chevys. But even I wasn't cynical enough to believe the lieutenant governor, goofy as he was, would go around blowing his opposition out of the sky. Fortunately, Marsha was on the ball enough to offer some information on the situation.

"Now, Lieutenant Governor Wally Oates, I understand that you and a delegation were on your way to Roundup today to attend a conference on child care."

Oates nodded sagely. "We got word of the crash sometime after we left Cheyenne, and, as you know, the interstate is just a couple of miles from here."

And then he and Marsha, standing in front of the fire-retardant foam-soaked King Air, reviewed the plight of Wyoming's latch-key youngsters while a local ambulance shrieked away bearing the Johnsons' smoldering remains.

No, I said to myself. No. This is not a conspiracy. Much as I may want it to be, to pep things up around here. It's not.

"You don't suppose, in your wildest dreams," I asked William, "that your brother James had anything to do with this?"

"No." William stood up and buttoned his jacket. "I mean, he's just not that nuts. Or that smart. I gave your secretary the other half of the retainer fee—you know Paul got the charges dropped? Our waiter swore we'd never left the Cheyenne Room during our dinner, and two of the busboys were in the parking lot having a smoke when we left."

"I heard. I'm not surprised." I began squaring piles of papers on my desk. "It still doesn't answer who sent the fax. Call me if you think of anything, and I'll let you know what develops from this end."

I dialed the Mirage in Las Vegas.

"James Hewitt's room, please."

"One moment." So he was still registered. The phone rang several times before he answered.

"Hello?" His voice came over the speakerphone.

I hung up and spun my chair around to look out the window, see what Buck was up to. See if maybe he was on his way into the saloon for a little mid-morning pick-me-up. I was definitely in the market for one myself.

"Mickey Giardino's on the line. Second call today," Linda said over the intercom. " 'Put the babe on the phone,' he said. What a great voice that man has." She laughed and said it again. "Put the babe on the phone. You'd better pick up."

"Morning, Mickey," I answered with a cheerfulness that I hoped he couldn't hear was forced.

"Babe," he said. "Where'd you go? One minute you're there and then you're gone. I wanted to be sure you made it home safe."

"More or less."

" 'More or less?' What's that? More or less."

"Somebody slipped me a Mickey, excuse the pun, in Clay's courtyard while I was on the phone."

"What do you mean? What're you talking about? You saying you were drugged?"

"Yup. That's what I'm saying. I was standing outside, talking on the phone, and some big goon dragged me into the bushes and gave me a shot and ran me out of town." I hadn't planned to mention any of this to Mickey, but, I thought, what the hell. I don't know anybody in Las Vegas. He knows everybody. I can be prideful and waste a lot of time for little, or maybe no, result. Or use what I've got, and improve my chances of getting some answers.

"I'll be in touch," he said when I'd finished. "One more thing. You got any leads yet on my Fabergés?" He said it like Fabberjays.

"I'm not working on your eggs."

"You are now, babe."

"Send me some pictures. I'll see what I can do."

The door swung open without a warning knock and I recognized the unmistakably languid, ambling shuffle of my deputy, Dwight Alexander. "You look like you've seen a ghost, Marshal," he said. "Let me rub your shoulders a little."

Just looking at Dwight always made me feel better. His sultry James Dean face, his roughed-up blond hair, his thumbs hooked through his belt loops, his fingers drumming incessantly on his buttoned fly, and his empty blue eyes with their knowing gaze that so far, in his thirty or so years of life, had been able to grasp only one concept: sex.

"My shoulders are fine, Dwight," I said. "Thanks anyway."

I fought back the one-dimensional images I used to have—before I met Richard and my life blossomed into a festival of unimaginable riches—of Dwight's tossing me up onto Marshal Earp's table like a rag doll, ripping my clothes off, and having his way with me. Now, my fantasies spanned the entire gustatory banquet—passing way beyond the realm of mere sex—to include such pleasures as Richard and I enjoying St. Marcellin cheese and burgundy for lunch on our private terrace at Gérard Boyer's place in Reims; or a spicy puttanesca and just-picked arugula salad and Chianti at the Marchese's villa in Porto Ercole; or luscious pasta e fagioli and roasted piglet at I Due Chippi in Saturnia; or lying in bed together for three days on a cliff above the Mexican Pacific making love, reading books, eating guacamole, and sipping rum; or sinking into a warm fur in the backseat of a limousine in a Manhattan blizzard and not worrying about missing your plane because it was our plane and wouldn't leave without us.

Compared to all that, Dwight was nothing more than an *amuse bouche.*

"I knew you'd say no." He sat on the edge of my desk and rolled an invisible bit of paper in his fingers. "Just thought I'd take a run at it."

"Sit in the chair, Deputy." I said.

"Right. Okay, here's why I'm here, ma'am. I hear you've got some showgirls coming to town."

"Where'd you hear that?"

Dwight grinned. "All the fellas are talking about it. Is it true?"

A loud whistle cracked the air outside. "Hey," Buck yelled from the street. "Hey, Lilly girl, get on down here. We got business."

John Wayne made a movie called *The Cowboys* about him and a bunch of inexperienced, innocent, preteen and teenage boys he pulled together to drive a herd of cattle across the range from somewhere to Dodge City or someplace like that. Naturally, Bruce Dern was the disgusting bad guy ringleader who tried to drown them at every river crossing, shoot them from every bluff, crush them by rolling rocks into every canyon and draw. But the kids hung in there and finally by the time they reached the railhead, they'd all grown up and turned into dependable cattlemen and tough range-tested wranglers. John Wayne was dead by then.

Anyhow, when I walked into the Golden Nugget Saloon with Dwight and saw Buck and Elias sitting at Buck's table with an open bottle of whiskey and four shot glasses, I felt like John Wayne with those wide-eyed boys.

"We hear you've got some showgirls coming to town." Buck's eyes twinkled.

"They're showgirls, not dance hall girls." I poured myself a shot. "And they're not coming to see you, they're coming for Lucky Johnson's fiftieth birthday party."

"She's *fifty?*" Elias said.

"Nevertheless," Buck, who had assumed the mantle of spokesman, persevered, "we want to be hospitable. Do whatever we can to make sure they're comfortable."

"That's right, Marshal," Dwight said and poured himself a hefty tot, but I put my hand across the top of the glass before he could pick it up.

"Sorry, Deputy. You're on duty and I believe you've got a prisoner."

"Aw, Jeez. It's just a witness protection guy. They're coming to get him at four." He slid back his chair.

I looked straight at him.

"I'm sorry, Marshal. I forgot. But do me a favor, at least let me meet them."

"I promise."

Wait until Suka gets her hands on you, I thought.

Elias and Buck and I proceeded to drink the whole bottle of whiskey and get totally hysterical about absolutely nothing. My day had been a complete waste of time.

Sixteen

Saturday Morning

Hear you've got some showgirls coming."
Art, the ranch manager, checked Ariel's
cinch. She grunted softly and turned to give him a dirty look.

"Yes. They'll be here Wednesday evening for Linda and
Elias's steak fry. You free?"

"You bet I am. Where're you and Romeo off to this morning?" He held my mare's head while I mounted.

"I don't know. Romeo, what do you think?"

Richard was listening to the conversation from aboard his
gigantic palomino stallion, Hotspur. "I don't care, but if you
two don't stop yakking, it'll be time to turn around and go
home for lunch."

Light had not even begun to hit the mountaintops west of

the valley and the sky still slept in its deep cobalt dome. Flat, cold moonlight bleached the ground.

"You plannin' to help out this weekend or you hung up with opera business?" Art squinted up at Richard through the smoke from his home-rolled cigarette, which punctuated his words like a conductor's baton.

"I never let opera business interfere with roundup. You know that, Art. Come on, sugar," he said to me. "Let's get up to the main camp before the biscuits are gone."

Richard might have been a Yankee, born and bred of rock-solid *Mayflower* stock, but something had put the frontiersman's glint in his eye and freed his soul, letting it make the leap to reincarnation as a full-fledged Westerner. It had been more than summers on his grandparents' ranch in Cody that made him change—lots of Eastern kids come West for the summer but they can't, or won't, or don't want to, shake loose of their native yacht-club, lobster-roll, clambake, Watch Hill ways. There's got to be an ache, a longing for room, for space to see the sky farther than should be possible. A lack of fear of openness—open country and open hearts. A trusting that your fellow adventurers will save your skin, dig you out of the snow, come for you against all odds, but until they do, you will be fine on your own—a self-sufficient survivalist. Just you, your horse, your dog, and your gun. That's all you need.

Westerners can go for weeks without saying a word. We figure, let the Easterners do the talking; they've got nothing better to do, nothing better to look at, no cattle to mind.

So this morning, as Richard and I set out for the high camp where the last leg of the cattle drive would begin with sunup, we clipped along in silence. Letting the chill air slice our lungs and our horses' footfalls make the noise. Richard had made the transition fully. From Easterner to Westerner. From Wall Street banker to rancher. From happily divorced and single to happily married. I glanced over at him, silhouetted against the dark dawn horizon—his hat pulled low, nose irregular, chin square, a dust bandanna loose around his neck, his carriage tall and straight in the saddle, his grip gentle on the reins.

I would do anything for him.

He would do anything for me.

We wound upward on the moonlit road until we crested the hill and saw the cook fires at the main camp. There were already a number of figures moving in the light of the flames. This was a big weekend—the start of the biggest ranching weekend of the year: roundup—when hundreds of head of our prized Black Angus cattle would be driven from all points of the ranch into the main corrals, loaded up, and shipped out.

The roundup was my most, and least, favorite ranching activity. I loved its history and tradition and the hard, physically challenging work as much as I hated the end result. Plus, I think the cattle knew what was happening. A number of them were already milling around and lowing, getting everyone else stirred up.

Cook poured us each a mug of coffee. There're lots of old jokes about how the cookie's coffee is so strong you can chew it and so forth. It's true. It's part of the tradition of the range. If the coffee isn't strong enough to make you choke, then it's coffee for sissies. You want decaf in Wyoming? Go down to Denver and get a latte.

And stay there.

Seventeen

Monday Morning

The last eighteen-wheeler pulled away after midnight Sunday leaving everyone physically and emotionally drained—but in spite of the constant activity, my head had never quite emptied of all thought. I never quite reached that blissful point of doing only what I was doing. And, as I stood in the shower early Monday morning, drenched with sunlight and hot water, the questions looped through my mind with an irritating taunt: Who shot Clay Parker? Who sent the fax? Who drugged me? And why? What would happen to the Land Use Bill now that Connie Johnson was dead and there was no one to lead the charge? Was the plane crash an accident?

I buttoned the tiny buttons on my ivory silk blouse, clasped a thick twist of pearls around my neck, and decided that, as far as I could tell, there didn't seem to be any answer but James Hewitt. Except that he had been at the country club dinner party, visible the whole time, according to all reports, although I didn't remember seeing him there. And, I reviewed for the millionth time as I zipped my skirt, he had been at the post-funeral reception at Clay Parker's house—drunk, belligerent, and again, very visible. He had answered his phone at the Mirage shortly after the Johnsons' plane crashed. Of course, he could have flown to Cheyenne late Thursday night, sabotaged their King Air, and returned to Las Vegas. That would be easy to find out if he'd flown on a commercial flight, but the Johnsons had not only their own planes but also private landing strips on all their developments. It would be simple for him to sneak in and out. Besides, Wyoming is so wide open, it would be easy for the entire United States Army to sneak across the state in broad daylight.

I picked up the phone and dialed.

"Yo," Elias's voice came through. I was sure he hadn't been to bed yet.

"I need you to do me a favor."

"Forget it. I'm on vacation. Besides, I'm not doing you any more favors. I'm just now getting so I can walk without limping, and the physical therapist says that possibly, emphasis on the 'possibly,' if I don't do anything crazy, *and* if I continue therapy three times a week, I just might, emphasis on the 'might,' be able to have three-quarters motion with my arm in another year."

"But . . ."

"And, how is it that I, who have survived firefights in the Laos jungle, rappelled down sheer cliffs into raging, tropical, snake-infested Cambodian rivers, and jumped out of helicopters into booby-trapped V.C. buildings—just to name a few adventures—have a sister who is more dangerous to my health than Pol Pot or Ho Chi Minh or a Somali warlord? No. The answer is *no*. N.O. I don't even want to hear what it is."

"It's right up your alley."

"No."

"Has to do with secret airstrips and plane crashes. Real life espionage stuff. But you don't have to fly anywhere. Unless you want to. This will be as safe as driving to the market."

"No."

"Come on, Elias. Help me out."

There was a long silence. I knew he had his eyes closed and was shaking his head.

"I'll give Linda an extra week off," I pledged. "With pay. You're going to Hawaii. I'll pay for the whole trip. Four Seasons in Hualalai or wherever. That is a *huge* gift. Come on, Elias, you don't leave until Thursday night. That's four whole business days. You can do this whole project with two phone calls and an hour in the helicopter."

"You are such a bitch."

"Grady speaking," a sleepy voice answered.

"Grady, Lilly Bennett here. I'm sorry to call so early." I glanced at my watch and realized it was already six-thirty in Las Vegas. Time to be up. "Do you want me to call you back?"

"No. No. That's okay. I was just lyin' here doin' nothin'." His Oklahoma accent was friendly.

"I need to ask you some questions about last Thursday night."

"Sure thing."

"What can you tell me about the gorilla who carried me to the car?"

"Well, like I told that fella last night"—Grady's bedcovers

rustled into the phone—"he was good-sized, not too big, not too small. Just average, I'd say. Said you'd had too much to drink and helped me load you into the backseat."

"What fella last night?"

"When I got home, a man from Mr. Giardino's office was waiting for me wanting to know the same thing. Seems like you've got some important friends."

"Yes," I said. "Seems so. What about his voice? Anything distinctive?"

"Well now, you know, Marshal, I think anyone not from the Panhandle sounds pretty funny. So I couldn't say. I mean he wasn't French or Japanese or anything like that. If that's what you're after. One thing I thought was kinda odd—he had on gloves. Black leather gloves. It was chilly out, but I don't think it was cold enough for gloves."

Black leather gloves. You always know, in cheap movies and television shows, when the husband leaves on his gloves while he's mixing the cocktails, it's not a good sign. Somebody—usually the wife—is about to get murdered. Unfortunately, she's generally so vapid, she never asks, for instance, "Dear, why are you making the martinis with your gloves on?" She never sees it coming.

I thanked him, gave him my number, and told him to notify me if anything came to mind. The minute I hung up, Linda called.

"How's that sunburn?" I asked her.

She'd gotten baked over the weekend. She'd been right there on the range with Elias every second, never failing, never flinching, heading back to the main ranch house a couple of times each day to make sure Marialita, Elias's cook, and her kitchen crew didn't need any last-minute help getting ready to feed lunch and dinner to the hundred or so hungry hands who rotated steadily in and out of the roundup. Linda would be the best thing that had happened to our family since my Chicago blue-blood sister-in-law, Mimi, married my brother Christian and became the ideal international corporate wife, and my own beloved Reeshard married me, and got me off the streets.

Like most Wyomingites, Linda had a built-in Bullshit Detector. She knew about ranching and she knew about men—and she'd never let either one of them get the best of her. She could see right through Elias. Right down to the little pointy toes of his cowboy boots. When I told her I'd invited some Las Vegas showgirls to her engagement party, she didn't bat an eye. She knew—in spite of Elias's big stud talk down there in the saloon with Buck, all the lies they told each other about all the women they'd handled and the ones they had lined up waiting for them—if one of those showgirls as much as winked at her beloved, he'd die of fright.

"My face is the same color as my hair," she said. "Don't forget, you're supposed to be at the Customs House at nine o'clock."

"On my way." I clipped on an earring. I looked extra sharp in an absinthe green suit with just a tiny speck of golden thread in the cord that bound the jacket and skirt. I was going to supervise delivery of a Renoir to a client. The work had been stolen from his family during World War II and had surfaced in my St. Petersburg antique store. The same greenish yellow as my suit appeared in the painting, and I thought it would look smart on television, because while I don't advertise or look for publicity, I don't shy away from it either. I'd had enough bad publicity—like appearing naked in that video with the judge—that now, when I know I'll be on television or in the papers, I take particular care to look my best. It was like putting money in the bank against that rainy day the judge's wife decided to release the tape. Everything is relative, of course, and as my body aged in real life, it remained slightly younger in the film, so maybe by this point, I'd be glad if people thought that—bad as I looked then—that was what I looked like now.

Last time I'd driven into town, I was wearing old jeans and a wool shirt and had ended up in Las Vegas. Today I wasn't taking any chances with my appearance. I was halfway through the Canyon—Baby balanced on the front seat with her paws on the dashboard, hoping to spot something to eat tossed out along the side of the road—when Elias called to report the NTSB had discovered what appeared to be table sugar and metal shavings in the propeller turbines of Frank and Connie Johnson's King Air. His call was followed immediately by one from Linda saying Tom Johnson wanted to meet with me and I was to come by their house at Sugar Hill as soon as possible. At least this time, I was dressed for the job.

As a matter of fact, today I felt ready for anything. Even a call from the Secretary of the Treasury saying that this was now a federal case—after all, Connie Johnson had been a powerful government official and her plane had been sabotaged, which made her murder an assassination—and, in spite of the fact that it was legitimately an FBI case, seeing as how I was already closely involved, the Secretary would tell me he expected me to lead the investigation.

Dream on.

Eighteen

In the oil and real estate glory days of the nine-teen-eighties, money hemorrhaged across the range and down the streets of Roundup like a gully-washer of greenbacks. Housing developments sprang up across Wyoming and Colorado and decimated the range like carbuncles. After the crash, it took years for those projects to sell out, but finally they all did, and now the grab-ass developers were at it again, with the A. L. Johnson Land Company leading the pack.

Their newest entry was the Sugar Hill Country Club and Ranch Estates. Ranch Estates, don't you love it? It is so indicative of what someone from Arkansas would build in Wyoming. The fact is, one either has a ranch or one has an estate, their only connection or similarity being that each has a residence.

An estate has a manor house and a ranch has a ranch house. We don't have estates in Wyoming. We have ranches, spreads, farms, and yards.

So I was especially interested to see what the Sugar Hill affair had to offer.

The whole damn place was surrounded by a fancy brick wall. And there was a security gatehouse with an armed guard. And it wasn't some Don Knotts, either. This guy looked squared-away and had a side arm in a shiny holster.

Now, when I was growing up, all this property had been owned by the Stafford family, and was called the Stafford Farm because they had milk cows. Molly Stafford and I had gone to school together and were good friends. In the fifth and sixth grades, we took turns spending weekends at her farm and our ranch. We rode our cow ponies all day every day and pretended we were in England and our horses were hunters and we'd try to make them jump fences and old fallen trees. Which was seldom successful. We would make those sturdy little pintos head for the obstacles at a dead run, our rationale being that if we got enough momentum, they'd have no choice but to sail over. They would become National Velvets, and we would be transformed into Elizabeth Taylors. Fortunately, we were good enough riders so that we seldom got thrown when they put on the brakes just seconds from what promised to be a glorious launch. Every time. The truth is, in all my years of riding, I've never experienced that thrill of soaring weightlessness as my horse took a mighty leap over a jump. Every now and then I can get Ariel to jump a log, but she has to think about it for a long time, and it can't be very big. On the other hand, she can power-haunch up and down rocky cliffs that would make a Thoroughbred lie down and burst into tears.

The point of all this is: The Stafford Farm had been basically flat, not much motion in the terrain, with big cotton-woods along the Dry Creek Irrigation Canal. So after the guard cleared me through the gate at Sugar Hill, I could not believe the change in topography. I literally could not believe it. It looked like the Adirondacks.

Shored up by escarpments of telephone poles, the golf course undulated with hillocks and bluffs, pools, creeks, and ponds. The "rough," traditionally trees and shrubbery and deep grass, was packed with enormous ten- and twelve-thousand square-foot gray stucco mansions.

Tom and Lucky Johnson's fieldstone, red brick, and stucco house sat at the top of a hill—a masterpiece of Rocky Mountain Gothic.

Lucky opened the door. "I'm so glad you could make it." She extended her hand. "Please come in. I fixed us a pot of tea."

The foyer and living room ran together, straight out to the deck. In spite of the glass Western wall and soaring ceiling, it was murky as a cave inside—a German beer house with black, hotel-lobby-style area rugs with a flowered pattern and over-sized nut brown furniture upholstered in deep burgundy bro-cade. Bottom line, the Johnsons had managed to reduce the most spectacular view on the face of the earth to a velvet paint-ing. The Wind River Range looked like a cheesy wallpaper mu-ral pasted over the big windows. Plus, the place stank of stale cigarette smoke.

Lucky looked wildly out of place, like a model on a quiz show whose smile never changes for the entire half hour. "Mind where you step. We just finished the house last week and there's still a stray cable here and there. It's taken ages."

I followed her across the living room to a fully loaded tea table.

"Milk? Sugar? Tom and Aunt Adelaide are going to be a

minute or two—they're on a conference call." She handed me a delicate white cup decorated with tiny colorful flowers. Her hands were graceful—pale with long fingers and smooth oval nails. "Would you like a tour?"

"Absolutely."

She led me into their bedroom, a bilious assemblage of mauve and silver—a stage set, done up to a mass market decorator's dream of mass marketable perfection. The only personal touch appeared to be a small blurry black-and-white photo on her dressing table. The Johnsons lived in a model home. And everything in it could be purchased at Wal-Mart.

We stopped by the sliding glass doors that led to the bedroom balcony, cantilevered over the eleventh tee.

"Where are you from?" I asked her.

"Las Vegas."

"No, I mean originally."

"Oh," she paused. "London. I was born in London."

Lucky turned and looked at me and for a second it seemed as though a veil had fallen away. I saw so much going on in her eyes, I wanted to sit down and talk to her for hours. There was that instant connection of *simpático*, understanding.

"How did you end up here?"

"That's such a long story." She laughed. "I can't imagine you'd be interested."

"I am. Very interested. I think everybody wants to know where showgirls come from. You aren't exactly the run-of-the-mill girls-next-door—how did you start?"

Her look weighed me with a mixture of shyness and skepticism. She gestured toward two lilac bargello wing chairs, and as she sat down, the image of this elegant woman in such a gaudy setting was so jarring I couldn't believe it. But we all have our reasons for doing things, for the decisions we make, and in spite of what Wayne Newton said about their being the queen bees, I think the life of a showgirl must be very hard. Sooner or later time runs out, your shelf-life has expired, and if you haven't made provisions, you're out in the alley with the rest of the week-old bread. An aging broad with extra skin starting to gather around her kneecaps. Lucky Johnson's life could have been much worse than this. Much, much worse.

She stirred her tea and laid the spoon gently in the fragile saucer. "I started dancing when I was three. Ballet school. And I had a real talent, a gift. By the time I was ten, I'd received a scholarship to the Royal Academy of Ballet, and at twelve I was part of the corps. Unfortunately, by the time I was fourteen, I was also over six feet tall." Lucky laughed. "Six three, actually. Which meant that when I was *en pointe*, I was almost seven feet tall."

"Wow."

"Wow, is right. Not much future for a seven-foot-tall ballerina, especially since most of the male dancers are no more than five eight or nine. It became obvious I could not continue. So, when I was seventeen, I went to work as a model in Paris, but I hated it. My life was dancing and I was lost in that world of models. Most of them have nothing going on in them except their beauty. Dancers compete with each other, but in the end we're part of a corps. Models are all free agents. It was a very difficult time for me.

"Then one day, a friend of mine said they were holding auditions for the Crazy Horse Saloon. Do you know the Crazy Horse?"

"Sure," I said. "Everyone does."

"I said no. I was not a stripper."

"She said, 'Crazy Horse girls are absolutely not strippers. They're all just like you. Classically trained, giant dancers.' But still, I didn't want to do it. I didn't want to think of what my mother would say. I thought it would probably kill her. Then three other friends called to tell me about it, and then the producer of the show himself called and asked me to come audition. So finally I did. And after two years, I became the principal dancer there."

"Can I ask you a very personal question?"

"Possibly."

"What was it like, the first time you were out there topless?"

Lucky smiled. "It was amazing. At first, before I went on, I thought I was going to faint I was so scared. But then, when I stepped onto the stage, into the lights, I'd gone to work. And the truth is, there's so much to think about. First of all, you're dancing and kicking in very high-heeled shoes, so whether you're fully dressed or not, one of the primary focuses is always not to fall off the stage. Plus, the headdresses can weigh as much as twenty pounds, so you're also concentrating on keeping your headdress from toppling and pulling you down with it. You just can't be worried about your breasts. They really become another part of your costume."

"Amazing," I said, knowing that if I had to go out on a stage with no top, I would simply have to shoot myself.

"You know, not to brag, but there are lots of tall women dancers in the world, but only a tiny handful of us can be showgirls. We not only have to be superior dancers, we have to be physically very beautiful—our faces and our bodies. These shows cost thousands and thousands of dollars to stage—the costumes are incredibly beautiful and lavish, and so, when you're out there in all your feathers and bijoux, and the audience is smiling up at you, what you feel is beautiful.

"Truthfully, the worst part can be the women in the audience. Some of them are so threatened by our nudity that they sit with their hands over their faces. It's really sad. It's not as though we were out there doing a bump and grind with men sticking tens into our G-strings, showing our all. But they are so insecure in themselves, they are humiliated by our physicality."

"How did you end up in Las Vegas?"

"Oh well, I moved to the Lido"—we could hear Tom's voice calling down the hall—"from there to Monte Carlo, and then to Las Vegas. Pretty common route. We'd better go."

"How long do you work out every day?"

"Six hours."

There were so many more things I wanted to ask her. I loved hearing her story, and in spite of what appeared to be candor, I knew she was telling me about half. The framework was authentic, but Lucky's sophisticated grace undoubtedly concealed a story of sacrifice and degradation. She could not hide how hard she was inside.

"One more question," I said as we stood up. "What has been the reaction to Frank and Connie's plane crash?"

The clear gentian eyes settled on me. "Frank and Connie who?" she said and turned away.

Nineteen

Lucky showed me the way to Tom's ground floor study, but she did not stay, and as I entered, I watched two men disappear down the hill in a golf cart. All I could see were their backs, but I could have sworn those were James Hewitt's trim, tight shoulders in a navy polo shirt, and Adam Garrett's hair underneath a black straw Greg Norman cowboy hat. Another cart was parked outside the door, plugged into the wall. A bag of clubs was loaded.

The room smelled faintly of nervous sweat and sweet aftershave. And menace.

Tom had on golf clothes—a multicolored striped polo shirt and baby blue trousers. He and Adelaide were waiting for me. She circled the round conference table like a barracuda, a predator in a reptile-print silk dress, running her arthritic, knobby hands across the chair backs. Her skin was dry, and I could hear it snagging the upholstery. Her big grouper eyes never left my face—sometimes it even seemed they were both on one side of her head—and the way they settled on me—that flat bloodless fish-eyed stare—made my skin crawl.

"Glad you could make time for us on such short notice," Tom said jovially. "We received word this morning from the NTSB that Frank and Connie's plane was sabotaged." He remained behind his desk at the far end of the room, like a picador in a bullfight ready to duck behind a screen if the bull got mad.

I stayed by the door.

"Someone put something in the gas tank," he continued when he saw I wasn't going to move. "Gummed-up the works."

"I heard. Doesn't look like you're too broken up about it."

Tom and Adelaide ignored the remark.

"We'd like you to find out who's doing these things," Tom said. "First, Clay Parker. Now, Frank and Connie. Seems like somebody's out to get us, or at least disrupt our business."

"Are you saying you'd like to retain me?" I asked, keeping my voice level, while Adelaide circled.

"Yes." Her voice cracked like a whip. "That's exactly what he's saying. Does he need to give you an engraved invitation?"

I turned to face her. "You know, Adelaide, I've never liked you. And I particularly disapprove of the business you're in. And I don't like your tone of voice. And, frankly, I really wouldn't mind or care if you and your entire family got wiped off the face of the earth. I might even join the line of people wanting to hold the gun. So thanks for the tea."

"Hey. Hey. Hey." Tom held up his hands. "Hold it. Damn it, Adelaide, we need some protection here. I'd at least like to hear what she thinks." He looked at me hopefully. "What's your take on all this, Lilly?"

"I think it's an inside job. Some member of the illustrious Johnson clan, some one of your lieutenants has run amok."

"Don't be ridiculous," Adelaide said.

"Who?" Tom asked.

"She doesn't know what the hell she's talking about, you dunce."

"Just a hunch." I grinned.

I quadrupled my fee.

"That's insane," Adelaide croaked. "It's usury."

"I know. But it's what it is."

"Maybe if you bought less expensive clothes you could charge less. Besides, you don't need the money. If you were a good Christian, you'd do this pro bono since the Cancer Institute is a beneficiary."

A good Christian. Don't you love it?

"I'm happy to recommend another agency to assist you, Ms. Johnson," I said. "If you want me to work on the case, this is how much it costs. I know it's high and I'll understand if it's more than you're willing to pay."

"It's ridiculous." She dug in.

"No problem. You called me. I didn't call you." I removed my dark glasses from my purse. "Good luck."

"Hold it. Hold it." Again, Tom thrust his arms in the air like Richard Nixon declaring victory. He had sweated through his shirt and rivulets of perspiration dribbled from beneath his toupee into his collar like dew down a mushroom stalk. "Now listen, Adelaide, we could be in some danger here. Clay and Frank and Connie, they're all dead. Murdered. I don't think they're coincidental. We could be next. Lilly has already been involved with this case. I want someone to get to the bottom of it, maybe even keep an eye on you and Dolly, and Lucky and me. Who knows what could happen next, what this person or people have planned."

"I don't need anyone watching me, you hopeless little pud," Adelaide sneered. "I can take care of myself. And that wife of yours is so tough, she could bring Baghdad to its knees."

"You take that back. Lucky's a wonderful girl."

"Get it through your thick skull, Tommy-Boy, she's no girl. She's pushing sixty if she's a day and she's nothing but a gold digger. How much money did she spend on this ridiculous house? Millions. And what did you get for it? A giant whorehouse."

"Don't push me, Adelaide."

I felt like I was on the set of the "Beverly Hillbillies."

"And if you want more truth, here it is: Your brother Frank Johnson was a troublemaker since the day he was born. And you know as well as I do that Connie was nothing but a stuck-up liberal Boston debutante. As far as I'm concerned, we're lucky they're dead."

"Aren't you even a little bit sorry?" Tom asked her.

"Not a damn whit," Adelaide declared. "And I won't pretend I am. The Land Use Bill is as dead as she is. With them gone, nothing can stand in our way. From where I stand, we don't need anybody's goddamn help or protection, because read my lips: Ding, Dong, the witch is dead."

I felt like spitting, and frankly, I was a little surprised they didn't. It certainly would have been right in character.

Tom spoke. "I'm hiring Lilly, and that's final."

"Suit yourself. You want to have these Bennetts looking

down their noses at you all day long, be my guest. You leave Dolly and me out of it." Adelaide slammed out, clomping up the stairs like a bulldog.

"Please sit down," Tom said when she was gone. "Let's get this worked out."

"Tom," I told him, "I'll only work for you if you are completely honest with me."

"Of course I'll be honest. Why should I lie? Our lives are in danger."

"What is James Hewitt's role with Johnson Land?"

"He's our lead consultant, a kind of closet lobbyist, on the Land Use Bill. It's no secret we've pulled out all the stops to get it quashed."

"Like putting sugar in your brother's gas tank?"

"No. No. No way we'd do anything like that. We're fighting this fight fair and square. We're under far too much scrutiny to pull any punches."

With every sentence, Tom Johnson seemed more and more Nixonesque. An individual so lacking a moral compass, so blinded by his love of money, he honestly could not tell the difference between right and wrong. And he was banked by two motivated manipulators: James Hewitt, who had a vision, a clear agenda for revenge, and Adam Garrett, a power-hungry influence peddler. Put the three of them together and you had a troika of formidable proportions. They would believe they could dominate the world. Wyoming, anyway.

Why should I care if they had protection or got murdered or not? My reasons were as selfish as theirs: I wanted to hit them where it hurt, in their pocketbooks. Take their money, the more the better.

And I didn't want them to win.

Twenty

One last thing," Tom said as I prepared to leave his study. "Lucky and I are having a party on Thursday night. You might have heard, it's Lucky's birthday and just happens to be the Grand Opening of Sugar Hill. We're bringing Wayne Newton and the entire floor show from the Stardust—putting it on in the ballroom over at the country club. I'd like you and Richard to join us. We have a lot of important people coming in for it. You'll be impressed."

"Thanks," I answered. "I'll check with Richard but I'm sure we'd love to come."

It wouldn't take any great brain to figure out the people who impressed me and the people who impressed Tom Johnson came from opposite sides of the universe. I'm impressed with parents who forgo soccer and lacrosse practice in favor of having dinner together—you only have a small window of time to build your family as a unit, and it starts when they're young and it starts at the dinner table, and face it, the chances of Little Johnny or Little Suzie being the next Pelé are basically nil, but the chance of building outstanding people is right in front of your nose. It's like these corporations who have to spend a kajillion dollars taking their executives off to Outward Bound for team building and trust. One of the reasons they have to do it is because these individuals have no idea about teams or trust because their parents didn't teach it to them at home because one child was at soccer, one was at lacrosse, and one was home alone playing video games and having potato chips for dinner.

Madeleine Albright impresses me, too, but I didn't imagine she would be at the Johnsons' Grand Opening of Sugar Hill Country Club and Ranch Estates, either.

"How big is Bennett Security?" Tom asked.

"Not huge, but we've never had an assignment we couldn't handle."

"That's what I wanted to hear. The three top girls arrive tomorrow, and I'd appreciate it if you could arrange for someone to keep an eye on them. It'd be a disaster if something happened. They'll have rehearsals and so forth, and the producer will be with them, but I'd like it if your people'd make sure they stay out of harm's way."

"What about Wayne?"

"He'll just fly in and out."

Rats. "Have your office fax me all the information and we'll handle it."

□ □ □ □

Lucky walked me to the car. I could tell there was something she wanted to tell me, but didn't know how to start. I asked her about James Hewitt.

"What about him?"

"What do you think of him?" I said.

She shrugged. "I stay out of Tom's business affairs, so I don't really know him very well. He seems nice enough, I suppose. When he's sober."

"Do you know he's trying to have his mother committed in order to sell her ranch to Johnson Land?"

Lucky's face colored. She nodded. "It makes me terribly sad. How could anybody do that to his mother?"

"Do he and Adam Garrett come here often?"

"Not that I know of."

She appeared totally detached—not just from her husband and his life, but oddly enough, from herself as well.

"Would you like to have lunch one day?" she asked tentatively.

"I'd love to."

"You would?"

"Absolutely," I said. "How about tomorrow?"

"That would be great. I haven't made any friends since I moved here. Women are very put off by me, as though they think I'm going to steal their husbands." Lucky laughed. "So far, I haven't seen one I'd want."

Starting with her own, I suspected.

Twenty-one

Elias stomped up the steps and burst through the door, his arms loaded with burritos and bottles.

"Snacks," he yelled. "Let me put this down so I can give you a squeeze, my little darlin'." He and Linda were perfectly suited—a couple of shy, self-conscious, road-worn, aging geniuses, as sweetly innocent in their love as Romeo and Juliet.

"What did you find out?" I helped myself. I hadn't had lunch and the rich, tangy fragrance of Marialita's fresh, salty taquitos and fiery salsa filled the air and made my mouth water.

"I don't think much of anything." Elias rolled open a burrito and ladled in about a cupful of jalapeño/tomatillo salsa. Then he rolled it back closed and ate practically the whole thing in one bite. "A dozen and a half private aircraft took off from Las Vegas between the hours of ten Thursday night and six Friday morning," he said through the beans. As he talked he poured most of a bottle of Cuervo Gold, a little triple sec, about a cup of fresh lime juice, and a few handfuls of ice into the blender, which he then fired up. "Twelve of them filed flight plans," he called over the racket. "Six for California, three for Chicago, one for Roundup—yours—one for Minneapolis, one for Toronto. None for Cheyenne or anywhere else in Wyoming. I confirmed arrival on all twelve. The other six were cleared for takeoff without plans. Any of them could have headed to Cheyenne."

"Do you know what kind of aircraft the other six were?"

He swiped the rims of three large bowl glasses with fresh lime and then twirled them in a dish of salt. "As best the controller could recall, there was nothing fancy. All twin engines. No jets."

"What about their tail numbers? Can't you trace them that way?"

"Nope. You can file or call in any tail number you want. The guys in the tower aren't going to check."

"You're kidding."

"No, I'm not kidding." He poured the margaritas into the glasses and handed them around. "Airports are airports. They aren't jails where you need passes to get in or out. All you have to do is call in and get cleared for landing or takeoff. If you want to file a flight plan so people know where you're going, that's up to you. Or you can file a phony plan. Or change it in-flight. You can do anything you want, as long as you get air traffic clearances along the way. *Bon appétit.*"

Honest to God, Elias made the best margaritas on the face of the earth. Not great enough to distract me totally, though. I was frustrated by how we could track a possible flight from Las Vegas. It was hard to believe planes just fly around and nobody keeps track.

"All right, all right," I said. "What about landing? Doesn't somebody write it down when a plane lands?"

"Well, sure if the field's open. But if it's not, you just land. If the lights are out, you click your radio button three times and the lights come on. It's a no-brainer. It'd be simple to fly into Cheyenne—it's dark from eight at night until six in the morning—sabotage Connie and Frank's plane, and take off again without anyone knowing the difference."

The phone rang. Linda answered, had a brief conversation, hung up, and turned on CNN in time to see an indignant Janet Reno in her red suit saying, "No one gets away with the assassination of an elected government official. We will track these people down and prosecute them. The Justice Department will seek the death penalty in this case. I have instructed FBI Director Louis Freeh to make this a top priority. The U.S. Marshal Service has been on the case since the accident on Friday, and U.S. Marshal Bennett and Director Freeh will be cooperating closely. Thank you."

We all swallowed our mouthfuls of tequila in one big gulp.

"Whoa," said Elias.

"God," I said, a warm, happy glow filling my stomach. "I hope to hell Jack Lewis is watching."

"He'll be in the bathroom by now."

The phone rang again. "Yes, she is," Linda said into the receiver. "May I ask who's calling?" She stood a little straighter. "One moment, please." She punched the hold button and squeaked, "It's Janet Reno."

I cleared my throat and smoothed my hair. "Marshal Bennett." My voice was crisp as could be—no margarita in sight. I knew she was calling to say that the statement had just been her way of public acknowledgment and thanks for what I'd done so far, which was basically nothing, and the FBI would take it from here. I could handle the rejection. I would take my big handshake, kiss-off, pass-the-baton-to-the-Big-Boys like a woman.

"Good afternoon, Marshal Bennett. I'm glad to catch you in your office. I won't take a lot of your time. Did you just see the news conference?"

"Yes, General Reno, I did."

"I understand you've been working on a wide range of possibilities in this case." A euphemism for nobody has a clue which way to go.

"Yes, ma'am, that's correct."

"Do you have any idea yet who's behind it?"

"No, ma'am, I don't. There are a number of individuals involved, some high-ranking politicians, some nobodies. It's possible that this murder and that of the old cowboy star Clay Parker are related because of Wyoming's pending Land Use Bill and the Johnson family's stake in it. It's too soon to tell."

"You know Director Freeh?"

"Yes. I know him well. He and I have cooperated on a number of cases. I admire him enormously."

"Well, apparently it's a mutual admiration, because he told me—I hope you're sitting down because this one's going in the record books—he thought we should leave the investigation in your hands."

"You mean the FBI would back up the Marshal Service?"

"Can you believe it?" She laughed.

"No. But don't ask him twice."

"Don't worry, I won't. Is that no-good, reprobate brother of yours, Elias, helping on this?"

I looked at Elias, who was smiling at Linda. He looked placid as a cow. I kicked Elias's leg and pointed at the phone.

"Yes, ma'am. He is."

"Good. Give him my best. He's saved our bacon a few times. That man is a true American hero."

"Yes, ma'am. He is."

"Anything you need, let Director Freeh know personally. He will cooperate to the maximum. And good luck, Marshal. We expect results."

"Thank you, ma'am." I answered, but by then the line was dead.

"What'd she say?" Elias and Linda asked at the same time, and when I told them, we all whooped and hollered and did high-fives and had another drink for good measure. Then I described my meeting with Tom and Adelaide Johnson, and Tom's request for protection for the dancers.

"But, actually," I said, taking a bite of steamy burrito smothered in salsa, "I think what's required here is surveillance on James Hewitt and Adam Garrett. I think James was pretending to be drunk in Las Vegas and made a big show out of confronting me so that people would remember it. Then, I think he got into a plane and hightailed it back to Wyoming. So, what I'd like for you to do . . ."

"Forget it, Lilly. Today's the start of our vacation. Linda and I are practically on the plane for the Big Island."

"You don't leave until Thursday."

I worked him. Hard.

"Special, *personal*, request of the Attorney General of the United States," I said. "She loves your ass."

He looked at Linda.

"We weren't going to do anything this week anyway," she said. "Except catch our breath from roundup."

140

"What do you want?" He finally caved.

"I just want you to keep an eye on Hewitt and Garrett."

He spewed his drink across the floor. "Is that all? What are you going to be doing? Getting a manicure?"

I looked at my watch. "Oh, I'm so glad you said that. I'm late."

"Give me a break."

I used the time under the dryer, while the color baked into my hair, to think. The word "family" didn't really apply to the Johnsons. I'd never met a more disconnected group—they were beyond dysfunctional. They were individuals who shared the same name and business interests and that was it. Otherwise, they were true barbarians—the sort who eat their young. If I wanted to feel sorry for them, it would be hard. I think the Pope himself, Christ's representative on earth, would be hard-pressed to squeeze out a tear on their behalf, no matter how devout they were.

I also wondered where I was going to gather up all the help I needed to keep an eye on the girls from the Stardust. Things this big simply did not happen in Roundup.

That night, it came to me.

Twenty-two

Tuesday Morning

Good morning, Mother," I said. "I hope I'm not calling too early."

It was six.

"Good Lord, Lilly," she said, once I'd explained what I wanted. "I can't be baby-sitting a bunch of girls like that. What on earth would I *do* with them?"

"I don't know. You're a smart woman, you'll come up with something. Believe me, this is a delightful group of ladies, and it's important work you'll be doing. I'd do it myself if I could," I told her, which was true. "You know, I'm working this case at the personal request of Louis Freeh and Janet Reno."

"She's a Democrat."

"For God's sake, Mother. Help me out. Forget I mentioned Janet Reno. Think about the showgirls. They're targets. You'll be in danger."

That got her. Snoop Sisters at Work. "What time did you say they land?"

Dwight was slouched in my chair spinning it around when I walked into the office. He jumped to his feet.

"Morning, Marshal."

"What's up, Deputy?" I put my briefcase on my desk with one hand and Baby with the other, where she stood like a statue looking out the window for Gal and Pal to drive up and the day's fun to begin.

"Well, it's kind of boring around the jail. No prisoners or anything. So I thought I'd see if you had any other kind of assignment for me."

I looked at him and smiled. "You know, Dwight. I think I have the perfect assignment for you." I picked up the phone and dialed. "Mother? I've assigned Deputy Alexander to assist you today. He'll pick you up at eleven."

"Oh, jeez, Marshal. I like your mother," he lied. Nobody but Dennis the Menace liked my mother. "But I was sort of hoping I could work with you directly for a change, maybe help you out with those showgirls. I hear they're coming in and Secretary Reno herself said you're in charge of their protection."

"I'm in charge of a murder investigation, Dwight. The showgirls are another issue altogether."

"Well, you know what I mean."

"My mother's expecting you at eleven, Deputy." I handed

him a slip of paper with my parents' address. "Stay sharp. Get the Suburban washed. Keep your eye on the ball. Be a professional."

"Yes, ma'am." He took the address from me and shuffled out of the office and down the stairs like a twelve-year-old going to the dentist.

"These arrived in the overnight." Linda laid a stack of eight-by-ten color photographs on my desk. They were of Mickey Giardino's Fabergé eggs, four exquisitely enameled, jewel-encrusted objects.

I studied them briefly. "Ship them to Demetriev in St. Petersburg," I told her. "If they come on the market, he'll be one of the first to know."

"Kaleen Warhurst called looking for Richard." Linda went down her checklist. "She said something had happened to her laundry at the hotel and she wanted him to call the manager. She was really rude. What's with her anyway?"

"She's driving everyone nuts," I said. "Thank God she doesn't have our home phone number because she leaves messages for Richard 'round the clock at his office."

I know Richard loves me, but deep down, I also know I will never relax, never assume a laissez-faire attitude with him about other women. I mean, this man was a seriously big catch, with a seriously big history with women to go along with it, and no way was I going to let my guard down. Kaleen Warhurst, in spite of her divaisms, was a very beautiful woman and possessed one of the most beautiful voices on the planet, and Richard—who himself claims to have perfect pitch, whatever that is—is a sucker for a pretty voice, which makes it all the more a miracle he fell in love with me: I could audition successfully for the role of Janis Joplin.

"Whatever you do, don't be rude back," I told Linda. "Or we'll never get rid of her."

At about eight, I called Lucky to confirm our lunch date. She was still asleep.

"Who?" she asked.

"Lilly Bennett. The investigator. We talked yesterday about having lunch today. Ringing any bells yet?"

"Oh, I'm so sorry," she groaned. "Morning is not my best time. You know, I can't have lunch. I completely forgot, I've got other plans. I'm so sorry, but maybe next week."

"No problem. Just give me a call when you want to get together," I said and hung up. For a girl whose calendar had been completely open, if she'd had a previous engagement, I think she would have remembered it. But then again, beauty and brains do not always go hand in hand.

I hadn't had a chance to review Elias's schedule with him—he should already be on his way to stake out James Hewitt, but when I dialed his car phone, there was no answer. Then I heard his Suburban slide around the corner. He gunned the engine and headed straight for Buck, who was standing in the middle of the street holding both his hands up in front of himself, giving Elias the bird.

"You are such a chickenshit," Buck started yelling at the top of his lungs. He was dancing around, jabbing the air with his fingers. "You couldn't hit the broad side of a fucking barn. You are a fucking chickenshit loser. Loser."

I hated it when they played Chicken. I knew they'd never hurt each other on purpose, but one of these days one of them would be drunker than he thought and pick the other off like a cat on a curb. Just bing him right into the next county like a big old cowpie.

Gal and Pal had their paws on the dashboard and were staring wide-eyed at Buck as they hurtled toward him at about seventy miles an hour until, at the last second, Elias slammed on the brakes and turned his wheel and entered a Hollywood-style spin, stirring up a cyclone of dust.

"Loser," Buck howled one last time before he dove for cover under the saloon sidewalk.

"You know," I said to Linda. "I was sort of hoping that when you and Elias decided to get married, he'd slow down a little. Maybe even grow up some."

"Your brother's not exactly a fireball, you know." Linda squared some papers on my desk and gazed out the window at her intended, who had on a pair of khakis, a navy blue blazer, and his Hill School tie. "As a matter of fact, if he went any slower, he'd be dead. And as for being grown-up—forget it. He's a case of arrested development if ever I've seen one. I think that's why I love him so much. He's seen so many bad things in his life, so much pain and fear and suffering, all he can see now is the good."

I didn't ask her if she'd seen his office in the cattle barn, where the Justice Department—for whom he claimed no longer to work—kept him supplied with so much seditious literature featuring militia group movement, armory stats, and militia poster boys *du jour,* he could walk right into one of their camps, infiltrate them in a heartbeat, and plot the overthrow of the government without blinking. All the while leading the feds right to them. He'd done it before and he'd do it again.

"And yes," she said as though reading my mind. "I know he does a little job for the government every now and then, but that's business. That's not his heart."

"Fair enough."

Elias helped Buck struggle to his feet and started brushing

him off. Sometimes Buck reminded me of Pigpen in *Peanuts.* They were now trying to see who could say the word "ass-hole" more times than the other. Shortly, Elias thundered through the door.

"Morning, my angel darling." He kissed Linda. "You look especially delicious today."

She blushed.

"Shouldn't you have been long gone by now?" I asked. "Your bird could have flown the coop."

"Nah. I gave his doorman my beeper number; if he does anything I'll know it. Besides, the doorman said he never leaves for the office before nine-thirty. Whose are these?" He picked up the photographs of the Fabergé eggs.

"Mickey Giardino's."

Elias dropped them back onto the desk. "Look like fakes to me."

"Right. I'm sure Mickey will be grateful for your expert opinion. Six million dollars later." I took my triple-magnification mirror out of my desk drawer and checked my makeup. "I'm going to pay a call on Adam Garrett. Let me know if you get anywhere with Hewitt."

"Sure thing." Elias was getting ready to kiss Linda, sort of circling her like an old bull examining an old cow. "I'm right behind you."

The day was crisp and beautiful, and after about five minutes, as I raced down Squaw Canyon toward the interstate, I saw Elias gaining on me, the big Suburban popping on and off my rearview mirror as it bull-dogged its way around the sweeping curves. In the distance, Roundup's whimsical skyscrapers twinkled like the Emerald City in the clean morning sun. My brother and I flew in formation down the empty interstate, until he turned off for James Hewitt's downtown penthouse and I continued on. Baby, who loved to go to town, patrolled the car's interior like an ensign on the bridge in a busy harbor, barking out warning commands to real or imagined passing dogs.

Twenty-three

Adam Garrett officed in a small, restored Victorian house on the edge of downtown. I circled the block a couple of times, getting the lay of the land, and when I drove down the alley past his parking area, he emerged from the back door. Dark glasses covered his eyes. Adam was sleek-bodied as an Italian model: tall and lanky, with a voracious grace. His face was strong and had improved with age. He was perpetually tan and his hands were large and square. His PAC money kept him in Armani.

Bottom line: Adam Garrett was cool.

I pulled onto the street and waited for him, praying he would exit the alley from the end I'd chosen. No such luck. After thirty seconds I pulled forward and looked down the narrow lane just in time to watch the rear end of his navy blue BMW 740-il disappear west on Cherokee Avenue.

Garrett was an easy tail, mostly because he was far too cool to believe anyone—other than the media, whose attention he cultivated more avidly than Martha Stewart cultivated her garden—would be so presumptuous as to track his movements surreptitiously, and also because he talked on the phone the whole time. Also, my Jeep Wagoneer was one of the most common cars in Wyoming, after the Suburban, which I personally think is too big. For me at any rate. The only difference between my Wagoneer and all the others was that I had a souped-up 5.9 liter engine under the hood—a three-hundred-and-sixty-cubic-inch gut-buster with two hundred and thirty-five horses. And even though Garrett's BMW could beat me on mileage, cornering, power, and speed, I didn't think Garrett himself could outdo me on skill. Or surprise.

We headed into the mountains, the morning sun at our backs. Fifteen minutes later, he turned off the highway at Henry's Park: a small bump in the road that boasted a biker's bar notorious for its Sunday afternoon stabbings, a couple of curio shops, a doctor's office, a convenience store/gas station, and a liquor store—Henry's—which had neon signs in its windows for every possible kind of beer. Real beer: Coors, Budweiser, Miller, Colt .45, and so forth, not that precious designer stuff all the kids think is so great. Garrett slowed and turned into the package store's small, dirt lot. He parked under a large tree on the far side of the building.

I pulled onto the apron of the gas station next door and called up my new best friend, Louis Freeh. I thanked him for the case and promised him he'd be the first to know if I needed any help. He and I had worked together a number of times when he was chief in Philadelphia and I was chief in Santa

Bianca. He made his big chops in the Pizza Connection RICO bust. I had just been getting ready to make mine in Pizza Pacific-Style when I had the unfortunate experience of being caught naked on video with the judge. My successor got the glory of hauling in the Asian dons I'd already trapped in my big net, while I slunk out of town.

"Actually," I said, "the only thing I'd really like you to do is send a fax to Jack Lewis requesting that he provide me with all possible assistance, should I request it."

Louis laughed. "He having a few problems adjusting to your living on his turf?"

"You could say that. Incidentally, I've been wanting to ask you how things are going in Russia? Getting any better?"

"Not really. We do whatever we can to help, but there is so much graft, so much corruption, so much crime, and so much money—real and bogus—there's not much anyone can do until it cools down a little. We're trying to help them keep the lid on, but the police themselves are pretty suspect. It's like Chicago in the thirties. How's your operation over there going?"

"Fascinating," I answered. "The payoffs alone are enough to feed hundreds of people a month. But it's a nice business, beautiful objects, lots of intrigue. High stakes. It's fun."

"Be careful. Russians are seldom what they seem."

We signed off and about five minutes later, Adam Garrett emerged carrying a brown paper bag from which protruded what looked like the dark foil caps of two bottles of Dom Perignon, except I was sure they weren't. Nothing like a little champagne with a twist-off cap to start your day in Henry's Park.

He opened the rear door of his car, laid the bottles on the seat, and removed his suit coat, which he hung on the rear hook. Then he pulled his hair into a ponytail, tied a bandanna around his head, and shrugged into a faded Levi's jacket. Finally, he disappeared behind the building and reappeared a minute or two later wheeling a Harley—a real hog with saddlebags and room for a friend. He tucked the champagne into the bags, fired her up, and took off like a bat out of hell toward Big Bear Canyon. No way I could keep up.

I followed his route, past the lake and around the bend, but by the time I entered the canyon, a ten-mile track of hairpin curves and high drop-offs to a roaring creek far below, Garrett was long gone. I kept rolling—operating on the assumption that, since he wasn't wearing off-road clothes, he would not have taken any of the small dirt paths that wound up into the dozens of steep gullies. At the end, the canyon broke out into Big Bear Valley, where the water slid low and windy through mowed hay fields, past a group of shacks still inhabited by die-hard hippies: Big Bear Commune.

Was Adam Garrett a commune kind of guy? Well, who knew. He was full of surprises.

I turned in, but as I drove slowly around the beaverboard parabola houses and fiberglass geodesic domes in which the earthlings lived with their children, who played in the dirt alongside Rottweilers chained to rusted-out VW buses, I knew I wasn't going to find former senator Garrett's motorcycle. These people had no money, no power, and no deodorant, and if Adam Garrett was possibly a little dirty as a businessman and politician, I knew he was personally clean. One has to be when one moves indiscriminately from one roll-in-the-hay to another.

I said good-bye to the commune and kept going. He could be anywhere, and what had begun as a simple tail had become a solitary drive in the mountains on a beautiful day. The valley was wide and gentle, one of the most majestic in Wyoming, with a beckoning vista of the snowy high range in the distance. At the end of the valley, the asphalt road became dirt, heading higher into the hills. I bumped onto the hard-pack, past driveways that disappeared into the trees—leading mostly to summer homes now closed for the season. The road was quiet, abandoned. Leaves still clung to the aspen, but they'd lost their golden orange and turned black and shriveled.

Just one more mile, I thought. Then I'll turn back.

Up the hill, through the trees, a glint caught my eye. It was the sun sparkling off the windshield of a white Taurus sedan parked in front of a pine-log cabin. Right behind it, poked out the rump of the hog.

WALLIS said the name on the mailbox.

The possibilities for whatever activity our esteemed former United States senator was up to at the Wallis homestead outside of Henry's Park were as unlimited as they were scandalously delicious: women, drugs, mobsters, boys. The possibility that whatever he was doing was *not* illicit never entered my mind. Where was the media when you needed them?

I circled back and parked across the road, took out my binoculars, and picked up my phone.

"Morning, Bill," I greeted the clerk in the Wyoming DMV office. "I need you to check a plate for me."

The Taurus was a rental, no surprise there. Then I called the registrar in the Fremont County Clerk's Office and asked for the name on the tax registration for that property in Upper Big Bear.

"That would be Margaret Wallis," the registrar said. The mailing address was a post office box in Henry's Park. "She's owned it since 1991."

"Thanks."

After I called Linda to tell her where I was and ask her to

call Hertz and find out who had rented the Taurus, I checked my Glock, chambered a round, slipped it back into its holster under my left arm, and headed across the road.

The cabin, which appeared so rustic from a distance, was actually a very solid, meticulous little house in the woods—a real Ralph Lauren Vision-of-the-West kind of deal. Wildly expensive, idealized, and charming. Two rocking chairs sat behind the rail of the long front porch. Smoke curled from a fieldstone chimney. The Rolling Stones rattled the windows.

Staying well into the trees, I crept around back, where the remains of a vegetable garden rested in tidy rows. A wooden picnic table and stone barbecue grill stood at the far end of the yard, and outside the back door, a basket overflowed with empty Dom Perignon and Kristal bottles.

I'm always nervous about dogs in situations like this. They can be a nightmare, ferocious and terrifying, and I always feel like a criminal when I have to Mace them, but I'd rather drop them in their tracks than have them drop me in mine, and they don't need five hundred stitches in their arms and faces from Mace. Fortunately, there weren't any canine signs at the Wallis cabin, no doghouse, no run, no old tennis balls lying around or holes dug in the yard.

I ran to the house, and crouched quickly behind the back-door woodpile. Someone had turned the music down as I made my dash, and my heart pounded with the possibility I'd been spotted, but after a minute, I heard voices speaking at a normal level. They were coming through the window just above my head. I slid up and peeked into what turned out to be the kitchen.

A woman, presumably Margaret Wallis, barefoot and wrapped in nothing but a thin, silvery silk kimono, was standing at an enormous old-fashioned wood-burning stove frying eggs and bacon. Long blond hair fell over her shoulders and loosely down her back, hiding her face. Adam, in an open kimono, was leaning on the doorjamb, holding a bottle of champagne in one hand and himself in the other. They were both laughing. I'll say one thing for these two: They were definitely in shape.

All I could think was how great the bacon smelled. Is that pathetic or what? I guess that's what marriage has done to me. Here I am looking at what could be a scene from one of the century's greatest porno movies, and all I can think about is how good the bacon smells.

Suddenly the back door flew open. I dropped to my knees as an empty champagne bottle was added to the basket. The screen door slapped shut.

"Anything new on your watch?" I asked Elias. I was sitting on an end-up log behind the woodpile. Voyeurism was just not my deal and actually never had been, even when I was single.

"Nah. Where are you?"

"Upper Big Bear. Adam and some woman are getting it on in a cabin for what sounds like the third time today. In an hour and a half. I think he must get monkey shots in Switzerland or something. I'm starving to death. Where are you? Anything happening with Hewitt?"

Elias was bored. "I'm at the club. He's still rolling for drinks. His tee-off time isn't for another twenty minutes."

"I'd better get dressed," Adam said.

"Will I see you later today?" Margaret asked. They'd finally gotten around to finishing their breakfast.

"I'm not sure, it really depends on how things go. I've got a lot on my schedule for the next few hours. Old constituents looking for handouts. Then a three-thirty with Adelaide and Nicky at High River. But after that, I'm probably available. What about you?"

"I was going to go home, but I think the idea of all these showgirls coming to town is making you a little too steamed-up. I think maybe I'd better stick around."

Adam's laugh acknowledged the truth of the remark. "Good-bye, dearest," he said finally. "I love you. Let me know what you decide."

"I love you, Adam."

Moments later, the wheels of the Harley grabbed the gravel and spun it onto the hard-pack. I poked my head around the corner of the house in time to watch it accelerate around the bend.

My pager went off. Elias.

"You'd better get down here as soon as you can," he said. "You won't believe your eyes."

"What?" I started for the car.

"Just get here. I'll meet you in the Ladies' Bar." He hung up.

Twenty-four

The parking lot at the Roundup Country Club was almost full—weekdays were as busy as the weekends these days, what with golfers, bridge groups, ladies' luncheons, and committee meetings—so I actually had to drive around to look for a parking place, which aggravated me a little. Doesn't anybody work anymore?

Finally, I just said to hell with it, pulled up to the front door, and handed Ernie, the doorman, a twenty, which was so totally against club rules that if Ernie had told on me, I could have gotten thrashed or something. But he and I were old buddies and he regarded me and my twenties as sort of an annuity. Of course, I could have flipped down my visor with my U.S. Marshal Service sign and claimed it was official business, which maybe it was and maybe it wasn't. But, frankly, I'd much prefer getting thrashed by Malcolm St. George, the everlastingly gassed president of the country club board of directors for tipping the doorman, than by Janet Reno, for misusing my official power.

As promised, Elias was in the bar eating peanuts and drinking a bloody mary. All the cocktail tables were full and an abnormal amount of noise poured in from the formal dining room, where lunch was in full swing. He ordered me a drink.

"You need to gird your loins," he said. "This is worth the price of two trips to Hawaii."

"Is it something to do with James Hewitt?" I asked, and took a big swig.

"Nah. He and his buddies played the front nine this morning and now he's in the Men's Grill in a gin rummy tournament. The guy is a total waste." Elias put down his empty glass. "Come on," he said. "This is something you must see to believe."

I followed him into the crowded dining room and there, at the large round table in the center, sat Mother, Dwight, and . . . the Showgirls.

"Is that the single greatest sight you've ever seen in your life or what?" Elias said.

Mother had on one of her lovely, old luncheon ensembles—pale pink with a white silk blouse and a hundred ropes of pearls. Dwight had on his uniform and a big smile. And the girls might as well have just walked off Prada's Milan runway, their dresses were so delicate—pale little slips that skimmed their bodies like thin water. They were all sipping champagne.

Even when it's packed, the country club dining room is generally as quiet as a tomb. Today, with everybody trying to pretend they weren't interested in Mother's guests, it was loud enough to wake the dead.

The showgirls had captivated everyone. Even without their costumes, arrayed as they were in beautiful, chic dresses and high-heeled, sling-backed pumps, they seemed to have plumage.

Elias and I said a quick hello, declined Mother's invitation to join her party, and returned to the bar. Dwight followed us.

"I think this is it, Marshal," he told me.

"Think it's what?"

"Suka," he said. "I think I'm having a *coup* deal, just like you and Richard."

"A *coup de foudre?*"

"That's the one."

I looked back into the dining room at Suka, the youngest and most exotic of the trio, and tried to imagine her and Richard in bed together. It was far too painful to contemplate. I hoped I didn't have to stand next to her when he was around. One of my upper arms was the size of her body. I didn't remind Dwight that this was the fourth girl in the last year who'd had this effect on him.

"That's wonderful," I said.

"She was Miss Universe."

"I know."

"But I don't want you to think she's not smart. She is. She was in the Israeli Army."

"That's great, Dwight."

"Well, do you need me to do anything else? Besides stay with your mother and guard the girls, I mean?"

"Nope."

"Okay, I'll get back to work, then." He grinned.

"Carry on, Deputy."

"That kid would be totally lost without you," Elias said. "You literally saved his life."

"You're right." I watched Suka look up at Dwight—the damaged and exiled son of a Grosse Point industrialist son of a bitch—and pat his empty chair. "If there's an earthquake tonight, it'll be those two. You know," I turned back to Elias, "Richard used to go out with her."

"Who?"

"Suka."

He studied me. "Don't worry about it, kiddo. When she's your age, she'll look like a Bulgarian charwoman. That pouty beauty will ripen like fruit and fall to the ground. Trust me. Richard's got an eye, he knew what he was getting. You're a Thoroughbred—she's naught but a plow horse. A spry, young, plow horse to be sure, but a plow horse, nevertheless."

"He also used to date Kaleen Warhurst."

"What in the hell is wrong with you today? She's a complete psycho. She's nuts. Do you know, one time, she was in her limo in Los Angeles and it was too cold. She calls her agent in New York and asks him to call the limo company to call the driver and ask him to turn down the air conditioning. Now, I swear to God, is that what you think Richard wants? Buck up, for Chrissake. Have another drink. Do you want a club sandwich or something?"

"What's on for this afternoon?" he asked once our sandwiches had arrived and we'd loaded them up with extra mayonnaise.

"I think I'll go down and talk to Adelaide and Dolly Johnson."

"That'll be fun." He sipped his drink and drizzled some peanuts into his mouth. "You won't have to look far, they're both upstairs at a meeting. And now, here comes Lucky. For a bunch of people who aren't even members, the Johnsons sure do spend a lot of time hanging around this club."

I spun around to look. Sure enough, Lucky Johnson was prowling across the lobby toward the dining room. She meandered through the tables where she greeted my mother and her showgirl best friends and sat down to join them for dessert.

Mother did not look happy.

Ten minutes later, Adelaide and Dolly descended the staircase at the far end of the bar. I kissed Elias's bearded cheek and followed Dolly's little James Bond BMW convertible down Cheyenne Boulevard. She was right on the verge of needing to be arrested for drunk driving.

Twenty-five

The receptionist at Johnson Land, La Donna Baker, didn't recognize me from my visit the week before when I'd claimed to be Letitia Vanderbilt. Of course, La Donna wouldn't know the difference between Letitia Vanderbilt and Evita Peron.

Her black and white hair was pulled tight into an exploding Roman candle on top of her head, making her look rather like a zebra-striped carrot. She was practicing touching the ring in her nose with the stud at the end of her pointed tongue. I hoped the stud would get caught and she'd have to go to the emergency room and have them both removed surgically after experiencing great pain. I don't know what it is about body-piercing, it totally disgusts me. I cannot bear it. The idea of self-mutilation is so abhorrent to me, I cannot look at it or contemplate whatever darkness lies behind it.

"I'd like to see Adelaide Johnson, please. Marshal Bennett."

"Sure," she said and picked up the phone. Her fingernails were black today. After a quick conversation, she hung up. "She says to tell you, you need to make an appointment."

"Wrong answer," I said, and started down the hall.

"You can't go down there," La Donna called.

"Watch me." I opened the door to Adelaide's office and walked in. She was at her conference table with Tom and Dolly, who was wearing dark glasses. They were all smoking.

"You can't barge in here and interrupt me this way." Adelaide looked over my shoulder to La Donna. "Call Security." She was as secure in her power as a Mafia don accustomed to ordering hits and having his orders carried out. But, like all criminals, she was only as good as her lieutenants let her be. The power all boiled down to: How much could she trust her henchmen? It is a precarious and dangerously unreliable backup system.

"I'd hold off on that, if I were you, La Donna," I said, showing my badge. "What you may regard as a busy schedule, Adelaide, I consider obstruction. I'd appreciate it if you would ask Tom and Dolly to leave."

"No."

"All right, then let's go down to the Federal Court House Building and talk." I knew I was never going to get anywhere in this investigation unless I could raise the stakes and therefore the paranoia level, starting with getting this bunch of Clampetts divided—if not physically then at least in their loyalties, assuming they had any, which I assumed they didn't.

"You can't talk to her that way," Tom said. He had immediately begun to sweat through his shirt. "We're paying you."

"Not anymore. Unfortunately. I loved the idea of those big fees, but I guess you missed the Attorney General's news conference yesterday. Your sister-in-law's murder made this a capital case—assassination of a government official. Surely you've heard. You need to buy yourself some other personal protection, because if you see me following you around, it'll be to see what you're doing, not to see who's doing what to you."

"I told you she was bad news." Dolly laughed nervously, and then went to work biting off a piece of cuticle.

"Well, then," Tom said, trying to be conciliatory, "how about if you excuse us for a couple of minutes? Let us wrap up this meeting."

"Beat it, you two," Adelaide said, which didn't surprise me. I suspected Adelaide ran the company on at least three Need-to-Know levels—one was public; another was what she and Tom did behind the scenes to make their political under-the-table deals and land-grabs; and the third was her own personal power trip, where she, and she alone, cooked the real books and greased the skids and the palms to get all those new sewer hookups and kickbacks. "I'll hear what she has to say right here. I'm not interested in having any trouble with the feds. Not that I can't handle it."

"You should have stayed away from her," Dolly said and slung her purse over her shoulder. "Don't say I didn't warn you."

"Shut up, Dolly," Tom said and then added on his way out the door, "I'll call Dick Sweeter."

"I don't need any goddamn lawyer," Adelaide snapped. "Just do as the woman says. Git. Now what the hell is all this about?" She had not moved from her chair at the head of the conference table, and now sat leaning toward me, like a quarterback about to receive a snap. "Is it more money? You didn't think those fees were high enough? You Bennetts think you're so high and mighty, you can waltz in and rip us little people off. We work like dogs for our money. We pay our taxes and build housing for poor people. Low-income families. Single parents. People you wouldn't know anything about. You and all your rich, fancy ways. We give back to this community. All you do is take. Why don't you just do your job and leave me be?"

In social situations, I fight back if I feel like it. For instance, if we were at a cocktail party, I might take the time to point out to Adelaide Johnson that there were responsible developers and then there were sackers, plunderers, looters. She was the latter. If she considered donating a hundred acres to the Cancer Institute so she could circumvent national forest laws and boundaries and terrorize Victoria Hewitt into giving up the Broken Arrow Ranch, as "giving back" to the community, she was misguided. Everything she did was motivated by self-interest and resulted in long-term damage to the public. I could have used my breath to point out that the Bennett Foundation gave away about fifty million dollars a year to institutions and individuals who weren't expected to give anything back. All we expected was that, hopefully, life would improve for them.

But this was business, not social, and the best thing to say was nothing.

I fingered a few objects on her desk—paperweights from insurance companies, pictures of her at groundbreaking ceremonies, the originals of the old black-and-white pictures I'd seen at the banquet: the Johnsons in front of Buckingham Palace; young Adelaide, with her scaly legs and mule teeth, standing with her brother and her parents next to an enormous

HENRY JOHNSON & SON LAND COMPANY sign. Some small thing resonated in me, some tiny zing of recognition, but I couldn't catch it in time. I spotted a roll of Life Savers.

"What do you want?" Adelaide pressed.

"I'm not really sure," I answered and helped myself to a lime one. "I know you were involved in Clay Parker's murder and the sabotage of Frank's plane. Do you want to tell me about it?"

"That's ridiculous. We were all sitting right there when Clay was shot and we were all in Las Vegas until Sunday night. I don't know the first thing about airplane engines. I wouldn't know where to start."

"No, but you have a lot of flunkies who do. What about James Hewitt? He's a perfect soldier in your land war: He's got a personal ax to grind, he's not any Rhodes Scholar, he needs a cause, and he needs strong direction. He's the ideal cultist. Someone you could, and do, manipulate to your heart's content."

"Why aren't you talking to James if you think he is responsible?"

"Because even if he did it, he's not responsible. You are. You're the mastermind. And I intend to prove it. The wall will tumble. As a matter of fact, a couple of little cracks have already appeared." I helped myself to a cherry-flavored Life Saver.

"What do you mean?"

"Did you know that Lucky and Adam Garrett are having an affair? And all this time I thought he was one of your loyalists. Too bad. I bet their pillow talk is something."

Old news, to be sure, but finally I'd gotten her attention. The expression in her lizard eyes snapped flat like metal Venetian blinds. Hard and reflective as polished steel. "Are you through?"

"Yup," I said. "I'm through for now. Have a nice day."

"Which way is Tom Johnson's office?" I asked a secretary outside Adelaide's door.

She pointed down the hall to an open door. "It's there, but you just missed him. He's gone for the day."

So much for hanging around to see if Auntie were going to get busted and hauled off to the clink. Talk about the rooks abandoning the castle and leaving the queen unguarded. This was check. Exactly the sort of unreliable backup support I was looking for and expected to find in the Johnsons: total lack of teamwork, virtually no cohesion, completely driven by self-satisfaction. I hoped I'd accomplished what I'd set out to with this visit, maybe break the logjam, stop the inertia, and I hoped delivering the news about Lucky and Adam to Adelaide, not Tom, would spur some action.

I waited in the alley across from the garage exit. Adam Garrett had said he had a three-thirty meeting with Adelaide and the Secretary of the Interior, Nicky Harmon, at High River Ranch, and within fifteen minutes, Dolly's little red car appeared. Adelaide had on wraparound dark glasses—the kind people with cataracts wear. She slumped low in the passenger seat and talked into the phone. As best I could figure out, Dolly's sole job at the Johnson Land Company was driving her aunt around. She accelerated smoothly onto the interstate, moved immediately into the far left lane, and pushed it up to about seventy-five.

Traffic was light and it was easy for me to keep them in sight. I stayed well back in the center lane and called Richard.

"How're Susannah and the Seven Dwarfs?" I asked.

His laugh was rich and happy. "She's off this afternoon, presumably torturing her hairdresser or manicurist. The director called to report that the rehearsal was going like a breath of fresh air without her. Did you know that Susannah means lily? Like lily the flower?"

"No, I . . ."

Suddenly a dark green Humvee appeared on my right and passed me as if I were going backward. It cut in front and I watched in horror as it roared toward Dolly's car and smashed into it, causing the little roadster to spin headfirst into the cement median wall and roll three times, end-over-end. The Humvee never stopped.

"I gotta go," I yelled at Richard and punched in 911.

Twenty-six

The accident's effect on traffic was monumental—it was literally a miracle that no one else was killed or injured when Adelaide, Dolly, and the BMW somersaulted across the highway like a big, red majorette doing handsprings with a flaming baton in her teeth. It was a gruesome, slow-motion sight, watching the car pinwheel high up through the air while Dolly's and Adelaide's arms and heads snapped back and forth like daredevils on a roller coaster.

Purses, phones, and a briefcase flew like birds set free from cages as speeding cars, trucks, and semis all slammed and swerved, dodging the flying, flaming debris. Traffic finally came to a halt in a multi-lane jam-up that would take hours to rectify.

I turned on all my blinkers and lights, stuck my official flashing gum ball through the sunroof, and drove as close to the wreck as I could. Then I leapt out and tried to get closer, but the fire was so hot, there was no way I could get near them. It didn't matter. I knew they'd been gone from the first slam into the concrete wall. Nothing in the world can save a living being from such a violent, high-speed crash—I don't care how many air bags the car has. Adelaide's black eel-skin briefcase lay near my foot. I tossed it into the Jeep.

Fortunately, we'd been close enough to downtown, emergency and rescue vehicles flooded the scene almost immediately. I returned to my car and closed my eyes to replay what I'd seen, working to remember every detail. The Humvee had a hard, not a convertible top. Color: dark, dark green, almost black, drabbed to give it a paramilitary look. Had I seen the driver? No, nothing more than knowing there was one. Anything distinguishing? No. License plate? I prided myself on my ability to reconstruct crime scene minutiae and I knew if I just sat there in silence for another minute or two, something would come to me. Finally, three of the six elements emerged: LVX. Three numerals followed, but three characters would be more than enough to get an ID, especially for a showboat like a Humvee.

I called my man at the DMV for the second time that day and within thirty seconds had my answer: James Hewitt. It had been about ten minutes since the accident.

"Goddamn it, Elias," I yelled into the phone. "What are you doing? All you had to do was keep an eye on Hewitt."

"What are you talking about. I've got him in my binocks right now. He just sank a twenty-foot putt. Guy's one hell of a golfer."

"What hole is he on?"

"Just finishing seventeen."

"Has he been on the course the whole time?"

"Yes. What's up?"

"Have *you* been there the whole time?"

"Well, I went to the men's room once, but I was only gone for about five minutes at the most."

"Stay with him. Somehow or other, he gave you the slip."

I put my foot to the floor and called headquarters downtown to let them know what I was up to.

"You want backup?" Jack Lewis asked. I had to give it to the guy, he was really trying to be professional, in spite of the fact he'd been handed his business on a public platter.

"I'd like a squad ASAP and a forensics crew. Other than that, I think I've got it handled."

I made it to the country club in record time, arriving at the eighteenth green just as James and his foursome were knocking their balls into the cup.

"Look who's here," James sneered as I crossed the green toward him, puncturing it with my heels. "Miss Fancy Pants. Don't you know any better than to walk on a putting green in high heels?"

I held up my badge. "James Hewitt?"

Elias fell into step next to me.

Hewitt smirked around at his buddies. "You all as scared as I am?"

I handed my handcuffs to Elias.

"James Hewitt, you are under arrest for the murders of Adelaide Johnson and Dolly Johnson. Anything you say can and will be used against you in a court of law. You have the right to an attorney. If you can't afford one, one will be appointed for you. Do you understand?"

As I spoke, Elias circled behind him and had him locked

down before he knew what hit him. Hewitt's friends watched in confused silence.

"What is this? Some kind of joke?" James's face had reddened with embarrassment.

"Do you drive a dark green Humvee, license plate number LVX-692?"

"So?"

"Would you please show us where that vehicle is, Mr. Hewitt?"

"What's all this 'Mr. Hewitt' crap? Take these things off me." He struggled against the cuffs.

"Would you please take us to your vehicle?" I was loving making this little turncoat bastard blush and squirm.

"Okay. But you have to take these off me first."

I stared at him through my dark glasses and waited a couple of beats. "The vehicle?"

He jerked out of Elias's grasp and started toward the parking lot. "I'll be right back," he called over his shoulder to his mute friends. "Order me a double gin and tonic."

He led us through the parking lot, keeping his head up, trying hard to look nonchalant, which simply is not possible with your hands cuffed behind your back. It's an unbelievably obvious posture, one that signals immediate trouble—stay-away-if-you-know-what's-good-for-you kind of trouble. Very, very seldom is a peace officer interfered with once a suspect is locked-in. Onlookers may be drawn to the scene, but they aren't there to interfere, they're there because they're glad it's not them.

And that's the way it was as we followed James Hewitt through the Roundup Country Club parking lot on this sunny October afternoon. Staff and kitchen help came from the service entrance. Some took advantage of the break to have a cigarette. Others wiped their hands on their aprons. Club members, holding bridge or gin rummy hands, gathered on the terrace outside the bar. Members getting into or out of their cars stopped and stared. James's three golfing buddies stood by the front door, unsure what to do next. James Hewitt had become an object—no longer human.

Was he aware of his change in status? Undoubtedly. But none of us spoke as he took us directly to his car. The front left fender was dinged and streaked with red paint. The hood was warm. James was shocked and indignant. The keys were in his pocket.

The squad car and forensics van arrived.

"What's going on?" James said. "I haven't done anything. I was playing golf."

"Watch your head," I said as I tucked him into the back of the Jeep. Elias joined me in the front. Baby licked James's face all the way downtown. Anything in the backseat was considered hers.

"Get this fucking mutt off me."

I told Baby to stop but she wouldn't listen. Little terriers really are untrainable.

Twenty-seven

Once Hewitt had been booked and taken to the lockup to wait for his lawyer, Elias and I joined the sluggish, rush-hour river of traffic and headed out to Sugar Hill to deliver the news.

This was one of the parts of my job I liked least. And most. Informing next-of-kin. Jack Lewis, who wanted a piece of this case so badly it was all he could do to keep himself from dropping to his knees and begging for it, had offered to go out and tell Tom and Lucky about the fatal accident, but understood when I thanked him and said I'd rather do it myself. Eyeball-to-eyeball delivery of the news is one of the most useful elements in an investigator's toolbox. It is a one-time-only, no-repeat-performance, split-second deal. That unique reaction when a family member or associate hears that someone near, but maybe not so dear, to him or her is dead.

Elias sat in the passenger seat, chain-smoking and looking out the window in angry silence.

"Stop beating yourself up," I finally told him. "The guy gave you the slip. It's happened to me dozens of times."

"I just don't see how he did it," he answered. "I never took my eyes off him except when I went to the head. I suppose he could have made a switch with someone at that point, but then, when would he have switched back?"

"What time did you go inside?"

"Right at three. They'd just teed-off on the fourteenth hole."

"The accident was at three-twenty-two," I said. "I guess he could've done it. Left the golf course at three, got downtown and into position by three-ten. It'd be tight, but not impossible, if the traffic all worked in his favor. Plus, he probably knew about the three-thirty meeting with Adam Garrett and Nicky Harmon at High River, so he knew when they'd be leaving."

I reflected on when I'd been waiting in the alley across the street from the garage entrance. Did I recall seeing the Humvee? No. But I hadn't been looking for it, either.

"But when would he have been able to switch back?" Elias continued. "I was there the whole time. And the course was almost empty this afternoon. If someone had come running across the fairway, I guarantee I would have seen it. You called at three-thirty sharp, eight minutes after the wreck. No way he could've gotten back in eight minutes, besides which, the second you called, I moved in tighter."

"There's only one solution."

"Like what?"

"He didn't do it," I said.

"Well, then, who did?"

"At the moment, we've got three obvious choices: Tom Johnson, Adam Garrett, and Lucky. Did I tell you about Adam and Lucky?"

"You mean coming out of the bedroom at Clay Parker's funeral?"

I nodded. "But if they were having a *serious* love affair, it would make sense for Adam or Lucky to kill Tom, not Dolly and Adelaide. Besides, Adam told that woman this morning how much he loved her. And he sounded like he meant it."

"Spare me," Elias said. "He's the kind of guy who would say anything. Senator Garrett has been involved with some very dubious projects and groups over the years. I know at one point, his banking records were subpoenaed and a Senate investigating committee tried to get its hands on some Swiss and Cayman account information."

"When was this?"

"Three or four years ago. You were still living in California. Probably wasn't big news out there. The Cayman banks told them to take a hike and the Swiss said they had no records of accounts in his name. The Senate can't subpoena his wife's records without strong cause, so it was dropped. He's always been suspect. One Armani suit costs about three thousand dollars—I know because I just bought a couple—and he's always had about a dozen of them, even when he was in the Senate. A United States senator makes what, about a hundred and thirty a year? After taxes and all, let's say his take-home was seventy, at the most. I can't see him spending fifty percent of his net income on suits."

"Do me a favor," I said absently, trying to picture Elias in an Armani suit. "Call up your spook friends and see what you can find out."

"Be my pleasure."

"Do me another favor and get Mother on the phone."

"Do I have to talk to her?"

"No, just find her."

He finally tracked Mother down at the Sugar Hill Country Club.

"You simply will not believe your eyes," she said. Her voice sparkled over the speaker. "They invited me to watch their rehearsal. The way these girls dance is unbelievable."

"Is Lucky Johnson still with you?"

"Yes, she's dancing in the show, too, as a surprise for her husband. Sorry, I have to go—the Adam and Eve number is coming up."

"Well," Elias said, "that eliminates one suspect."

"Tom had more than enough time after he left the office to drive to the club, get James's car, do the deed, and switch back. Adam? He and Nicky Harmon were supposed to be together— it'd be a pretty good alibi because Harmon loves his entourage. Even if he and Adam disappeared off into the trees at High River to have a secret meeting, they wouldn't leave the property. They're probably still out there waiting for Adelaide." My pager buzzed at my waist. I checked the number. "Would you dial up Linda for me?"

"Who was your slave last year?" Elias lit another cigarette and stripped down the match, leaving a Haiku of black streaks on his pant leg. He threw the stick out the window.

"Don't be a jerk, Elias."

"I finally got the info from Hertz," Linda reported. "The car was rented by Margaret Wallis. Address is in Henderson, Nevada."

"Where's that?" I asked.

"It's part of Las Vegas."

"Find Grady and ask him to check her out."

"Sure thing."

"What the hell kind of a house is this?" Elias asked when we pulled beneath the Johnsons' Tara-sized porte cochere.

"Bad," I answered and got out of the car. Elias told me he'd wait in case the phone rang. I knew he wasn't coming with me because he couldn't stand bad news, even if it was someone else's. Besides, although he'd been deputized, he didn't have any official obligation to accompany me. He was such a chicken sometimes.

It took Tom a while to get to the door. "What do you want?" he growled.

"May I come in?"

He stepped aside to let me pass—I practically had to dog-paddle through a sea of Aqua Velva—then closed the door and led me into the living room. Outside, the sun was setting brilliantly, really putting on a show, but strictly impersonal light came through the dark-tinted windows.

"There's been an accident." I watched him closely.

For a moment there was no reaction, then a look of unvarnished anger. "What in the hell has Lucky done now?"

"Lucky? No. It's Adelaide and Dolly. They've been killed in a car accident."

"What?"

"Adelaide and Dolly are dead."

"Adelaide and Dolly?" His confused and shocked reaction to his aunt's and sister's deaths seemed completely genuine.

"Let's sit down," I suggested.

"Wait. Wait." Tom pinched his nose and squeezed his eyes shut. "I need to find my wife. Where is she?"

"Over at the clubhouse."

He called and told her briefly what had happened. I could hear her screaming practically all the way across the golf course.

"Goddamnit, don't get so upset," Tom yelled back. "Of course we won't cancel the party. Don't worry about it. Nothing is more important than your goddamn birthday. We'll bury them next week. It's no big deal—just all my family's fucking dead. But why think about them when we can think about you?"

Lucky's sobs, which could melt a glacier, seemed to be melting Tom.

"Oh, honey, I'm sorry I snapped at you." He mopped a bandanna around his neck and up under the back of his toupee. "I know how hard you're working on this. You come on home, now. Your daddy loves you."

Once he'd hung up, I asked where he'd gone from the office. The car wash. He had the receipt to prove it: three-ten.

"I'll ask the Roundup Police Department to provide you with protection," I said.

"Thanks."

He never even inquired as to what they'd done with the bodies.

Twenty-eight

know this is a long shot, but see what you can find out about Suka."

"You mean as in the showgirl Suka?" Elias asked. "Why?"

"I've been thinking. Dwight said she was in the Israeli Army. Those Israelis are tough, and they have long memories. What if she was a helicopter pilot? What if the rumors about Clay Parker were true and he *was* a Nazi? What if she was the one who killed him because he did something to her family in the war? What if she's an agent for the Mossad? It's possible."

We'd reached Elias's car in the country club parking lot. The silent scorn coming from him was deafening.

"Well?" I asked. "Don't you agree it's possible?"

"It's also *possible* you need to be on Prozac. I think you've left the launch pad."

I ignored him. "While you're at it, see what you can learn about Martine and Lana."

He patted my hand on the steering wheel. "All right. If you say so."

I could tell he thought I was pathetic. *I* was starting to think I was pathetic.

By the time I got back to the station, James Hewitt's lawyer had arrived. Thankfully, my old friend Paul Decker could not defend him because James Hewitt's brother, William, was already his client-of-record in the matter. I was glad Paul couldn't take the case because if he had, he probably would have won; he usually did. I wanted James to lose. Go down. Big time. Whether he'd murdered any of the victims or not, he still deserved to fry.

The session went as expected. James denied ever leaving the golf course, and in fact, his alibi was pretty darned ironclad, starting with what Elias told me about not taking his eyes off James the whole round except for one five-minute period, information I did not pass along to James and his attorney. Then, after a brief huddle, the attorney—as a demonstration of his client's innocence, good will, and eagerness to help—consented to let me question James not only about his whereabouts in regard to the Clay Parker and Frank and Connie Johnson murders but also as to what he knew about the whereabouts of Tom Johnson and Adam Garrett during the periods the murders occurred. No new information emerged. These guys were sticking together like glue.

At seven forty-five, I called Richard at his office. He sounded as beat as I was.

"Let's meet at El Gallo," he suggested.

"What a great idea. I'm on my way."

El Gallo Tuerto—The Crazy Rooster—was a small road-house at the entrance to Crazy Squaw Canyon and served the best, freshest Mexican food on the face of the earth. In the summer, the deck that hung over the creek was always packed, but tonight, in spite of the sunny day, the sky had clouded up and looked like snow, and the restaurant was almost empty.

Richard was already at a table for two in front of the fire-place when I arrived. The air was rich with the scent of burning piñon. Two sangritas sat on the table. A sangrita is a small rocks glass of tomato juice, orange juice, beef bouillon, a double shot of good tequila, a big blast of hot sauce—the hotter the better—a large slice of fresh lemon, and a small jalapeño. No ice. It is similar to drinking fire. We hatched them fast, and ordered another round, along with platters of guacamole, tacos, enchiladas, refritos, and tostadas.

I was so tired and overloaded, all I wanted to do was sit and stare at Richard. Then I realized he looked pale and preoccupied.

"Are you all right?"

"Fine. I want to hear about your day. What's the gouge?"

"Well." I leaned back in the rawhide barrel chair, and let the fiery tequila relax me. "I think James Hewitt is basically out of the picture. Unfortunately, during the questioning this evening, even I believed him. There was a big powwow at High River scheduled for three-thirty and he wasn't included. He's nothing but a flunky in the Johnson group—just there to deliver his mother's ranch."

"Not the murderer?"

"No. He doesn't have the wit to pull off these crimes on his own. He's too mentally disorganized. He may be able to talk a good game, but each one of these hits was professional, almost military in its precision: The shooting of Clay Parker— it was quick in, bang-bang, out the door, into the helicopter, bing-bang-boom. The killer not only knew how to run and shoot but also how to fly an advanced aircraft."

I specifically didn't mention my fledgling suspicions about Suka, they were so outrageous. If I was right, I'd be a superheroine. If I was wrong, which was very likely, no one except my brother would know, and we already had so much on each other, he'd never tell.

I continued. "The sabotage of the King Air? That took specific, technical knowledge. This individual had to know just how much or how little sugar and steel to drop into the tank to make sure the plane got off the ground before the engine fell apart—that it didn't just grind to a halt on the runway. The hit-and-run this afternoon? Cool as ice. The Humvee must have been going a hundred, and it takes considerable skill to bump another car at that speed and keep going. It didn't even wobble. This is an extremely professional operation."

The waitress brought us a third round of drinks. Thank God they weren't vodka or I would have been completely wasted.

"What about Mickey Giardino?" Richard asked when she was gone. Some of the color had returned to his face.

I shook my head. "These aren't mob hits, either. They don't go to this kind of effort. They just blow their marks away. We know they did it. They know we know they did it. They're proud of their style. It's old. It works. It's cheap. No. This is some other faction and I can't figure out what's behind it. I'm down to two viable suspects: Tom Johnson and Adam Garrett—either one of them is fully capable of contracting for the crimes."

"I can't believe Tom Johnson would bump off his whole family."

"Are you kidding? After what I've seen the last couple of days? He'd do it in a heartbeat. They all would. There's also a side-shadow: this Margaret Wallis person. I'm waiting to hear from Grady in Las Vegas, see what he's learned. I think that's about it. Okay"—I stretched—it felt good to get the kinks out of my back and shoulders—and slumped back in my chair—"your turn. What happened with you today?"

"I'm really glad you're sitting down."

All my antennae shot into the air like Cindy Lauper's hair. "What?"

"Kaleen Warhurst filed a paternity suit against me this afternoon."

"What?" I screamed and started to laugh. "Are you serious?"

We both got completely hysterical. We laughed until we were sick.

An hour later, I was lying in the bathtub when the ten o'clock nightly news came on—KRUN-TV's big red, white, and blue graphic filled the screen, and trumpets blasted as the camera swished and swooped like a teenager's homemade, hand-held video-camera commercial, before it finally came to rest on Marsha Maloney's perfect face.

"Local stories top our news tonight."

The hokey exploding graphic with the word CRASH! stamped across it filled the screen behind the anchorwoman's head.

"Tragedy struck the Johnson family again today as Adelaide and Dolly Johnson, two more members of one of Roundup's leading families, perished in what witnesses are calling a bizarre hit-and-run on the interstate. At approximately three-twenty this afternoon, close to downtown, a military-style vehicle traveling at a high speed forced Dolly Johnson's small foreign convertible into the cement median. Cowboy star Clay Parker and State House Minority Leader Connie Johnson and her husband, Frank, were earlier victims in the crime spree that seems to have targeted this powerful and generous family."

"Excuse me while I barf," I said.

Marsha continued on with the fact that James Hewitt had been detained, questioned, and released due to a strong alibi and lack of evidence, and then she added a bunch of editorial hogwash about the danger the wonderful Johnson family appeared to be in, and why weren't the authorities, in general, and Marshal Lilly Bennett, in particular, doing anything about it, especially since Attorney General Janet Reno and FBI Director Louis Freeh themselves had pledged to provide all support necessary to find the killers.

"Give me a fucking break," I said to the screen.

"In other news, Marshal Bennett's husband, opera impresario Richard Jerome, had his own encounter with the law today when soprano superstar Kaleen Warhurst slapped him with a paternity and abandonment suit."

Marsha had trouble keeping a straight face.

Richard was sitting on the edge of the tub shaking his head, and I thought I was going to drown I was laughing so hard. The phone rang.

"Can you believe this," I yelled into it, thinking it was probably Elias.

"No, I can't," an unfamiliar voice said. "What exactly in the hell is going on out there?"

Oh, Jesus. It was Janet Reno. Oh, God. I sat up. Straight.

Twenty-nine

Wednesday Morning

Y ou swear to God this isn't a publicity stunt?" I asked Richard as we set out on our dawn ride.

Snow flurries had whipped through overnight and coated the landscape with a flawless dusting of powdered sugar. In the rising sun, the distant range looked like smooth, glossy peaks of meringue, their rocky cliffs and ridges temporarily hidden. The air had a wintry, tasteless bite, making the horses want to go—they snorted impatiently and danced up the road sideways, kicking up their heels and prancing in the snow, fighting as we kept them reined in.

"It sounds sort of like the kind of thing you'd do to sell more tickets."

"I wish I were so creative," Richard said. "Paul Decker said he'd be able to get the whole thing dismissed."

"You're using Paul? Isn't that sort of overkill for this? You didn't murder her."

"Not yet anyway." He grinned over at me. "Paul's the best, and you know I believe in going straight to the top. He'll make this business disappear fast."

"How can you be so sure? I mean, you did have an affair with her. It's possible the child is yours."

"I had a vasectomy fifteen years before I met her. You're right, though. It's one hell of a way to sell out a show nobody's wanted to see. Until yesterday, we hadn't been able to give the tickets away. Now I have a hunch we'll be adding performances."

No grass growing under Kaleen's feet.

When I got to the office at seven-fifteen, Linda's desk had vanished beneath a mountain of creamy roses whose centers were such a delicately pale, heart-wrenchingly tender shade of pink it made you want to cry. The fragrance was exquisite.

"They're Bridal Bouquet." Linda laughed. "Have you ever seen anything so beautiful?"

"Never."

Today was the day of their engagement party.

"Look." She held out her left hand shyly, like a college girl showing her engagement ring to her sorority sisters, but trying not to brag. "He gave it to me last night."

It was Grandmother Bennett's ring: a big square-cut diamond set in platinum, flanked by triangular aquamarines the color of Linda's eyes. Linda's hands were ranch wife's hands—strong and sinewy, red and rough, showing their years of hauling and lifting, calving and scrubbing. The ring suited her perfectly—it was as square and sturdy and dependable as she was.

I hugged her. "I've always wanted a sister—I'm so glad it's you."

That is not to say I didn't love Christian's wife, Mimi, but she wasn't really the sister type—Mimi was more Athena than Juno. She could hurl thunderbolts faster than anyone I ever knew, except my mother.

Linda could catch them.

Her left hand had the ring. Her right? About a hundred pink message slips. None from Janet Reno. Thank God. My backside still stung from her claw marks. But, just as bad, the top message on the stack was from Louis Freeh.

"I'm getting some heat from the Western Region," he said.

"I imagine." My gut was locked into a lead ball and a steel band tightened like a tourniquet around my chest. I could not lose this case now.

"What can I tell the AIC?" the director asked. "What have you got?"

Crap. I didn't have anything. I didn't answer.

"Look, Lilly, you've got to hand me something or I'm going to have to invite my boys and girls to the party. I know in detective work it's standard procedure to work through a process of elimination, but as far as I can tell, your suspects are all getting eliminated physically. That's not the goal."

"All right," I said. "Here's what it looks like from here." I laid out my theory—which even as I said it, sounded more and more unlikely—about Adam Garrett, Nicky Harmon, and Tom Johnson contracting for the killings. "If you start putting a bunch of agents on this now, it'll blow the whole investigation. You can't work as efficiently as I can, and no matter how hard you try, it's conceivable we could have a leak—I mean that's how you all back there in Washington disseminate news, isn't it? Leaks?"

"Not out of this Bureau." The director bristled.

"But we're talking about a high-profile former senator and possibly the Secretary of the Interior. It could come from his office, and if word leaked that these gentlemen are active and viable suspects, we'd have our hands full of so many media types and Philadelphia lawyers, we'd get buried."

Thankfully, I thought I'd scored. Louis was quiet for a minute. "How long?"

"Seventy-two hours?" I suggested.

"Forty-eight. Whatever it takes."

"Done."

We hung up and I stared out the window. I'd gotten forty-eight hours to bring this to a head—and when Louis said forty-eight, he meant it, there was no wiggle room in the number—and I had bubkes. Generally, after a while, pieces begin to pull together in the cosmos, shape themselves into some sort of cohesive clump, like gathering together a ball of pie-crust dough. But right now? It was still like trying to catch feathers.

Adelaide's briefcase, which I'd rescued from the flaming highway, sat in the middle of my desk. I took out a screwdriver and popped the lock. The case was stuffed with documents. At first glance, it was all the usual business correspondence, nothing pertinent to the national forest shenanigans that Adam had no doubt orchestrated, or to the Broken Arrow Ranch land grab. Only one document stood out. A bill from a Dr. Kenneth Schmidt for five thousand dollars. Services rendered was all it said. His office was out west, toward High River. What I had so far was nothing, so maybe this was something. Maybe it was more nothing.

"Linda," I called through the door. "Did Grady ever call back?"

"No, ma'am."

I picked up the phone.

"You do like to wake people up, don't you, Marshal?" the Las Vegas chauffeur said.

"To tell you the truth, it's hard to figure out when people in Las Vegas work and when they sleep," I said. "Besides, it's six-thirty in the morning, you should be out of bed by now."

"Yes, ma'am. Except I just went to bed at six. I had a group of ophthalmologists last night. They're notorious for staying out late and not tipping." He yawned. "Well, like I always say . . ."

"Now, listen, Grady," I interrupted. I was in no mood for a bunch of Farmer's Almanac Benjamin Franklin country fair backwoods bullshit. "Things are starting to heat up here, and I need a couple of quick answers. What did you find out about Margaret Wallis?"

"Well." His laid-back Oklahoma style was about to make me jump out the window. "Not anything, exactly. That address you gave me isn't a residence."

"What? That's not possible. Hold on a minute." I punched the Hold button and yelled out to Linda, "Would you reconfirm that address for Margaret Wallis with Hertz."

Seconds later, she yelled back that the address she'd given me was the one Hertz had given her. "Also, Ms. Wallis turned the car in at Roundup International at six o'clock last night. And I'm already calling United and Frontier to see if she took any of their flights to Las Vegas."

"Excellent. Also, get Dwight over here." Then I returned to Grady, who'd fallen back to sleep. "Are you absolutely positive that was the address you checked?"

"Yes, ma'am. It's a 7-Eleven. Both sides of that street are strip-mall shops."

Hell. It took all my self-control not to slam down the phone—I told Grady I'd be in touch.

Never, ever, in my career had I felt such pressure to perform. This had turned into a nationally visible case. The Attorney General and the director of the FBI had gone out on a limb for me—on CNN. They'd abjured their own systems, procedures, and policies based on my reputation. If I didn't deliver, it would be a professional disaster for all three of us. But, for them, it would be worse: I could stick my head under my pillow at the ranch and not come out until I felt like it, but they could not hide. This mess would stick all over them.

My stomach was in flames. I stormed into Linda's office.

"Where in the hell is Dwight?" I couldn't keep the snap out of my voice.

"He said he couldn't come over right now." She peeked over the top of the roses.

"Really. Do me a favor, call him back and tell him to get his butt out of his chair and into my office in three minutes or I'll put him on disciplinary leave, which, you might point out, will go into his record. Without pay." I knew that wouldn't faze him even slightly since he had almost as much money as I did, but I couldn't think of anything else to say.

I dialed Elias, who was supervising the scrub-out of the barn for the party. "Stay with Adam Garrett today and stay in touch."

"Can't. I've got to get things squared away for tonight."

"Don't give me any crap about this, Elias," I bit. "I need your help."

"Right."

Dwight got to the office in two minutes, instead of three,

and I could see why he hadn't wanted to leave his jail house. His whole face and neck were purple—aubergine splotches with rosy borders. Dwight was one giant hickey. And he was walking like he had a poker up his behind—very gingerly, sort of a stiff shuffle. I could only imagine what the rest of his body looked like. He was definitely in pain.

I burst out laughing. "What in the world has happened to you?"

Dwight's square, handsome mouth crooked into a grin. "Oh, boy. They don't call her Suka for nothing." He settled uneasily into a chair. "I'm in bad shape, Marshal."

"I guess you are. I'd love to take the time to hear about it, but I need you to get back to town and look after Lucky and the girls today."

Dwight looked as if he might cry. "Oh, please, don't make me look after them anymore. That Suka is crazy. She almost killed me. My body looks like I'm a Dalmatian. It was like being mauled by a mountain lion or a vampire or something. I probably should have gone to the hospital and gotten a shot on the way home, she bit me so much, but I was too embarrassed."

He really was pitiful, but that wasn't my problem.

"Look, go by Dr. Gregory's office in town, have him check you out. He'll give you some salve or something, and a shot if you need it. The future of our whole district depends on you and me right now, Dwight—we've got forty-eight hours to make an arrest—and you've just got to suck it up."

"I hear you." My deputy hoisted himself to his feet like a hundred-year-old man. "You can count on me."

"Thanks. I knew I could. Suka and Lucky are the ones I want you to tail. Mother can watch the other two." I pulled on my black shearling jacket and dark glasses. "Let's go."

Thirty

Dwight tiptoed back down the street to the jail and I stuck my head into the saloon, but Buck wasn't there.

"He's getting a haircut," Ecstasy said from behind the bar. "For tonight."

I bit my tongue to keep from telling her she, herself, could use not only a haircut but, more important, a hair wash. But she and Billy weren't coming to the steak fry/square dance. They'd been invited but couldn't make it. What in the world, I wondered as I climbed into my Jeep, do you imagine they're doing instead? Listening to Bob Dylan eight-tracks and picking bugs off each other?

Bennett's Fort grew smaller and smaller in my rearview

mirror until I rounded the cliff into Crazy Squaw Canyon, where the sun burned across the skiff of snow that iced the rocky walls. The road, however, was dry, and I made good time to Mustang Road on the far side of town. I located Dr. Kenneth Schmidt's office in a well-kept, small, white brick building. He obviously had a lucrative practice—INTERNAL MEDICINE—the sign read.

It was barely eight-thirty, but patients already filled the waiting room, sipping coffee, eating miniature corn muffins, and reading the morning papers. A couple of them looked at me and some vague recognition passed their faces, but they couldn't quite place me, although my picture was right there on the front page. Dopes.

The receptionist sat behind an open sliding-glass window. She had a large stack of multicolored folders on her desk.

"I'd like to see Dr. Schmidt, please." I showed her my badge. "Official business."

"Um . . ." she said. I think she was ten.

"Um?"

"Okay. Well, let me go get him."

"I think it would be better if we met in his office," I explained. "Not here in the reception room."

"Okay. I'll tell him." She vanished up a short flight of stairs and around a corner. Moments later she was back. "Come on up."

The doctor's private office was comfortably furnished with cowboy prints and diplomas. He'd attended Stanford Medical School. Nice. There was a picture of what I assumed was his wife. She had a beautiful, strong profile, and steel-gray hair pulled into a bun. She was posed before a sunlit backdrop of golden aspen leaves. The door opened and he entered. A handsome man of more than sixty, I'd say. Gray hair, blue eyes, long, lean body. A slight limp and a sure handshake. Tortoise-shell-rimmed glasses. I liked him instantly.

"Your fame precedes you," he said, taking the seat behind his desk. "I hope whatever this is can be quick. I've got a number of patients."

"I'll take as little of your time as possible." I pulled out the receipt for services rendered I'd found in Adelaide Johnson's briefcase and pushed it across the desk to him. His demeanor changed subtly and instantly. I detected a slight tremor in his hand as he slid the paper toward him. "What can you tell me about this?"

Dr. Schmidt took off his glasses and rubbed his eyes. Then he spun his chair around and looked out the window.

"Doctor?" I said.

Finally, he turned to face me. He put his glasses back on. "I think I should call my lawyer."

Although this response is always a possibility, of a hundred million things Dr. Schmidt could have said, calling his lawyer was way down on my list of expected replies, and I needed to make a couple of quick decisions. What could his involvement possibly be? Was he the killer? Was the limp from arthritis? Or an accident running from the scene of a crime? If it were arthritis, he could not be the killer, because our killer was agile. But he was the right height. And he appeared to be in good shape. Did I want to promise him immunity right here on the spot? The clock was ticking, and I now had less than forty-eight hours. All my judgment and expertise came into play. This was a very tough call.

"Why?" I said.

"I'd rather not say." He picked up his phone.

"Wait a minute." I held up my hand, palm toward him. "Hold it. Doctor, you know as well as I do that you are completely within your rights to have your lawyer present, but you may be jumping the gun a little. I don't know why you think I'm here, but I'm looking for the killer who's targeted the Johnsons. Now, if you still want to call your lawyer, go ahead. But I personally have a feeling if you'll tell me your whereabouts last Tuesday night, you'll move way to the bottom of the suspect list."

I was thinking, this would be just my luck, to have some guy so guilty about overbilling his patients, or billing them for services not rendered, or cheating on the travel and entertainment line of his federal income tax form, that I'd sink into a big mess of red tape and my whole career would come to a screeching halt.

Dr. Schmidt's relief at my words was palpable. He opened his large calendar portfolio and swept the pages back a week. "I was at Christ and St. Luke's, a patient was having a baby."

I wrote that down. "How about yesterday afternoon between the hours of three and four?"

He flipped the page back. "I saw patients all day up until six."

I wrote that down. "Good, now, based on those alibis holding up, which I'm pretty sure they will, you are not a suspect, officially or unofficially. And I've got to tell you, Doctor, I can spend a lot of valuable time checking you out, but I know you are not the killer."

He nodded his head. "You're correct. I'm not. But," he blurted out, "she was blackmailing me."

"She who?"

"Adelaide Johnson."

"Over what?"

"A case several years ago. A patient died and it was my fault. I could have lost my practice. My license. Everything. She was the only one who knew, and she never mentioned it until last year when she showed up on my doorstep and said there was something she wanted me to do for her. She offered me a great deal of money."

"She was blackmailing you *and* paying you? Isn't that odd?"

"Adelaide was always all business. Always made sure there was a paper trail that worked to her benefit. She would have turned her payments to me into my blackmailing her for some trumped-up reason or other. That receipt you found is a drop in the bucket." He looked at me and I saw his eyes had filled with tears. "My wife, Lucy, was dying. I was desperate. I needed the money."

"Tell me," I said.

"Lucy died six months ago, anyway. Adelaide's money didn't make any difference and I suppose what I tell you won't make any difference, either." He stopped to gather himself back together.

"Please."

"Victoria Hewitt has been my patient for more than thirty years. Do you know her?"

"Yes," I answered. "My whole life. I know her well. At least, I used to. She's not in such great shape, now. Her mind is gone."

"The truth is, there wasn't anything wrong with her. Adelaide has been paying me twenty thousand dollars a month to drug Victoria. Turn her into a paranoid schizophrenic. It's ironic you'd show up here today, because the final hearing is this afternoon at two o'clock. I'm supposed to sign the committal papers that will put her in St. Mary's for the rest of her life."

"Which will clear the way for the High River Ranch project to go forward," I said. No wonder James Hewitt was so eager to cooperate yesterday: his entire raison d'être was coming down at two o'clock today. He probably saw it as the biggest day of his life, a double play: He'd get even with his mother and endear himself to his new family—the Johnson clan—or what was left of them—forever. He couldn't see that once they had his land they'd chuck him into the wastebasket like a bunch of flyers for yesterday's open house.

"Is she a totally lost cause?"

The doctor looked at his hands and shook his head. "I'm not sure. We're in unknown territory."

"Dr. Schmidt," I exhorted him, "if there's any chance Victoria is salvageable, this is your opportunity to rectify your actions. You can save her and you can save her ranch. And you can save yourself, starting now."

He didn't seem so much reluctant as he did befuddled. His age had swept over him like a crushing wave.

"Please, Doctor. If you can fix it, do."

"Please, God, don't let it be too late." He picked up the phone and dialed the number from memory. "Laird? Dr. Schmidt here. I want you to stop Mrs. Hewitt's medication immediately. That's right. Immediately. Do not give her her ten A.M. dose. *No more Dr Peppers.* Do you understand? I'm on my way over right now."

Dr Peppers? I almost laughed out loud thinking about Victoria in that moldy house screaming for another Dr Pepper.

"Dr Pepper?" I asked when he'd hung up.

"She loves them and they're a perfect mask for the LSD. Tiny, regular doses keep her borderline delusional."

"Do Tom Johnson and James Hewitt know about your agreement with Adelaide? Do they know what you've been doing?"

"I doubt it."

I doubted it, too. If Adelaide didn't tell Tom about little things, I was certain she wouldn't share with him something as major as drugging Victoria Hewitt.

"Where did Laird come from?" I asked.

"Victoria hired him years ago as her personal trainer when she was still able to work out, and he's just stayed on as her de facto nurse and companion."

"So you trust him."

"Absolutely."

"Here's what I want you to do," I said.

Thirty-one

I hadn't been back in the car for more than ten seconds when Elias called.

"What's up?"

"I'm at the airport. Adam Garrett checked in for United's eleven o'clock shuttle to Las Vegas."

"Stay with him."

"No."

"No?"

"No," he shouted. I had to hold the phone away from my ear. "I'm not going to take off today and leave Linda alone for our engagement party, and that's exactly what will happen. I will follow this clown to Nevada, he'll spend three days fucking around. Somehow or other, I'll get shot or stabbed or blown up, and I'll lose my life or a limb, and worst of all, I'll lose Linda, and the answer is no."

The fact is, the guy had a point. "All right," I said.

"All right?" He couldn't believe I'd let him off without a fight. "All right? Are you sure?"

"Yes. Have you gotten anything back on the showgirls yet?"

"Should have everything this afternoon. Between their false names and the U.S. Immigration Service, it's complicated."

"I appreciate whatever you can get. I'll talk to you later." I punched in Richard's number as I sped toward the airport. "What are you doing?"

"I'm busy working," he said impatiently. "What are you doing?"

"Want to have an adventure?"

"I have plenty of adventures right here at my desk, thanks. I'm pretty adventured out at the moment."

"No, I mean a real one. Come to Las Vegas with me."

"When?"

"Right now. Meet me at the hangar."

"You're serious."

"We'll be back in no time, and you can work on the plane. I won't bother you."

I bit my lip to make myself keep my mouth shut and give him a chance to consider.

"What the hell," he said. "My lawyer said to stay away from Kaleen, which means I can't attend the rehearsals. I can do these calls and paperwork on the road. Yeah, I'll do it. I'm on my way."

"You are so fine."

□ □ □ □

The little Lear was gassed up and ready to roll, and after take-off, we each retreated into our own world of business. Richard, to contract negotiations for artists—none of whom he had been intimate with—for future seasons; and me, back to trying to figure out, as Janet Reno had so succinctly put it: What the hell was going on.

Getting up forty thousand feet in the sky clears my head, gives me vision, literally and figuratively. Not only can you see hundreds of miles, your brain, if you let it, will open up and give you the full dimensionality of a problem. Deliver the ball. All you have to do is listen.

I sat back, closed my eyes, and examined the evidence and action to date. I wondered if, as in many cases, there were possibly two separate but parallel situations, one merely coincidental to the other.

Out of the ether of the jet engines' screaming white silence, the possibilities revealed themselves.

Possibility One was the High River Ranch project and all its surrounding skullduggery: This included James Hewitt's vendetta against his mother and brother, surreptitiously aided and expedited by Adelaide's poisoning of Victoria. The involvement of a number of government officials—some more elevated than others—was another factor, but when you got right down to it, their corruption was not very unusual for a project of this magnitude. Every land development deal is done under the table, with money changing hands with the elected and appointed powers-that-be, whether they're zoning board members or presidents.

Possibility Two was the Johnson family itself. What if this were a vendetta against them, personally? Say Clay Parker's murder was just to set the stage. Throw us off the scent. Frank and his wife: dead. Adelaide: dead. Dolly: dead. Who was left?

Tom and Lucky. Were they responsible? Or the next victims? Who stood to gain? Tom would gain the most. I was positive Lucky had a tight and generous prenuptial agreement, no matter what happened to Tom, be it death or divorce. But if Tom were behind the killings, wasn't it a little obvious? Who else stood to gain? Why was Adam Garrett going to Las Vegas? Maybe we would find the answers there.

I opened my eyes and looked at the vast nothingness of the land grow closer. Moments later, we touched down and screeched to a halt next to the Luxor's Great Pyramid and Sphinx, which sit practically in the middle of the runway.

Grady met us at the plane. "Where to, boss?"

"The main terminal."

Richard stayed in the car while I raced to beat the eleven o'clock shuttle from Roundup to the gate. It was docking when I arrived. McCarran's concourses and gate areas are so jammed with slot machines—they fill every available square foot of airport space—passengers practically have to fight their way through them to the trams that run to the terminal. Concealed behind a row of Lucky 7s, I waited until Adam Garrett strode out of the jetway. As before, he was an easy tail. He was such a strong presence, the people who didn't look at him were in the minority.

I watched from the other end of the tram car while a stranger spoke to him in an animated way for the entire ride. Adam appeared to take it all good-naturedly, smiling at the man from behind his mirrored Ray-Bans. What an awful way to make a living. Almost as bad as being a member of the media. Politicians give, media types take. Both do it all in public. They've traded class for clout.

One time, I read, Colorado's senator, Ben Nighthorse Campbell, was on a flight to Washington from Denver when another passenger walked up and started berating him about something. Senator Campbell went ballistic, yelling at the guy to leave him alone, just because he was a public servant didn't mean he was public property, he had as much right to privacy as anyone else, and so forth. I didn't blame him a bit.

Adam exited the airport quickly and jumped into the first available cab. We took off right behind, and Grady stuck to his bumper for the few short blocks to the old Zanzibar Coast Casino—one of the few remaining relics of the Strip's golden days.

Grady whistled.

"What?" I asked.

"This is where it all happens."

"You mean happened," Richard observed, taking in the chipped stucco on the old facade, the grimy indoor-outdoor carpeting on the driveway, and the overflowing ashtrays at the glass front doors, which were slick with fingerprints. "This place is on its last legs."

"No, sir. Happens. This is where the bosses meet."

Richard looked at me and rolled his eyes.

"Come on," I said. "Put on your shades and let's go."

Thirty-two

The transition from our cool, dim, quiet car through the casino doors and into jarring noise and thick cigarette smoke, was almost disorienting. The place was mobbed with grungy types shuffling around the stained and sticky floor from slot machine to slot machine, their hands black from the coins they dug out of plastic tubs and dropped like automatons into their staked-out rows of one-armed bandits. They didn't even have to take the time to pull the arm anymore, all they did was push a button. A spinning light and clanging bell on top of each machine announced when a jackpot had been hit, and from the looks and sounds of it, the Zanzibar Coast was an easy mark.

Way off to the side at the end of the vast lobby was the

rocky, cavelike entrance to the restaurant—the Blue Grotto. Adam Garrett was just disappearing into its dark, gaping mouth. We followed.

"May I help you please, sir?" A tuxedo-clad maître d', a tiny man with a pencil mustache, stepped around his podium-desk and blocked our way. The dining room itself was hidden behind a wall of fake rocks draped with fake moss and red plastic hibiscus.

"A table for two," Richard said.

"Do you have a reservation, sir? We are completely booked."

"No." Richard palmed him a fifty.

"Please wait one moment and I will see what I can arrange." He stepped behind the wall, leaving us with a view of the coat-check room and an unplugged cigarette machine.

I could feel the eyes all over us. Camera eyes and living eyes. Virtually everything is watched in Las Vegas. Every breath. Every move. Every glance. Not only do the casino floors swarm with undercover bosses and chicks, most visitors are unaware that the ceilings of all the casinos, dining rooms, cocktail lounges, hotel corridors, and lobbies are false. And one-way transparent. A whole other floor of people is on catwalks up there, looking down on the activity, watching the dealers, the gamblers, the deal makers, the hookers, the customers. The human eyes are backed up by surveillance cameras located every few feet, which feed back to monitors that other, bigger bosses study. Nothing goes undetected.

So I knew, as Richard and I waited for admittance into the Blue Grotto, that we were being studied. I also knew that whoever was doing the studying knew exactly who we were.

The maître d' reemerged smiling and gathered up two thick, leather-bound menus and a large wine book from his stand. "Follow me, please, sir. And madam." His manner was courteous and deferential.

As its name implied, the Blue Grotto was dark; however, nothing was blue or bore any relationship to a secret cave hidden by the tides—booths upholstered in black leather; dim, smoky light from golden sconces with twenty-watt bulbs reflected off black-and-gold flocked wallpaper; black-and-gold patterned carpeting. The ceiling had sparkles in it. Two long, empty tables for large parties ran down the center. As we followed along, I noticed a waiter taking a drink order from Adam. All I could see at a glance was that he was with a woman who had lots of blond hair and dark glasses. She looked like Madonna. I assumed she was Margaret Wallis.

Richard ordered a bottle of champagne.

"What the hell," he said. I think Kaleen Warhurst's lawsuit was having a greater effect on him than he cared to admit.

When our eyes became accustomed to the dark, we could begin to see faces at the tables across from us. The clientele was made up entirely of older men and younger women, except for one table, which held four men in business suits. One of them stood up and approached us.

"Babe," he said. I hadn't recognized him in the murk. It was Mickey Giardino. "Why didn't you tell me you were coming to town?"

I introduced him to Richard.

"You are some kind of lucky guy," Mickey said.

"Yes." Richard's jaw was tight.

"May I?" Mickey indicated the empty place at the end of our table, sat down, and snapped his fingers. A waiter was there instantly with a demitasse of espresso. "What brings you to our fair city? You here about my eggs?"

"No," I answered. "Is this your casino?"

"You could say that." Mickey dropped three sugar cubes into the coffee. "I have a number of interests." His eyes stayed on Richard as he stirred. "How about if you stay in town for a couple of days as our guests. All comp. We'll put you up at the Mirage, big suite, big line of credit—all comp. This place," he indicated the room with a small tilt of his head, "is not for you."

He and Richard continued their staredown. Two big bulls starting to paw the dirt.

"But I guess you knew that," Mickey said. He removed a flat gold cigarette case from his pocket, opened it, and offered the cigarettes to us before helping himself. "Nobody in the outside world smokes anymore. Do they?" The question was more of a statement, neither expecting nor requiring a response. "I heard where Janet Reno and Louis Freeh handed you the keys to the country. You here on an official visit?"

I nodded. "What is Adam Garrett doing here?"

"Free country last I checked."

"No, I mean here in this room?"

"This is a private kind of room. He's a member you could say. Lots of important men come here—they like the privacy."

"Who's that he's with?"

"I'm not too sure," Mickey said. "He's here with her occasionally, but she's not a regular girl, if you know what I mean. I can find out for you. Is he a focus of the investigation?"

I ignored the question. "Do you know a woman named Margaret Wallis?"

Mickey looked at me with his dark eyes and tapped his index finger on his lips. "Rings no bells," he said.

I could see it had been a mistake to invite Richard. He and Mickey hated each other's guts and this was turning into a big testosterone face-off. Mickey was possibly lying and definitely being obstructionist, showing Richard that he wasn't going to let some dumb chick interrogate or intimidate him. And Richard was looking at Mickey and remembering I'd said that the most erotic night I'd ever spent in my life was with Mickey Giardino. He was getting madder. And madder. And madder. At Mickey. And me. He was steaming.

And I'm thinking, maybe I shouldn't have been so forthright in the first place, telling Richard about the one night I spent with Mickey. But hey, it was *years* ago. And what about all of Richard's lovers—including Kaleen and Suka? Both of whom were practically sleeping right on our doorstep, I might add. Already I was building my defense.

However, there was no changing the immediate situation. I had to find a way to work with it.

"Mickey." I put my hand on top of his and looked directly into his eyes, forcing him to turn them from Richard. "This is a big investigation, very wide-ranging. But to my knowledge it does not include you, nor any of your buddies, nor any of your businesses. And, as you yourself just pointed out, I have the keys to the country." I didn't add that I only had them for about forty more hours. "I'd appreciate your help. The fact is, if you don't help me, I'm going to have to request assistance from the local feds, and I really, really do not want to do that because it will add an element that would be overkill and cumbersome. I know you have all the information I need at the snap of your fingers."

Mickey had not gotten where he was because he was stupid. He was one of the smartest, most powerful, most-feared businessmen in the country. A virtual kingpin. No way would he risk bringing the local feds—who now basically lived on every casino's premises—into his inner sanctum because he didn't like the federal marshal's husband.

"I'm telling you the truth, babe. I'm not sure what her name is—Margaret Wallis doesn't mean anything, but she and Garrett have been seeing each other a long time."

"You've never been introduced?"

"Sure. Dozens of times. But her name? Do you have any idea how many girls I meet every day? And she's not what I would call the pick of the litter. I mean she's not bad but," he shrugged, "she's old. What's to remember?"

This remark gave me a brief thrill of satisfaction. Out of all the girls Mickey had met over the years and probably all the wild nights he'd spent at hundreds of boxing matches, he'd still remembered me.

"Is she a dancer?"

"Nah. She showed up in Vegas a few years ago, never has had a job I know of that drew any attention to herself. Garrett flies in to see her about once a week, but she never goes out with him in public—like at Clay's funeral for instance, she wasn't there. Could be he supports her. Do you want me to get her name and introduce you?"

"Not just yet, thanks."

"You let me know. In the meantime, I'll get my people on it, see what I can find out." Mickey swallowed the last of the sweet coffee. "Lunch is on me. Have whatever you want."

He stood up and so did Richard. They shook hands.

"Stay on those eggs, babe." Mickey kissed my hand.

"Interesting guy," Richard said when he'd left.

Thirty-three

I picked up my menu and frowned at Richard over the top of my reading glasses.

"What?" he asked innocently.

"I thought you two were going to start lifting your legs on each other. God."

" 'God' what?"

"Forget it."

The menu had been carried to Las Vegas from the Stork Club in the fifties and never revised. It was the Holy Grail of decadence, loaded with what *Gourmet* magazine calls "Forbidden Pleasures." And although we could have had cherrystone clams casino or escargots bourguignon to start, followed by lobster thermidor or abalone d'oré stuffed with crab in a cream sauce or veal scallopini or a tournedos of beef with crab legs, asparagus, and bacon, and concluded with baked Alaska or crêpes suzettes, we kept it simple—small filets and sliced tomatoes.

One hour passed. Two. We'd long since finished the champagne and each drunk an entire pot of espresso.

"What in the hell are they doing over there?" Richard asked since I had the better view of Adam's table. While I couldn't see Adam, I could see a small slice of the blonde, who seemed to be doing most of the talking. She was counting something on her fingers. Counting what? Months till the baby came? How many payments Adam had left on his contract with her? Minutes till the next murder?

"Want me to show you?" I joked.

"No, I've got to leave. I've got to get back to work." Richard had gotten very testy and I wasn't exactly having a ball. "This was a bad idea."

We tried to call our respective offices on our respective phones, but the Blue Grotto had been blocked to outside communication.

Finally, the lovebirds drifted past, not looking at either one of us, and Richard walked out so closely behind them, I thought he was going to step on their heels.

They climbed into a white Corvette convertible that idled at the front door. The woman smiled at the valet and did not offer him any cash—meaning they knew each other. Meaning he was on her payroll, for whatever that was worth. She climbed behind the wheel and tied a scarf over her head. The hair looked like a wig. Adam lowered himself into the passenger seat and we followed them back to the airport. She gave him a big kiss good-bye. End of rendezvous.

"All right," Richard said enthusiastically. "Let's go."

"No," I said. "I can't."

"Excuse me?"

"I want to know who this woman is. I'm staying."

"What?"

Adam was walking into the terminal and the Corvette was pulling away. I didn't want to lose her.

"I'm sorry, Richard," I said anxiously and kept my eyes on her car. "But if you want to go home, you'll have to take United, bacause I've got to stay. And you need to decide *now.*"

Richard saw the sports car moving off and immediately grasped the situation. He climbed out quickly. "Be careful and I'll see you at the party. I love you, darling. You make sure nothing happens to this girl," he said to Grady through the open window.

"Yes, sir." With that, Grady floored the big sedan and laid fifteen feet of high-quality German rubber along the lines of passengers checking in curbside. Out the back window, it looked like Richard's boots were in flames. He was waving and so was I, but he couldn't see me through the darkened windows.

"I love you," I called, but he couldn't hear me either.

The woman got onto the interstate and joined the traffic. Grady stayed relatively close behind, but unless she'd memorized our license plate, there was no way she'd know we were tailing her because practically every other car on the road was a white Town Car owned by Bell Transportation.

I'd done a little business over the years with the Las Vegas chief of police and had had plenty of cocktails with him at numerous police conventions, so after twenty seconds of hellos, I asked him to check out her license for me. He knew better than to ask why I wasn't calling the local FBI office for the info. All law enforcement officers appreciate the concept that

power and control are ninety percent perception and ten percent weaponry and that I didn't want them to know I needed
any help doing anything. Even the slightest whiff I might not
be able to handle the task and my thirty-seven remaining hours
would be out the bottom of the hourglass before I could blink.
This sort of assignment was an incubator for enemies.

"Hold on," he said.

I sat back in the comfortable seat and drummed my fingers
on the ashtray as Las Vegas, which, now that we were away
from the Strip, could have been any city in the western United
States, passed us by.

We were cruising out of town, headed north.

"Registration is in the name of Margaret Wallis." He repeated the address we'd had earlier in Henderson.

"But that's a 7-Eleven," I told him.

"Must have a mailbox service in it," he said.

"You mean it's legal to get your driver's license and regis-
ter your car to a post office box?" I asked.

"This is Nevada," he answered. "You can do anything you
want."

"Does she have a record?"

She didn't.

"Are we almost to Henderson?" I asked Grady as we
passed the entrance to Nellis Air Force Base and picked up
speed.

"No, ma'am. Henderson's south of town."

North of Las Vegas is nothing. That is no exaggeration.
Literally nothing. And I couldn't tell if she'd accelerated because she'd spotted us or because of the big emptiness, but after
a while, ours were the only cars on the interstate and we were
traveling at one hundred miles an hour. She exited onto Highway 93 and pushed it up to a hundred and twenty. Grady

stayed back, but unless she was blind, she knew we were tailing her. I glanced at my watch. Five o'clock. We'd been driving for over an hour. The car's external temperature gauge said it was still ninety-six. How did people live in this climate?

Margaret turned onto a two-lane, leading us deeper into the desert, and then she really put her foot down. And she disappeared.

"Forget it," I told Grady. "Let's go back."

"Yes, ma'am, I think she's got us."

He turned the car around in the middle of the highway and aimed it toward town. Ten minutes later, we ran out of gas.

Where were we?

Nowhere.

Our phones didn't even work.

We were on the dark side of the moon.

Thirty-four

No gas. No phone. No air conditioning. The good news was that the sun was setting so it would cool off, except in what seemed like seconds, the temperature had dropped to forty-five. It was freezing.

We started walking.

It takes a lot to give me the willies—hitchhiking in Nevada can do it. And did. I even had a weapon and I still had the creeps. Highway crime-scene images filled my head—torture/slasher/mutilation slayings that are worse than a human can imagine. Killings people read about in the papers or hear about on the news: "Two bodies were found on Highway 93 late last night. They appeared to have died from knife wounds." But readers never see the pictures of the victims. Sometimes they see the bodies being wheeled away under white sheets or tucked neatly into body bags, and they think, "Oh, that person was stabbed once right in the heart, and his heart stopped right then and he was dead, and under that shroud, except for that one wound, everything looks normal." They cannot even begin to imagine what a nightmare those corpses are.

I started seeing my body found on the desert floor, unbroken strings of ants—that from a distance would look like thin lines drawn in black ink—crawling silently out of my nose and mouth and eyes and ears, carrying away my brain, sinuses, and gums, one ant mouthful at a time. My fingernails broken and my beautiful wedding and engagement rings gone, found days or weeks later in some cheezy pawnshop, sold to feed some lowlife's drug problem or to buy more bullets. At least, I thought, I hope I'm dead by the time they cut off my breasts or carve some satanic message on my forehead and chest and butt. And I was glad I didn't have pierced ears so they couldn't rip away my lobes when they stole my earrings. I prayed they wouldn't break my teeth with their gun butts, softening up my gums so they could force themselves into my mouth and I wouldn't have anything left—neither teeth nor will—to bite them with. I prayed that whoever found Grady's and my bodies wouldn't find a broken vodka bottle inside me. Or worse, Grady's chopped-off penis.

I pictured Richard and my parents and my brothers at hearing the news and knew, right off the bat, they'd all blame Richard for leaving me alone in Las Vegas, but after a while they'd agree I'd always been uncontrollable and forgive him. Would they find the instructions I'd left for my funeral? That I wanted all Casablanca lilies because they were my favorite but I'm allergic to them so the only time I'll be able to enjoy them is when I'm dead. Would they find my music list? Andrew

Lloyd Webber's *Requiem,* Widor's *Toccata,* Roy Rogers's "Happy Trails." Would they remember that I wanted to be there at my own funeral, in my coffin—closed—and then cremated and sprinkled on the hillside across the river?

I started to cry. Who gave a shit anyway if everyone in the Johnson family got murdered? Who cared what Janet Reno thought? She was just an appointee. What was I doing here? My whole family was back at the ranch do-si-do-ing in celebration of my beloved brother's engagement and I was hobbling down an abandoned Nevada highway in a tight pair of Charles Jourdan pumps.

Night fell and no headlights appeared on any horizon. I stepped in a pothole and tripped and fell and skinned my knee and snapped the heel off my shoe and twisted my ankle. I was pretty sure it was broken.

"You got to look at it this way, Marshal," Grady said as he helped me to my feet. "It's too cold for the snakes to be slithering around, biting our ankles."

I cried harder.

The two of us walked side by side down the center of the empty highway in the deepening twilight. It was absolutely freezing. Finally, after God knows how long, we saw car lights and Grady almost got killed flagging down the rusted little maroon Mazda.

So this was how it would end. Murdered by a Mazda driver. I'd always wanted to go the way Pamela Harriman did: of a heart attack in the Ritz Hotel swimming pool in Paris.

"What are you folks doing out here?" a cheery lady's voice asked. "You could get murdered or something. Come on. Get in. You must be cold as hell. What happened? You all run out of gas or something?"

Yes. Yes. Yes.

She was a dealer at the Bellagio on her way to work.

Okay. Maybe I got a little carried away, but I knew what the possibilities were. Sometimes, I think I know too much.

I'm going to get that bitch, Margaret Wallis, I vowed as the little jet broke from the ground, and I swallowed a big gulp of Jameson. She would pay for this. Big time.

Thirty-five

About half an hour from Roundup, I finally succeeded in getting Richard on the phone. The party was loud in the background until he went outside.

"You're missing a lot of excitement," he said. I could tell he had a cigar in his mouth and was slightly loaded.

"Oh?" He had no idea.

"We just broke up a fistfight between Tom Johnson and Adam Garrett. Adam and Lucky were dancing together and Tom thought they were getting too familiar, so he punched him. Then the two of them really went at it. Tom's toupee went across the room like a . . ."

"Don't say it," I said. "I get the picture."

"Your father's the one who broke it up."

"No way."

"He stepped in and grabbed them by their throats and told them if they couldn't act like gentlemen, then to get the hell off his property and never set foot on the place again."

I was speechless. My father was *never* confrontational. He was a total behind-the-scenes kind of guy. He must have really been angry.

Suddenly my mother was on the phone. I guess she'd ripped it right out of Richard's hand. I think everyone at this party was completely smashed.

"Where are you?" she shouted.

"In the plane on my way home."

"You get back here and fix this mess. You and your damn . . . damn . . . *Democrats.*"

In her lexicon, it was the worst epithet possible.

"And what on earth gave you the idea that Victoria Hewitt and her butler could move into our guest rooms? She's as nutty as a fruitcake and he looks like Cro-Magnon man with that sloping brow and crazy hair."

I'd completely forgotten I'd told Dr. Schmidt to get Victoria and Laird off the Broken Arrow as soon as he could and move them to my parents', where I knew they'd be safe. I started to laugh.

"It's not what I'd call funny," Mother said, except I could hear laughter begin to creep into her voice. "I was just getting ready to get in the tub—I was supposed to attend a Junior League luncheon, well, that went right out the window—when Manuel came up and said there was an ambulance, a doctor, a nurse, two crazy-looking people, and a mountain of Louis Vuitton luggage at the front door. So I went down and there's Victoria with this entourage."

The line got statick-y.

"When will you be here?" It was Richard.

"Soon," I told him.

"Good. This is too much fun for you to miss."

"Come on, Ricardo," I heard a woman say in an insinuating sort of way. "They're forming up a new line."

Ricardo?

Line dancing—one of my faves. I'd been so busy with my own problems, I'd completely forgotten that prima showgirl Suka, the exotic, erotic *sauvage* who'd sucked out practically all of Dwight's blood and who was one of Richard's former lovers, was at the party, too. And now there was someone calling him *Ricardo?* What exactly did he mean by "too much fun"?

"You know your brother doesn't like us to use the strip at the ranch except in case of emergency," the captain told me.

"This is one, believe me."

Then we were flying over the Circle B. Everything as far as I could see was pitch black except the light pouring from the open barn doors, reflecting off the cars parked along the road. And old Ricardo was in there bucking and clapping with one of the rodeo girls.

The lights on the landing strip magically came on—now I knew it was because the captain had clicked his radio button three times—and we screamed down the valley, flying the break past the barn, turning into a steep left bank, and touching down like greased lightning. To keep his Marine pilots happy, Christian had painted the strip at the ranch like a carrier deck; there was even a "meatball" of landing lights. Marines fly like wild animals. It's something in their souls. Their skill and precision in executing exquisite carrier landings, real or imagined, is second to none. I don't know how they found the Circle B in the first place in all that dark.

Richard was waiting for me at the bottom of the stairs. "What happened to you?" he asked as I limped off the plane with my bloody knee and ripped skirt and grimy face and broken shoe. "Are you all right?"

"Remind me never to go to Las Vegas again. You have no idea," I answered. "But it's all right now that I'm looking at you." He had never looked so good.

"Come on, I'll run you up to the house so you can change. The party's really rolling."

The fact was, as I stood in the shower and let the hot water pour over me, I didn't care about the party. All I wanted to do was get in bed and feel sorry for myself and get back on the case at the crack of dawn. Adam Garrett and his mystery girl were at the top of my list.

"Come on, babe." I could see Richard through the foggy glass shower door holding a towel. "Get a move on."

Babe. Give me a break.

For the last two days, Elias and his crew had scrubbed the cement floor in the barn until it looked like new, and rubbed the wooden stall dividers with cedar oil so they gleamed with a beautiful burnished glow. The wranglers themselves had scrubbed up like new pennies and looked like movie stars lined up against the box stall gates, in their tight, ironed Wranglers and clean white shirts and bandannas and good hats. They held long-necks of Coors and blushed at their polished boots when one of the girls walked by.

The horses, which peeked out between the cowboys, seemed singularly disinterested in the raucous goings on. If they couldn't eat it, they didn't care. A low stage had been erected and the cowboy band, square dance caller, and girl singer were going to town.

"Glad you could drop in," Mother said as she promenaded past on my father's arm. She had on a blue suede skirt, a white blouse embroidered with red, blue, and yellow flowers, and red snakeskin boots. It was sort of like seeing Claudette Colbert dressed up as a cowgirl. My father, on the other hand, was Gary Cooper. A born and bred cowhand, through and through. "Did you see who's here?" Mother's eyes twinkled.

Just then, the song ended and new squares formed, so Richard and I hurried to join in. I love square dancing, but it's not like line dancing or the two-step or fox-trot or samba or rhumba or tango, where you've known the steps all your life and just go along, and if you trip a little every now and then, miss a step or two, no big deal. No. In square dancing, in spite of the fact that all you want to do is laugh and you get winded so quickly you think you're going to die, you have to listen and concentrate or you can screw the whole thing up for everybody, so I hadn't really had an opportunity to see who-all was at the party, and now the only people I could look at—and then just for a brief passing promenade or twirl or do-si-do— were the other dancers in our square—sixteen of us in all: four small squares of four. We formed up quickly, sharing our four-square with Buck and the showgirl Lana, who had on skintight black jeans tucked into high boots and a loose, rouge velvet Navajo Indian blouse caught with a concho belt at her waist. No bra, of course.

I glanced over my shoulder at my parent's square, and in addition to lots of guests I recognized but didn't know— friends of Elias's and Linda's—I spotted Tom and Lucky Johnson. Tom had a Band-Aid over his left eyebrow, a black eye, and a split lip.

"Greet your partner," the caller called and sawed on his fiddle and tapped his foot.

Richard and I stepped forward, then back. Buck and Lana repeated the steps.

"Greet your other partner."

"I like your haircut," I said to Buck as he bowed and I curtsied.

"She is the nicest girl I've ever met. In my life," he said.

"Swing your partner and do-si-do."

We wove and swung around the room, bowing, twirling, kicking up our heels, laughing, happy, changing partners with giddy swings, afraid not to listen, afraid to make a wrong step, turn the wrong direction, and have the caller yell at you—I felt like Scarlett O'Hara doing the Virginia Reel at the War Bond dance, getting handed off from one handsome soldier-stud to another—Richard, Buck, Elias, Christian, Dwight, William Hewitt, Adam Garrett (who had no marks from the fisticuffs at all) and . . . Wayne Newton.

"Well, hello, there," he said.

What?

Then he was gone and I was back to Richard and we still had about ten more minutes to go. There was no time to think about it. Wayne Newton at the Circle B. How cool was that?

The barn rocked with the band and the fiddle and all the light feet. We girls all looked and felt as beautiful as if we'd each been chosen to be the Homecoming Queen at our college dance—the guest of honor, Linda, who'd tied a pink ribbon around her head to hold back all that gorgeous red hair, could not stop laughing. Mimi, Miami McCloud Hewitt, Suka (who appeared to have forgotten all about Richard once Dwight appeared in her life), Adam's plump wife Susan, and my good friend Pitty-Pat Palmer, a former Miss Texas who was always on the lookout for a new husband and who had, naturally, snagged Wayne, and didn't care that he was already married.

We danced and danced, and I thought, why would I go off and chase after a bunch of third-rate bad-guy losers, who can kill each other off for all I care, when I have this? Why not just do this all the time?

"I'm going to take myself off the case in the morning," I told Richard. We were outside catching our breath. "I don't have anything but this mystery woman, Margaret Wallis, and I'm not the person to track her down in Nevada."

"Why not?"

"I don't know anyone, I don't know the territory, I don't *like* the territory. Too many snakes. I'm letting my pride get in the way and slowing down the process. If I keep going, I'll start looking bad. Unprofessional. A bigger team will get more done."

"I understand."

Later, we stood by the barn doors and watched Elias and Linda telling their guests goodnight and receiving their congratulations. I have never seen two happier people in my life, except for Richard and me. Even Buck, who never wanted anything to change, especially his relationship with Elias, was happy. Of course, that might have had to do with the fact that Lana seemed genuinely to like him. We watched him help her into the high cab of his Ram pickup and hand her the seat belt.

By one-thirty, everyone was gone.

"Here's the info," Elias said and handed me a sealed envelope. "Some pretty interesting stuff. I think you'll want to read it right away."

"Thanks."

By one-forty, I was sound asleep. I didn't open the envelope and I didn't wash my face.

Thirty-six

At two twenty-six, the phone rang and I flew about ten feet off the bed.

"Bennett," I said, my voice sharp, my head clear. I was awake, ready to go. Years of experience train police officers that some sleep, even half an hour, is better than none, and you can always do more than you think you can.

"Sorry to disturb your beauty rest." It was Jack Lewis, who sounded as though he'd just stepped out of the shower and smacked on some Mennen "Thanks, I Needed That" Skin Bracer. "But we have a situation here. Seems Tom and Lucky Johnson were stopped at a light and someone blew him away."

It took me a second to grasp what that meant—the last Johnson was now dead.

"I thought you assigned someone to protect them."

"He told us he didn't need our guys to follow them to the party—I mean, that Range Rover is practically land-mine proof—and we're shorthanded, so I said fine."

"How's Lucky?"

"In shock but unharmed."

Jack gave me the address.

"I'm on my way. Try to keep her at the scene if you can. And send a squad by Senator Garrett's house. I don't want them to go in, just watch to see if there's any activity."

"Is this surveillance or protection?"

"Call it whatever you want."

"Right," Jack said. I knew he was being cooperative because he was gladder every second this wasn't his case. The thing stank worse than Yasir Arafat's feet.

"Want me to come with you?" Richard asked halfheartedly. I could hardly hear him from where he was speaking with his head under his pillows.

"No." I kissed the back of his neck. "But I need to take your car. Mine's at the airport."

"Help yourself," he said as he and Baby dropped back to sleep.

I splashed some water on my face and pulled on my middle-of-the-night crime-scene uniform—a black turtleneck sweater, black slacks, black wool jacket, thick-soled Robert Clegerie walking shoes—and closed the door softly behind me.

The flashers and halogen lights of a dozen police, emergency, rescue, and media vehicles had turned the corner of Cheyenne and Main into a movie set, as local residents, some with parkas over their bathrobes, gathered behind the police barricades.

Tom Johnson was still strapped into the passenger seat of

Lucky's black Range Rover, but most of the windshield was gone. His face and chest looked like raw hamburger. The acrylic toupee drooped like a furry Beanie Baby over where his bandaged black eye had been. It appeared the killer had jumped up onto the hood of the car and blasted him point-blank through the windshield. No other windows were broken. The driver and passenger doors were open and the car's headlights still burned. Someone had removed the keys from the ignition and laid them on the console.

"Has anyone checked the phone?" I asked Jack.

"No one's checked anything."

"Good. Thanks." I reached in and pressed the Send button on the phone. The last call had been to 911.

Down the street, through the open rear doors of a brightly lit ambulance, I could see Lucky sitting inside, wrapped in a gray blanket, chalk-white and shaking like a leaf. Her wide-open eyes watched my every move.

"What happened?" I asked Jack.

"Call came in to Roundup Emergency at two-twelve. It was Mrs. Johnson screaming that her husband had been shot. She was completely hysterical."

I circled the car, ending up back at the front. Scuff marks and notch-soled footprints were visible on the hood, and I could picture the same black-garbed killer who had shot Clay Parker scrambling up there lithely, firing off two fast rounds, and disappearing into the night. I wondered it if would turn out to be the same sawed-off shotgun that had killed Clay Parker. It had to have been a major weapon to inflict this much damage. I wondered it it had been Suka, then realized I'd left Elias's envelope of information on my dressing table.

"Officers are working the neighborhood right now. They haven't found any witnesses yet, but they're on it."

We were right at the edge of downtown and while the neighborhood wasn't the best, it wasn't the worst, either. It was a reclaimed slum and had a mixture of black and white, young and old, poor and upwardly mobile. If anyone had seen anything, they'd say so. These people worked hard to keep their neighborhood safe, and for the most part, it was. Tom Johnson's killing had nothing to do with them. No neighborhood kid had done this.

"Any report from the Garrett resident?"

"Dark and quiet. No activity."

I took a moment to study Lucky from where I stood outside and recollect things she'd said and done in the few days I'd known her. I didn't know much about her, but enough to know she would not be sorry Tom Johnson was dead. She'd been present or accounted for at every family disaster during the last week. Was she involved or the next victim? Unfortunately, I had no opinion, no conclusion, my mind was open.

"Let's go talk to the widow," I said.

Jack and I entered the ambulance bay, closed the doors, and sat down on the bench opposite her. Jack switched on the video recorder. Lucky appeared clammy and dry-mouthed. Her eyes were glassy and her energy was off the charts. I knew she was unaware that her whole right side—her hair, her face, what I could see of her clothes under the blanket—was decorated with bits and clumps of Tom's bone, brain, hair, and blood.

"Oh, God, Lilly." She spoke in a rush. "I'm so glad you're here. I can't even believe what happened."

"Tell me everything you remember." I reached across and took her hand. "Everything."

She glanced nervously at Jack and back to me. "Well, let me see. We were on our way home from your party, or rather, I

mean, your brother's party. And I told Tom I would drive
because he'd had too much to drink, plus that fight with
Adam." She started to drift away. "What a silly thing to do."

"Keep going, Lucky. Everything you can remember is important."

"You're referring to Adam Garrett?" Jack asked.

"Yes." Lucky nodded. "They'd had a fight because Tom
thought he was being too familiar with me, although he and his
wife are our closest friends."

"Okay." I tried to get her back on track. "So you're driving home. Is this the regular route you would take?"

Lucky nodded. "Do you suppose it's all right if I have a
cigarette?"

"I don't think you can smoke in an ambulance," I said,
frustrated by her babbling. "Oxygen and all."

"Oh, right."

"Why wouldn't you stay on the interstate to go home?"

"It loops so far out, it's quicker to cut crosstown."

"So, you're coming down Main Street and stop at a red
light?"

"Yes. And then, out of nowhere, I saw this thing right in
front of us. This big man. On the hood of my car. Right outside
the window. I saw the gun flash and I screamed and covered
my face. And there was an explosion." Lucky's face contorted
with the recollection and she began to cry. "Glass exploded
everywhere. It sounded like it was going to go on forever. And
then . . ." She broke down completely. Who could blame her,
with her husband like ground round in the seat next to her.

On television, this is the time when one cop says to the
other, Maybe we ought to let her rest. But Jack and I both
knew, in reality, cruel as it may be, this was when you had to
get all the information you could. When it was freshest, unvar-

nished, nonselective. When it gushed out in torrents. And when—on the chance the bereaved turned out in fact to be the perpetrator—it went on the record and couldn't be changed without a lot of shoring-up, back-filling explanations.

"Do you remember anything at all about this person?" I asked.

"Nothing. It was a flash and then the explosion."

"One or two explosions?"

"I don't know. It could have been two. It was so loud." She seemed to sink deeper into her shoulders. "I'd really like to go home."

"I know. I'm sorry we have to put you through this. Just a couple more questions. Do you remember what the killer was wearing?"

"Black. All black. He even had a mask. One of those horrible ski masks with tiny slits for the eyes and mouth."

"Gloves?"

"Yes. I think so."

"Did it look like the same person who shot Clay Parker at the banquet?"

"Possibly."

"You said it was a man, but could it have been a woman?"

The question surprised her. "I'm not sure. I suppose it could have been. But it would have to have been a very big, strong-looking woman."

"After you screamed and covered your face, and when the explosions were over, did you see the killer again?"

Lucky shook her head. "No, everything was quiet."

"Is there anything else you can recall? Do you remember what you were thinking?"

No answer.

"Do you have any idea how long it took you to call 911?"

"I think it was right off."

"Lucky, who's Margaret Wallis?"

"Who?" She appeared confused.

"Margaret Wallis. Who is she? She's having an affair with Adam Garrett."

Jack was looking at me like, Huh?

Lucky closed her eyes and shook her head. "I don't know what you're talking about. I must be in a dream or something. A nightmare."

"Could the killer have been Adam Garrett?"

By now Lucky and Jack were so baffled, they both looked at me as though I were crazy.

"Adam isn't a murderer, if that's what you're thinking."

I didn't know what I was thinking. I was grabbing at straws.

"Where can I find her?"

"Find who? I don't know what you're talking about. Can I please go home now? You're making me feel like I'm the one who shot Tom."

"We'll have someone drive you." Jack helped her to her feet, put his arm around her shoulder, and led her outside. I watched them go. Something tugged at my brain, just the way it had that afternoon in Lucky's dressing room and then a day later at Adelaide's office. What was it? Nothing. I needed to keep listening.

"Double her protection," I said to Jack when he returned. "I want someone watching her every move."

Lucky never said she was afraid the gunman was going to shoot her, too.

Thirty-seven

Thursday Morning

By the time I left the murder scene, the sun was up and I'd already had ten cups of coffee and about a dozen doughnuts. It was a little after six. I decided to call on former Senator and Mrs. Garrett.

The Victorian urban neighborhood still slept in the dawn chill, but lights burned downstairs in the Garretts' big two-story house. A patrol car idled in front and the officer rolled down his window as I approached.

"All quiet," he reported. "Front and back."

"Thanks." I rang the bell and was immediately greeted by the sound of large dogs barking.

Adam, looking fresh from the shower and dressed in a

business suit, opened the door and shooed back the two black labs. "This is unexpected," he said. He was holding a steaming cup of coffee.

"Tom Johnson has been murdered."

"You're not serious." Adam frowned. "What about Lucky?" He asked when he realized I *was* serious. "Is she all right? What happened?"

"She's naturally very shaken up but she's at home now. May I come in? It's cold out here."

"Oh, of course." He stepped aside and held the door open. "Please. Do you want a cup?" He led the way into the kitchen, where a full pot of coffee sat on the counter.

"Who is it Adam?" a sleepy voice called from upstairs.

"It's nothing, Susan. Go back to sleep." He turned his attention back to me. "What happened?"

"No, thanks," I said, purposefully not answering his question. "I'm all coffeed out." I removed my notebook and glasses from my jacket pocket. "I won't be here long. I've just got a few questions. What time did you leave the party?"

"I think it was about twelve-thirty. We were among the first to go. Susan was tired and wanted to go home."

"Where were you at two o'clock?"

"Home in bed. Asleep. You don't honestly think that I've had anything to do with these murders? Besides, Tom was a close friend and business associate."

"No, sir, I don't. But I do think you are somehow involved."

"Do I need to call my lawyer?"

"Not yet." I closed my book. "But do me a favor, don't leave town."

"Sorry, but I'm taking a nine o'clock to Toronto for an

afternoon conference, and unless you plan to arrest me, I'm going to make that flight and be back home in time for Letterman."

I didn't have any way to make him stay. I didn't have any hard evidence, and if you're going to tell a major elected official—former or not, they all had serious clout—not to leave town in a murder investigation, you'd better have your stuff totally together. Which I didn't.

"You aren't going to tell me how he was killed, are you?"

"You can see it on television. Have a good trip."

"Good morning, Bennett Security International." Linda's voice was crisp and snappy over the phone.

"How are you feeling?" I asked. The sun poured through the windshield into my eyes as I headed to the office.

"Terrific. How are you feeling? You're the one who's been up all night."

"Tell me about it. Is Elias around?"

"He's right here, sitting on the edge of my desk."

"Put him on, please."

"You know we leave for Hawaii tonight," he said before I'd even had a chance to say hello.

"This is just some simple surveillance. You can take Linda with you if you want, but I need someone to keep an eye on Adam Garrett, fly up to Toronto and back. The flight's at nine and you just have time to make it. I don't know if he and this Margaret Wallis person have anything to do with the Johnson family murders or not, but I'd feel better if you kept track of him."

Elias put his hand over the receiver and I could hear him and Linda consulting. "Where is he?"

"He was at his home on Pine Street, but I imagine he's left for the airport by now."

"Okay, I'll do it. Linda's going to stay in the office with Wayne."

"Wayne who?"

"Newton."

"Wayne Newton's in my office?"

"Dropped in to tell you good-bye. They're all heading back to Vegas since Lucky Johnson's birthday party tonight is presumably canceled."

"I'm on my way."

"Could you believe that stuff on the showgirls? I thought you'd be all over her."

Hell. I'd completely forgotten about the envelope. "Tell me what it said. I left it at home."

"If I'm going to make that plane I've got to leave right now. I'll call you from the car."

"In a nut shell," Elias reported, two minutes later, "Suka's real name is Anna Leopold. Born in Russia, her family was refusenik, emigrated to Israel in eighty-four when she was ten. And she was never in the Israeli Army, that claim is fake. Serious résumé enhancement."

"Okay."

"Martine is Martine Duvall. Parisian. Has a fourteen-year-old daughter. Frank Johnson was her sponsor to come to the U.S."

"As in Frank and Connie Johnson? Do you think she had anything to do with any of this stuff?"

"No." Elias slurped his coffee. "She's never been anywhere near any of the crime scenes."

"What about Lana?"

"Denied access. She was Sam Giardino's girl and the files are sealed."

"Do you know what hotel they're in?"

"Hold on, I'll call Linda." Seconds later he was back. "Wayne says Suka and Martine are flying back to Vegas with him this morning—they were still asleep when he left the Grand, so they're not going anywhere until he does. Lana's with Buck."

I made a U-turn and headed straight back downtown to the Roundup Grand Hotel. And when there was no answer to our knocks, the manager opened the doors to their rooms and they were empty.

Thirty-eight

Wayne Newton is a complete charmer. He, Dwight, Buck, Lana, and Richard were in the saloon having breakfast when I got to Bennett's Fort. Lana was snuggled up next to Buck.

"She's spending the weekend," he told me when I sat down between him and Richard. Dwight was practically face-first in his eggs, he was so exhausted.

"I'm sorry we didn't get to spend more time together," Wayne said to me. "And I'm sorry to meet your husband. Sorry I like him."

"Me, too." I kissed Richard's cheek. I was so hungry I thought I'd die and had just dug into a plate of pancakes, bacon, and fried eggs when my pager went off. It was a Nevada number. I put down my fork and went outside to return the call.

Mickey Giardino. "Babe," he said. "I think I might have something for you. That chick who was with Senator Garrett yesterday? That was Margaret Wallis."

"I know."

"What you probably don't know is that she and Lucky Johnson are sisters. Identical twins. Mary and Margaret Wallis. They were a big act in Monte Carlo—the Mirror Image—but then they disappeared. Boom. Right off the face of the earth. Something happened to Margaret's face—some guy slashed her into sukiyaki or something—so she quit dancing. Never danced in Vegas. Always stayed in the background. Worked as a flight instructor at one of the local fields. Mary changes her name to Lucky, becomes a big star, and no one even knows about her sister. That's it. Maybe it helps. How you doin' with my eggs?"

I had sat down on the wooden bench outside the saloon's swinging doors and was trying to get my breath. The ball had pulled together and was now hurtling through space at the speed of light.

"Babe?" Mickey was saying, "You there?"

"Yeah, I am. Thanks, Mickey, I'll get back to you."

I punched in numbers like crazy. Called Jack and told him to alert the watch on Lucky Johnson's house stat and make sure she didn't leave the premises.

Called Louis Freeh and told him everything I knew about Martine Duvall and her relationship with Frank Johnson. Brought him up to speed on Margaret Wallis and provided her license plate and post office box address. Tried Elias a hundred times, but his line was busy.

I ran back into the saloon. "Sorry," I said to everyone, "but I've got to go. Things are happening."

"Wait." Richard stood up. "You've got my car. Give me a ride to the office."

"Come on," I told him. "But you'll have to come to Lucky's house with me first. You drive."

Elias finally called from the plane.

"These seats are nice," he said. "They give you a back rub."

"I'm happy for you. Is the senator on board?"

"Yup. Chatting up the stewardesses. Doesn't even know I'm here. I'd like a bloody mary, please," he told the flight attendant.

"Stay in touch."

We were halfway to Lucky's when Jack called. "She's not here."

"What?" I couldn't believe my ears.

"No one's home. Place is locked up tight."

"How in the hell did that happen? Didn't you have someone on her?"

"There's a back drive," Jack said. "A servants' entrance down the hill our guys didn't see until the sun came up. She must have given us the slip that way—probably walked out the back door right after she walked in the front."

Where would she have gone? The cabin in the mountains? No, not now that she knew I knew about Margaret Wallis. She did not know, however, that I knew they were sisters. Las Vegas? No. Adam was going to Toronto, that was my only chance.

"Linda," I yelled into the phone—it was noisy in Richard's car with the top down—"go up to the house and get my passport and meet me at the hangar."

"Yes, ma'am."

"Change of plans, darling. Drop me at the airport."

I made three more fast calls. One to make sure the plane was available and had a crew ready to go. Another to Jack to tell him to start checking every possible flight connection from Roundup to Toronto looking for either Lucky Johnson or Mary Wallis or Margaret Wallis. And another to the control tower at the executive airfield. The controller confirmed the Johnson Land Company's Gulfstream Four had taken off at five-twenty. The flight plan indicated they were going to Los Angeles.

"Can you confirm that?" I asked.

Moments later he was back. "The flight plan was canceled shortly after takeoff."

Lucky was gone. Vanished into thin air. And I had a feeling Margaret was right there with her. Everything fit perfectly. Lucky was present at, or had solid alibis for, every murder. The killer was her sister. Lucky just told her where to be and when. The tall, agile shooter at the country club who flew away in our helicopter while Lucky was at the head table with her husband? Margaret. The big thug who'd drugged me and who knew how much sugar and metal to dump into the engines of Frank and Connie Johnson's King Air while Lucky was in Las Vegas with her husband? The flight instructor, Margaret. The person who stole James Hewitt's Humvee and drove Adelaide and Dolly Johnson into the cement divider while Lucky was at a dance rehearsal with—of all people—my mother? And the person who knew exactly which stoplight to wait at in downtown Roundup to leap onto the hood of the car and blow away Tom Johnson while Lucky sat behind the wheel. God. It was perfect.

But why?

Linda was waiting at the foot of the air stairs into the Gulfstream Five. "I brought all the passports, including mine." She held out Richard's and my little blue booklets. "I'm coming with you."

I looked at Richard over the tops of my glasses. I knew he wouldn't do it, he had too much other business to take care of and I think he was still a little p-o'd that I'd shanghaied him to Las Vegas.

"Don't worry about it," I said without waiting for him to say no. "I understand. I'll call you as soon as I know anything."

"Hell, no," he said. "I'm coming with you. Last time I left you on your own you got lost in the desert."

We were soon under way. Wheels up at ten-ten. Toronto-bound. Wheels down at ten-eighteen. Back in Roundup.

"We have a pressure gauge that isn't working," the pilot explained. "Shouldn't be more than a couple of minutes."

Back in the air at eleven. We were way behind, and I felt the killers slipping from my grasp like sand.

An hour into the flight, Elias called.

"What in the hell are you doing in the G-5? Linda and I are taking it to Hawaii tonight."

"We're headed for Toronto."

"There is no conference in Toronto," he said. He sounded totally dejected. "And remind me to kill you when I get home."

"Why?"

"He's getting on a flight to Rome."

"Well," I told him, "you'd better get a ticket."

"Linda and I have reservations at the Hualalai and that's where we're going. No way I'm going to Italy."

"Linda's with me."

"Where? On the plane? Put her on."

I handed Linda the phone and went to the cockpit to tell the crew it looked like we needed to head for Leonardo da Vinci.

Thirty-nine

Friday Morning

Fortunately, Louis Freeh had pulled rabbits out of his hat and cut through the Italian Airport Authority's notorious red tape. A sedan met us at our plane and delivered us to the main terminal. We were all at the gate when the Air Canada flight from Toronto arrived at five-thirty Friday morning.

Adam Garrett was the first passenger to emerge from the first-class jetway, looking fresh and rested, as opposed to Elias, who stumbled out after him, looking as though he'd been hit by a car. Initially, Adam couldn't believe his eyes.

"What are you doing here?" he said to me.

"I've got a few more questions. They've set aside a special room for us to talk. If you don't mind accompanying me."

"You don't have any official capacity here." Adam was off-base, getting huffy. "This is Italy."

"I am a United States Marshal," I said evenly. "My job is to enforce the laws of the United States. That mandate applies to the planet. And we have some pretty clear treaties with Italy that enable me to be here. I only want to question you. I think you may be in over your head."

"I don't know what you're talking about."

"I hope you're right."

We'd started to draw a crowd.

"Listen, Senator, the press is going to start showing up pretty soon, and I know you don't want your picture on the front page of the *New York Times* and the *International Herald Tribune* being greeted by the law in Rome where, I'm also pretty sure, no one knows you are." I took his arm and led him toward a side door, down a flight of outside stairs, and into a cramped, smoke-filled office where we were joined by a diplomatic aide from the American embassy, an embassy attorney assigned to Adam, and two dapper Italian chief detective inspectors.

"Where are Margaret Wallis and Lucky Johnson?" I began.

"I don't know. I suppose Margaret's in Las Vegas and Lucky's at home."

"Don't play games with me, Adam. You are in so much trouble you wouldn't even believe it. They are sisters—Mary and Margaret Wallis—and they have murdered every single member of the Johnson family. Not to mention Clay Parker. And you're obviously on your way to meet them. You're an accomplice to those murders."

"Wait a minute," Adam said. "What in the hell are you talking about? I had nothing to do with any of that. And I mean nothing. What do you mean Margaret and Lucky are

246

sisters? That's not true. They don't even know each other. And if you want to know the truth, I've just had my wife served with divorce papers and I'm meeting Margaret, not Lucky. Lucky Johnson has nothing to do with me. I didn't have anything to do with any murders and neither did Margaret."

I laid it all out for him, and by the time I was done, every bit of color had left his face. He looked as if he belonged in Madame Tussaud's, especially when I told him I thought he was probably the next and last name on their list.

"Will you cooperate?" I said. "Will you take us to them?"

"You bet I will."

We piled back into the Gulfstream and took off for a little strip on the mainland across from the island of Monte Argentario in southern Tuscany. It was ironic they had picked this region as their hideaway since Monte Argentario was one of the few places in Italy I knew at all. One of the towns on the island, Porto Ercole, was the home of my client, the Marchese Cortini, whose no-good cousin in Saturnia was always stealing his Titians and Canalettos.

Twenty minutes after takeoff we touched down and emerged into a velvety morning. An Alfa-Romeo sedan was waiting for us. I took the wheel and we zoomed off across the causeway with two vanfuls of carabinieri and two unmarked sedans behind.

"Go right. The villa's in Porto Santo Stephano," Adam said. He was still in shock and probably extremely depressed as we wound our way along the coastal cliffs and then up the narrow road over the top of the island. We made a sharp turn into a private enclave: CALA PICCOLA, the sign said. PRIVATO. And twisted down a steep hill to the parking area for a small hotel that had closed for the winter.

We waited there while commandos took their positions around the villa grounds. These women were extremely dangerous. No one was taking any chances. Adam, Elias, and I tugged on bulletproof vests and put our jackets back over them. Richard and Linda would wait in one of the sedans.

Far below, beyond a high hedge of oleander bushes, the Mediterranean sparkled in the sun. Small islands lay offshore looking like Bali Ha'is in the morning mist.

"In the summer the hydrangeas are as big as basketballs," Adam said wistfully, apropos of nothing.

Shortly, we received word that all was ready and we set off again with Adam at the wheel. Elias was lying on the backseat and I was crouched in front.

"Here it is," Adam said. "Margaret and I bought this villa last summer."

We turned through almost hidden marble pillars onto a rocky drive, the sea now closer beyond the red tile roofs of the villa complex.

When the car passed behind a small side building, Adam slowed enough for Elias and me to jump out, then continued to the main house while we dashed through the cover of a small grove of olive trees and took up positions on either side of the front door. The air was the freshest I'd ever breathed in my life, and I gulped it into my lungs, forcing my heart to slow down. I leaned into the wall and watched Adam drive up.

He tooted the horn. The front door flew open and Margaret, wrapped in a white terry cloth bathrobe, raced to greet him. Elias grabbed her arm and flipped her face-down onto the ground before she knew what hit her. She never made a sound.

I took Lucky, who was right on her heels and just starting to yell, "Surprise!"

Except, it wasn't Lucky. It was Suka.

Forty

"Is he here already?" I heard Lucky call from upstairs. "He really made good time."

Footsteps fell on the narrow stone stairway as she and Martine came down. I was there to greet them with my big Glock pointed right at Lucky's face. A maid came out of the kitchen and screamed.

Within seconds, all four women—who were completely in shock—were shackled and seated at the dining room table. Elias radioed the all-clear and I started to read them all their rights.

Adam could not contain his anger.

"Is it true?" he interrupted. "Did you kill all those people, Margaret? Did you lie about everything?"

"Let me remind you," I said, quickly. "Anything any of you say can be used against you."

"Yes. I did." Margaret answered defiantly. She looked him right in the eye. Talk about sang-froid.

"Were you going to kill me, too?"

She didn't answer.

Now that I had a chance to see her and Lucky together—they sat very close to each other, shoulders and thighs almost touching—I could tell they were twins, their bodies and gestures were identical. But, just as Mickey Giardino had told me, someone must have battered Margaret's face into oblivion, because it had been totally rebuilt. In spite of the faded hairline scars, she didn't look ugly at all; to the contrary, she was striking. She just looked nothing like Lucky.

"What are you talkink about?" Suka asked. "What is happenink?"

"What is happenink," I said, "is this merry band of homicidal maniacs is under arrest for six first-degree murders. Elias, will you do the honors?" I handed him my video recorder.

"With pleasure."

Then, once more for the record, I read each one of them their rights. Lucky and Margaret understood. Suka said she didn't understand anything that was happening, and Martine just sat and cried.

"They didn't have anything to do with it," Lucky said. "They just came along for the ride."

"Do you mind telling me why?" Adam asked.

Margaret looked at Lucky, who shrugged her shoulders. "It's sort of complicated."

"We're all ears," I said. The video hummed quietly.

Carabinieri filed in and circled the room, their weapons locked and loaded. I knew if there were one false move, they'd shoot. When it comes to law enforcement, these people do not screw around.

Lucky spoke first. "All of us have an unhappy history with the Johnson family. Margaret's and mine goes particularly far back. Our mother was the company's secretary in England."

Suddenly the question that had been knocking against the back door of my brain was answered. The out-of-focus black-and-white photograph of the Johnson Land Company's English office staff in front of Buckingham Palace. The photo had been on Adelaide's desk, and a blown-up section of it had been on Lucky's dressing table.

"That was your mother in the photograph," I said.

"Yes," Lucky answered. "The Johnsons opened an office in London in the early fifties. Mother had just gotten her secretarial certificate and they hired her. We were just babies."

"Our father had been killed in a car wreck," Margaret explained. "So she had to go to work. There was no money. England was still reeling from the war."

"When we were about five years old"—Margaret spoke angrily—"one day, out of the blue, they closed the office with no warning and left the country. Mother had nothing. No job. No money. Nothing. They didn't even pay her back wages."

"I'm sorry your mother lost her job," I said. "But that's not enough reason to murder the whole family."

Lucky's eyes passed first over the cadre of dashing young Italian policemen in their dark khaki jumpsuits and navy berets, and then over her buddies, before they came to rest on mine. "Of course not. That was just our first taste of how the Johnson men felt they could treat women. Those people were cruel and vicious; they thought they could get away with anything."

"Tom Johnson is the one who did this to my face," Margaret spoke quietly.

"You don't have to tell," Lucky said.

"It's fine. I'm happy to tell. I want them to know what he did and why he deserved to die." Margaret pulled off the blond wig. Her bald head was a patchwork of thick, ropy scars that crisscrossed like a heavy-gauge, pink and white net across her scalp and down her neck. "It happened in Monte Carlo. Lucky and I were at the top of our career. We were the most highly paid showgirls in the world. Tom Johnson was staying at the Hotel de Paris, and he invited me to go to dinner with him after the show. We knew who he was—that he was part of the same infamous Johnson family from Wyoming that had ruined our mother's life—and while it was our policy never to go out with members of the audience, we decided it would be a good opportunity to get to know a little more about him. He was our sworn enemy."

"*Antichristo.*" Suka spat the name.

"So, I went," Margaret continued. "He had rented a car and picked me up in front of the casino. We sipped a bottle of Dom Perignon on the way to dinner and on the way back, he pulled over to look at the view. I wasn't a child, I knew what was coming. At least I *thought* I did. Except that what he wanted was so disgusting, I refused, and he slapped me. I slapped him back, which made his toupee fall off. He was such a ridiculous-looking man to start with, and then, without his toupee—you can imagine his shock that a woman would have the nerve to slap him—I couldn't help it, I started laughing. He reminded me so much of a sweaty Porky Pig with his pink head and big buck teeth, I couldn't stop. It was a mistake. He turned into an animal. He beat my face with his fists and then broke the empty champagne bottle and ground it into my head. Fortunately, I was unconscious by the time he pushed me out of the car and down the hillside."

252

"He slashed up her face," Lucky said. "And then, he scalped her. By the time the authorities found her the next afternoon, he was long gone."

"Everything you've told me for the last two years has been a lie," Adam said, stone-faced, having realized he had just left everyone and everything behind for someone who didn't exist.

"I'm sorry, Adam," Margaret said.

"No you aren't."

"Why didn't you press charges?" I asked.

Lucky snorted out a laugh.

"Marshal." Martine's voice was soft and her French accent deep. "Women have very little power, especially women like us. Because we make our living showing our bodies, we have to be especially careful who we go out with, what we do, because we are very, very vulnerable. If we get in trouble, people who don't understand our world say, 'Of course, she is a dancer, a stripper. She probably deserved it.' We are not like that. We are not whores. When Tom beat up Margaret? People would say, 'just another girl.'

"You know." She looked at her hands, which rested calmly, one on top of the other, in her lap. "The same thing happened to me with Frank Johnson. I didn't even know Lucky and Margaret. I knew the legend of Mary and Margaret, how famous they had been in Monte Carlo and how one day at the peak of their fame, they vanished, but I am younger than they are, and by the time I started dancing, they were gone.

"I was the principal dancer at the Lido, and we had a large group of American businessmen in the audience, which was not at all unusual. And some of them always wanted to meet us, take us out to dinner, hoped to get us into their beds. But the majority of us did not ever go." Martine bobbed her head from side to side with typically Gallic resignation. "There are always a few girls who are loose, but I was not one. I had a good background and also a little daughter. I always went straight home after work.

"The morning after Frank came to the show, I began to receive gifts, which was also not at all unusual. But these were ridiculously lavish gifts: diamonds, sable coats, cashmere shawls and blankets, dozens and dozens of roses. Something every day for a week. Very old-fashioned, with charming little notes. 'You are the most beautiful woman I've ever seen in my life. Please just meet me for a coffee.' That sort of thing. So I met him, and after a while, we began an affair. He convinced me to move to Las Vegas so we could be closer. Also, I wanted my daughter to grow up in America. When I arrived there, I spoke little English and I didn't know anyone at all. He was always telling me how dangerous Las Vegas was and how the men were sharks. I became totally dependent on him. At first, he seemed like a nice man, but deep down, he was a sadist. Ugly, sadistic, incredibly cruel. By the time he began abusing me, I was so weakened in my head—he had destroyed my self-esteem so completely—I could not leave." Tears streamed down Martine's face. "Because of him, I cannot have more children. I thank God every day for my darling little girl, Aimée. Lucky and Margaret saved my life."

"We met Martine a few years ago and helped her get away from him," Margaret explained. "That's when we formed the pact."

"And me!" Suka said. "Don't forget about me."

As if anyone could.

"Clay Parker promised to get me into the movies." Suka had risen to her feet and circled the room, passing very close to the young carabinieri, examining them as though she were trying to decide which one to tackle first. "He was the announcer at the Miss Universe contest. I thought he was a big star. How did I know he was just a wash-up? A nobody. A sickening old drunk. He deserved to die for what he did to me, and I would have killed him myself if Margaret hadn't offered to do it for me."

"You killed all of them?" I asked Margaret.

"This was Lucky's and my plan." She had not replaced the wig, and the gruesome starkness of her head turned her face into a series of hard angles. "We worked on it for years. Originally, we were just going to kill Tom. I wanted to make him suffer a lot more than I had—take him prisoner and stake him out in the desert or something equally grim. He got off easy; that gunshot was pretty painless for him."

"Didn't he recognize Lucky as one of the famous twins from Monte Carlo?"

"Of course not," Margaret said. "Women have no faces for him. We're just—women."

"I don't know what it is that has gotten into some men," Lucky said. "Somehow, somebody is raising them to believe that women are their property. Their chattel. That they own them, and if something doesn't go according to plan, they have the right to beat them, or mutilate them, or kill them. When we met Martine and she finally confessed what was happening with her life and who was responsible, that's when we decided to get rid of the whole family."

"And Clay," Suka added.

"And Clay," Lucky conceded. "But Suka and Martine didn't have anything to do with the murders."

"What about Adelaide and Dolly?" I asked.

Lucky looked at me with those steady blue eyes that seemed to see so much. "You met them," she said evenly. "Don't you agree the world is a better place without them?"

I chose not to answer that question. "And Lana?" I asked instead.

"Oh, she's just a friend. She was just along for the birthday party. Today is our fiftieth birthday." Lucky and Margaret smiled broadly.

There was no fear or regret in either of them. It was re-markable. They had the clear-eyed gaze of fanatics. Crusaders.

"In case you're interested, we've been extremely well paid. You'll find all the A. L. Johnson Land Company accounts are empty. Every penny is gone. Poof."

"What did you do with it?"

"None of your business," Margaret said.

They were happy as cats with cream.

The time had come to wrap things up. The police officers helped the women to their feet and led them away.

Forty-one

There wasn't much more to do once the last van had chugged up the hill with its glamorous load. I called the Marchese, who was kind enough to invite Richard, Elias, Linda, and me to lunch at his villa on the opposite side of the island.

Three hours later, on the way back to the airfield, we stopped by the police station. Suka and Martine were already gone. They'd been released quickly and fled as fast as they could back to Las Vegas to try to save their jobs. Adam had gone to his villa and taken the phone off the hook. I wondered if he would return to the United States to testify or just sit and stare at the sea and make his life in Italy.

□ □ □ □

I do not recommend breaking the laws anywhere, but especially abroad. Prisoners in America think our detention facilities are bad. Ha. They have no idea what bad can be. Our oldest prisons are two hundred years newer than some in other countries. Everything in the movie *Midnight Express* about the jails in Turkey is true. Times ten. In many countries.

That is not to say the whole police station in Porto Santo Stephano is medieval. Parts of it were built in the nineteen-fifties and the communications capabilities are completely twenty-first century. Everything else is original equipment. The toilets alone are enough to keep you a law-abiding citizen. The espresso, however, is excellent.

Once I'd completed my paperwork in an office decorated with murals of past carabinieri marching through the snow in navy coats with red trim and three-cornered hats, armed with rifles and bayonets, as though they'd just driven Atilla back over the Alps, I went down a narrow stone stairway to the holding cell to say good-bye to Mary and Margaret Wallis. By then, they'd recanted their confessions and would admit to nothing.

"We know the law," Lucky said. "We aren't American citizens and we didn't understand our rights."

"Okay, have it your way, ladies," I said. "Happy birthday. I don't think it's going to be much of a party."

"These gals are smart," I said as Richard drove us back to the airport. "This case will be gigantic. Some big showboat lawyer will represent them, and he'll get them off."

During the afternoon, a storm had blown in off the sea and the rain was coming down in buckets. It was cold and dark. The four of us were soggy, tired lumps as we climbed onto the plane. We dreaded the trip home. There was a fax waiting for me onboard, a terse note from Dimetriev in St. Petersburg.

Located the missing Fabergés. It read. *Fakes.*

"Told ya'," said Elias.

"I'd better call Mickey," I said. "He's going to be mad."

We rolled onto the runway.

"He'll get over it," said Richard, uncorking a bottle of champagne. "Call him tomorrow. Everyone's completely exhausted, and needs a break. We're already over here. Let's go to Paris."

Epilogue

You wouldn't have believed it." Mother's voice echoed over the phone.

I was lying in bed in our suite at the Ritz, watching the sun set on the garden. We'd been there for a week and had no plans to return home anytime soon.

"Suka, Martine, and Lana all called and invited your father and me to Las Vegas to see their show. You know, I think this thing between Lana and Buck is serious. Anyhow, they put us at the big table at the end of the runway and all the dancers knew who we were, so they all kept winking at us. I sent you a picture."

"I got it," I said. The color photograph showed my parents smiling out of a high-walled, horseshoe-shaped booth, holding drinks with paper umbrellas in them. They looked darling. Two elegant seniors—slightly hard of hearing, vision not too sharp, backs not quite as straight—having a ball. In Las Vegas of all places.

"You should see this show. I've never seen anything like it in my life. The costumes are unbelievable, and after about the first five numbers, they take off more and more of their clothes. By the last number, which Suka stars in, she had on a body stocking that was so sheer, you couldn't tell where the stocking ended and her skin began. It really looked almost as though she were nude."

"Mother. She was nude."

For a moment there was dead silence, and then she began to laugh. "Are you sure?"

"Positive."

"Have fun, darling," she said. "I have to go tell your father she didn't have any clothes on. He won't believe it."